ALORA CARTER

TIES
OF
SHADOW

TETHERED HEARTS

Thank you to my husband for many great quips and quotes, and for always being my greatest advocate, protector and friend.

To my BBC, you kept me going when this book felt heavy and my arms were tired. Thank you for carrying the load with me.

To my kids, the original wild animals. You are bright lights in my darkest days.

Trigger Warning

As always, my books have some mature themes, and don't pull back from darker aspects of life. In this book, the main trigger would be an alcoholic father, with a scene of rage, shame, and knocking a woman backwards. It is portrayed as vile, and unacceptable. A woman is asked to sacrifice for her nation and is injured. Three dead bodies are shown, but not their deaths. The battles are magical and distant mostly, and the rest are battles against spiders and other creatures. There are a lot of italics, not my favorite, but you'll see why soon.

As always good wins, love triumphs, and it all ends Happily Ever After.

Contents

1. The Storm — 1

2. Marked — 8

3. Father First — 17

4. Racerbristles — 27

5. The Ball — 36

6. The Shade — 46

7. Hide Yourself — 51

8. Prosperity Requires Sacrifice — 59

9. Nowhere Else To Go — 69

10. Introductions — 77

11. Bathtime — 86

12. A Tour — 92

13. The Solarium — 101

14. Under the Mountain — 112

15. Storms Rumble — 119

16. Potions — 134

17. Bitterroot Caverns — 146

18.	The Way Home	156
19.	Decide	166
20.	Darkness Within	174
21.	Trials	182
22.	Not the Mines	196
23.	Caverns and Chaos	208
24.	Badness and Weakness	217
25.	A Brief Castle Break-In	227
26.	My Father's Workshop	235
27.	Run or Fight	242
28.	Freedom of Choice	255
29.	Restoration	266
30.	Light at the End	271
Ties of Frost		278
Tethered Hearts Series		280
Acknowledgements		281
Also By Alora Carter		283

Chapter One

The Storm

The shadow storm swept in out of nowhere, drenching my clothes and basket with sticky, inky rain. The forest floor darkened with the black fog that billowed from the hot ground as toxic drops struck the surface. The seers had forgotten to mention this one.

Dashing behind the spiny bark of a razewa tree, I cowered, ducking and holding my basket over my head as I waited the tantrum out. The Shade was never angry for long, although it seemed like he was angry more frequently these days. If he could simply get over himself, that would be great—his storm was delaying my work.

Searing wind from the east ripped through the trees, their branches creaking ominously in the palace's flaming retort as the infernus prince reassured us with his fiery magic. What measly shadow could withstand a flame? As always, Prince Leon stood on the balcony platform, surrounded by galers, their wind magic extending his burning reach. I could almost make them out if I squinted. The billowing black clouds rippled as thunder roared, buffeting back the hot wind. Dust flew into my face from the cracked earth. I quickly checked on my necklace—safely tucked inside my shirt—before wrapping my cloak around my mouth.

Another drop of the black rain fell onto my cheek, stinging as it landed and tacky as I wiped it with my fingertips. The storm was worsening. I glanced up at the shoddy canopy the razewa provided, studying the rolling black magic before quickly looking down to protect my eyes. I couldn't stay here. The herbs I needed were nearby, just beyond the meadow, and we were running so low on supplies for the potion. The queen had looked so frail that morning; I couldn't give up on her because of a stormy inconvenience.

Pulling out my luz lamp to ward off the dark and bolster my courage, I started to run deeper into the leafy forest, heading toward the rocks and the pines. It was close to the border of our lands—too close to the edge—but I'd been here before. It was fine. The Shade hadn't found me then, and he wouldn't find me now, preoccupied as he was in his fight against Leon. Lightning crackled, flashing a stark contrast to the black trees and bleaching for a moment the sickly rain.

I slid to a stop when I reached the racerbristle bush, relieved to see it still standing. But my heart sank as I touched it. The leaves crumbled between my fingertips, and the branches snapped off and disintegrated to ash in my hand. Another ruined bush. The rain pelted harder. I fought the urge to throw the basket in frustration. It had been so hard to find this one last month. They were rare to begin with, temperamental to grow, and exquisitely sensitive to environmental changes like, for example, shadowy rains and billowing winds. What were we going to do now? What was *I* going to do?

The rain burned hotter, superheated by the fire, and stung my arms despite the sleeves covering them. I had to find cover fast. I sprinted again, this time ducking across the border into the darkened woods of the pines. Pine needles cushioned my flight beneath the black fog, and the trunks were so close that no light, and therefore no rain, could penetrate through the boughs. I'd find no herbs here, but at least I'd be protected from the harsh weather. I pulled my mother's necklace on top of my clothes; it cast a tiny glow before me, barely sending light a foot ahead. The coiled gold of the necklace burst like the sun from the glowing yellow stone within. Two longer sunbeams wrapped upward around the chain, and two longer ones trailed down the center of my chest while the other rays sprayed outward. A charmed gift from my mother, it had been brighter when I was a child but was now dimmed with age. Still, it produced enough light to comfort me at night. Although now, alone and in the dark, it didn't seem quite enough. I held my lamp higher, wishing Father had let me take a lamp with more luz. This lamp was already dimming, nearing the end of its twenty-four-hour glow.

My skin prickled, and the hairs on the back of my neck rose. The darkness pressed in like arms around my chest. My traitorous thoughts slipped to the Shade's manor somewhere beyond the forest—down a canyon and into the depths of death, if the seers were to be believed. Not here. Not the reason I felt like I was being watched. He was Death personified—a scourge, a menace. And all too close.

I backed up slowly toward the reach of the storm, torn between wanting to remain dry and safe from the rain and my inner senses screaming a warning. Then I heard a growl. A black wolf paced forward from deeper within the shadows, his silhouette backlit by a pulse of lightning. Wolves never came this far from the mountains.

"Nice pup. Handsome pup," I crooned, willing my voice to stop wavering. "I was just leaving. Have to get back, you know." I glanced down at the basket and pulled out a soiled strawberry. "Want one? It is...well, it *was* delicious." The wolf stepped forward and growled again. "No? Next time." My nervous laugh increased the tremor in my hands.

He lunged forward, and I spun and ran for my life.

"Bad wolf," I panted, ducking around the trees. "Very bad wolf."

He leaped, and I scraped my hand against a trunk; the momentum whirled me in a half circle just barely out of reach as he lunged. Some of the roots fell out of my basket, but I couldn't stop to save them. The wolf twisted and clamped its jaw over the hem of my dress, jerking me backward. I yanked hard, and his sharp teeth—the only whiteness in all the shadows of the forest floor—bit through, taking a piece with him. I stumbled at the sudden release and took off again.

Glancing over my shoulder, I didn't see the arching roots that coiled like a thousand arms from the base of a hemty tree. My toe caught on the elbow of a twisted root, and I flew through the air. I landed hard; the wind knocked from my lungs. I gasped, waiting for the air to enter back in, but the growling approached behind me.

Panic gripped my chest as I started crawling backward. A branch snapped on my right. I ripped my gaze from the beast to see a stranger emerge from the dark forest and step between me and the wolf. The wolf tilted his head one way and then the other as the man approached, his hands stretched out to either side. Then, the man gave a flick of his finger in a shooing manner. The wolf huffed once, pinned me with a glare, and then ran into the forest.

Relief flooded me, but when the dark stranger—a forester?—turned to me, the sense of danger returned. Dressed in dark leather, a long, thick coat brushed his calves, with belts across his torso. His face remained darkened under his hood, his eyes hidden, and his features shadowed by the weak penetration of light through the canopy above us.

"You shouldn't be in this forest." His voice was low, like the thunder around us.

I struggled to sit up. "I know. I was hiding from the rain. I'm sorry. So sorry."

I rose to my feet, and he huffed. "It isn't my forest."

"Still sorry. I'll just—" I pointed my arm to the right, toward where I thought the castle was. "I'll go back now."

Reaching up, his left hand clamped around my wrist. My stomach clenched in glacial fear. But then he pulled my straight arm a few degrees until it was aimed in a different direction. "That way."

"Sorry. Yes. That way."

I reached for my basket, my heart thudding the cadence of my nerves. "Thank you, sir."

I stepped and tripped again over the cursed roots. This time, I landed directly against his chest, my hands flung wildly, grasping at his wrist. The basket clanged against his side. My fingertips landed on the strap of a belt across his chest. His right hand reached to steady my shoulder but slid up to my neck as I fell forward. His fingertips threaded my hair as his thumb swept along my jaw. His warmth was electric. My skin prickled from his touch, which heated my marrow. This was too intimate for friends, much less strangers. My cheeks warmed, and I stammered as I pulled away. His eyes remained shadowed, but he tensed at our touch. "So sorry. Again. A thousand apologies. Thank you and sorry and bye."

I rushed past him, careful of the roots this time, as I headed in the direction he guided me. The weight of his gaze lightened as I put distance between us. The pines thinned. The rain lessened. And as quickly as it started, the storm and magic disappeared, and the forest was still. I paced through the shrubby, deciduous forest, heading back toward the town, and turned—only then looking behind me for the man or the wolf. But nothing stirred.

My heart kept up its rapid rate as I sneaked quietly onto the dirt street, wincing at every shuffle, crack, or scuff I made. What had I been thinking? I would never go back to the pines. I would stay out of that area. Go home tonight and remain below anyone's notice. Unseen by the forester, the wolves, or my father. And I'd also, somehow, avoid Leon. I held my lantern close, feeling foolish for needing its meager comfort. Glancing up, I tried to steal some more joy from the light tower of the castle. Beams of yellow poured from the hoard of luz behind the glass, glowing brightly to provide hope to a dark and tired city. I shivered from the residual dampness of my ruined dress and paused to breathe in the scene. *The prince and king lead the nation with light and hope.*

Then why did I feel so hopeless? I looked down at my sad, sad basket. Everything was ruined. The herbs I'd found near the creek were quickly drying; the strawberries and tubers that had remained in my basket were sooty and wrinkled. I grimaced as I held up a wilted wild carrot, blackened by the Shade's rain and cracked from the heat the prince had used to save us once again.

I studied the wrinkled orange skin; the scent of acrid charcoal wafted from it. "So sorry. Your life ended too soon, little one. It would have been better if I had left you in the earth until the storm had passed." I tilted the pathetic thing, wondering if I could somehow recover its essence, but who was I kidding? I was no washer who could rehydrate it; I was barely an herbalist, barely a lady, barely...anything. I set the carrot near a slimy, struggling caterpillar on the ground. Maybe the creature could be saved with the small offering. I shuffled through the rest. The baked herbs could be rinsed and dried again. And the roots could possibly be fried in oil if we cut off the bits where the rain had burned the surface. I closed my eyes and pressed my thumb against the bridge of my nose. Hours of work lost. Chef would be sad. Father would be furious. The queen would worsen yet again.

I couldn't quit just yet. I wouldn't quit. The soil beneath me was cracked and blackened. Too dry for anything to grow. Carefully not looking back toward the pines, I trudged to the south, curling under the village, downhill. Maybe I could still find something untouched by magic. Resigning myself to the search, I trudged on, hoping for just a few more ingredients to soften the blow of Father's disappointment.

Chapter Two

Marked

"Aelia, you're late. Though the seers did say you would be." Chef didn't spare me a glance as she took my basket. "Wandi, get over here. Stop admiring your mark, girl. It's not going to fade." Chef called to the washer at the sink as she rifled through my finds. Tossing the lot into the water basin, Chef heaved the now-empty basket back into my arms, finally taking in my filthy, oily—and likely horrifying—appearance. "Caught in the storm, aye? Bad luck. Even worse luck was your disappointing find." She gestured to the soiled plants. "Wandi, salvage what you can." The girl, perhaps a few years younger than my eighteen, pulled some water from the basin and wrapped tendrils around the leaves and roots. She was careful to flash me the light tan star-shaped mark on her wrist, her hand rubbing it periodically as she worked. Though her cheeks were bunched by her beaming smile, I recoiled.

That was a bond mark. Someone out there had a matching mark on them too—marking their potential to soulbond. If they met again, the mark would expand in various designs, and the bond would knit them together. Forever. Trapped.

How awful.

Wandi beamed at me when she noticed me staring. I tried to smile back, but I suspect it looked more like a grimace by the way she winced and turned away to manipulate the water around the herbs. Chef eyed me, shaking her head slightly. We had disagreed over the marks before.

She sighed, then tilted her head for me to follow her. "Were there no racerbristles?"

Turning away from the doomed servant, I wiped my hands on a towel. "I found the bush from last time, but it was dead. Brittle. I don't think it could withstand all these storms." I withheld my thoughts that, though the Shade was bad, the heat was worse for the plants. Prince Leon's magic made it hard for anything to grow in the castle gardens—so close to his fire. Racerbristles were uncommon in the wild and only bloomed every few weeks. Unfortunately, their roots, leaves, *and* flowers were components of the only healing potion able to keep the queen alive. The gardeners and washers worked under the canvas awnings day in and day out to keep the few bushes we did have alive—barely. But the cultivated racerbristles weren't enough, so I searched endlessly for more. The bushes preferred the edges of the forest and moist, windless air—hard to find when the canopies were charred crisps and the air heated by flames.

Chef grimaced. "The healer and king will not be pleased to hear this news. The queen fades even now."

I ducked my head, feeling the weight of the queen's dependence on herbal cures and my efforts to obtain them.

Noting my guilt, she patted my shoulder, then casually brushed away the crumbs she'd accidentally left behind. "Maybe we'll have you look on the other side of the mountain..."

"Yes, Chef," I murmured.

She sighed heavily as her curls wrapped around her round, weathered face. Chef's worry lined her features for a moment longer before she stiffened and regarded me again. "Go now, Aelia. Get cleaned up. Don't be late for dinner. Prince Leon is honoring the Mastersons tonight before their bonding ball."

"Yes, Chef."

She rolled her eyes and smiled as she batted at me with a towel. She hated it when I deferred so much to her, given my station. I smiled back and raced to my room. Pulling the tacky clothes off, I filled the tub with hot water—a luxury thanks to the lesser washers and inferni employed by the castle. I scrubbed at the oily shadows until my skin was pink and raw and my white hair had returned to its natural snowy shade. The water had turned as gray as the storm as I stepped out. I considered my soiled clothes and tossed the lot into the tub. A good soaking would be useful for the stains I would have to try to get out myself.

By night, I was Lady Aelia, a noblewoman; by day, Aelia, the magicless—and therefore useless—working woman. I'd save this mess for later when I had more time since I had no maids to assist me.

Tapping my lips, I stood before the wardrobe and reached for one of my nicer gowns. The green would look fine with my hair. It's not like anyone looked at me anyhow. I pulled out my mother's necklace, with its curling, sweeping rays of the sun. It looked pretty against the shining fabric, though the slight glow was soon too overpowered by the castle's luz lamps to be appreciated. It was still a small comfort if I had to celebrate a soulbond.

Soulbonds were a highly valuable cage that romantics honored, seers tried to matchmake, and all the other girls dreamed about. I knew better. A soulbond had ruined my father, killing him as decidedly as my mother, even though he was still here, walking and breathing. Poor Wandi. Given the details and distinctness of the unnatural mark, she would undoubtedly find her match soon. She must have seen him and touched him in order to trigger the magic...or rather, the curse. Couples could work their way out of the relationship, of course, if it didn't suit them. But the seers all claimed that bonds were the mark of one's true love and everlasting happiness.

Right. My father. The beacon of joy.

I struggled with the ties on my dress and swept up my white hair in the only style I could quickly do myself so I wouldn't arrive late or be embarrassed. King Harold, the regent, technically, let me and my father stay in the castle since we were useful to his queen, but as I had no magic of my own, I was a source of judgment and derision to both him and my father. The nobles always had the strongest magic. Except for me. So, I was in no man's land—too noble to be out in the city, too weak to deserve a lady's maid.

Slipping into my shoes, I dashed down the corridor, arriving as King Harold entered the hallway. I dipped into a curtsy, ignoring his scowl, and gracefully, meticulously minced into the room toward my seat. King Harold was announced amid trumpeting fanfare a few moments later, and we stood until he waved for us to take our seats. The room fell into murmurs, polite laughter, and warm remarks, all of which roared to a cheer when Prince Leon entered the room.

King Harold threw out his arms, greeted his son in a back-beating embrace, then pulled back to regard him. "Oh, my boy, what a wonderful display today. You are an asset to our nation and our lands! Keeping that filth away from us—a true hero!" The king turned Leon toward us, grasping him in a sideways embrace.

"The prince and king lead the nation with light and hope!" the table guests chorused.

King Harold continued, "Day in, day out, light or dark, you defend our great city and these very walls. Your magic is immense, and you use it for your people like a true leader. Prosperity requires sacrifice, which you demonstrate daily to our people."

Prince Leon dipped his head and beamed at us with a radiant smile. Radiant like his fire. Radiant like my face as I ducked to obscure my blush. It should be illegal for talented people to be attractive—worse yet, he was also powerful and charming. He was dressed in red attire, his sleeves capped with yellow flames that climbed down his arms artistically. His blond hair swept toward the sky in small spikes. The nobles' daughters rose and flitted to his side, twittering in their pastel way, each speaking the language of eyelashes and coquettish fan-waving fluidly. I rose in greeting, as did the men, but found my seat more quickly than the rest.

He rounded the table, greeting the nobles and congratulating the Mastersons on their match. Lady Marva Keller had a zigzag on her forearm, while Lord Henty Masterson's mark was on the back of his hand—their skin stained by the curse of the magic. Both looked flushed with excitement and regaled Prince Leon with stories from their courtship and their anticipation of the completed bond tomorrow. The prince moved with such confidence and ease, celebrating them as expected. His gaze caught mine, and his smile brightened a fraction. It was all I could ask for.

The prince and I had been friends since childhood, when Father and I had moved here. We were close in age, but as he grew up, our friendship grew apart. Ours was a subtle friendship, quiet and out of the view of our peers. I didn't need his public acknowledgment of our closeness. I knew who he had been as a child and the depths of our friendship outside of the court. He had his reputation to preserve, and I didn't want to tarnish it with my weakness.

"Lady Aelia." Lord Brynett's quiet words startled me, and I dropped my fork. I quickly gathered my composure as I turned. "Your father, is he well? He has missed several of the last dinners."

I glanced toward my father's seat, empty beside me. "Indeed, my lord, he just needs rest from his studies. He endlessly searches for ways to aid Her Majesty." The lie was well practiced, and no one ever sought to clarify or seemed bothered by the same answer stated a hundred different ways.

"Lady Aelia," King Harold called. "Won't you move down a seat so Lord Turnblat can sit beside Lord Brynett?"

I stood quickly, tucking my hair behind my ear in my surprise. I curtsied. "Yes, Your Highness." I shifted down to the end of the table as Lord Turnblat and Lord Jerrund moved up into my father's and my seats. I pulled the strands of hair I had left down in front of me, stroking them twice for comfort. I could eat here as well as there. My role was to serve the kingdom.

When I glanced back up toward Prince Leon, however, I was surprised to find Lord Brynett still staring, his jaw slack and his gaze fixed on my neck...or my ear. Did I miss something?

"My lord?" I asked, shifting in my seat as I bunched a bit of fabric between my fingers beneath the table. But he just pointed at my head with a furrowed brow. I brought a napkin to my chin and dabbed at my lips.

Lord Jerrund, who had just seated himself, turned sharply, acknowledging my existence for the first time in several months. "Egads, lass, are you sick? Cursed?"

My lips parted. Lord Jerrund was always a bit gregarious, but this was surprising. "I...no? I'm not cursed. What is it?"

"Your neck. What did you do? It looks like it's rotting away!" Lord Jerrund leaned away, standing to gain distance. The entire table was now staring. Placing a hand upward, my fingers followed my collar-bone up to my jawline, where I felt residual evidence of the shadow magic behind my jaw by my beauty mark.

I pulled my hand away, studying the blackness on my fingers, my throat tight. "Forgive me, my lord. I was in...in the garden...when the shadows fell."

Lord Jerrund sniffed haughtily as he straightened his jacket and resumed his seat, unembarrassed by his outburst. "Your lady's maid should be put out on the streets for missing such a thing. The inattention!"

Prince Leon cleared his throat, and the table fell to a respectful silence. "Perhaps so. Lady Aelia, go tidy up. Discuss this with your maid, or I shall have to."

My cheeks flared as hot as a sunburn under the weight of his gaze. I rose, curtsied, and swept out of the room. Yes. Me and my maid. The prince knew I had no maid, but no one else did. My father and the king regent were convinced that I would be fine on my own. Fine indeed. I paced back to the room and studied myself in the mirror, turning my head unnaturally to find the spot. Of course, I had missed it. I had a small mark tucked into the natural shadow below my ear, a mole that arrived when I was seven. The mark had been covered by a smear of black acid rain and was now irritated. I closed my eyes, clenching against the wave of shame. So much for being quiet and unobtrusive. How could I embarrass the prince in this way?

Grasping a cloth and dipping it in the cold, sudsy bathwater, I leaned toward the mirror to scrub away all evidence of my foraging. The cloth darkened, and I rinsed it again, but a thin line, swirling around the dark center circle and up toward my ear, remained. How much shadow goo could hide behind an ear? The skin around it turned red as I scrubbed, but it persisted. I cleaned several more rounds but made no headway; the cloth no longer darkened, but my skin refused to release the last bit of grime. With a grunt, I threw the cloth at the mirror. It was hopeless. Or maybe I *was* cursed, and Lord Jerrund was right all along.

It appeared I would not be returning to dinner, so I slipped down to the kitchen through the servant passages to grab some food and some help. The bustling form of Chef was kneading the bread dough for the morning. With dinner well underway, the room bustled with staff carrying new dishes, leaving soiled ones for the washers, and rushing around in a frenzy. Chef's hair danced to and fro over her forehead as she kneaded. I hated to disturb her. "Forgive me, Chef, do you have any oil I could use, please?"

Without turning, she pointed to a shelf. Grabbing a tall glass bottle, I doused a clean cloth and began rubbing anew. Her clomping steps warned me of her arrival. "Child, child, you have to leave the ear attached! Give the thing to me." Taking the saturated napkin, she pushed my head, tilted it to the side, and threw my hair behind me. Then she froze.

With a frown, I turned toward her, but her face had paled to the shade of the flour that dusted her cheek. Shaking herself, she dabbed the area twice, then stepped back again. She coughed. "It's only an irritated beauty mark."

"So I'm not cursed?" I said, smiling to lighten the tension. Chef stumbled and nearly knocked against a nearby pot.

"What?" she laughed with too much air. "Who would say such a thing? It's only a mark, like the one on my arm. Hard-earned and lovely, they are." Her eyes pierced me as she turned back. "All the same, better leave it alone. Let it heal." She tapped her hands against the table. "Is that why you left the dinner?"

Nodding, I twisted the rag. "Lord Jerrund and Lord Brynett saw that I missed some of the shadow filth from earlier. Made a scene." I tossed the rag into the laundry basket. "And Prince Leon told me to get my maid to fix it."

Her face softened with empathy. "Ah, dear girl. Prince Leon has a hard job, you know. Saving face in front of his father and people. I'm sure he didn't want to upset the Mastersons." She took some food from the ready dishes and made me a plate, wrapping the rolls before passing it back. "You'll be alright. But head back up to your room for now. Tend to your da when you're done. Keep your hair down so you don't go messing with it."

She paused and placed a hand on my cheek with a confused expression before turning me bodily and pushing me out the door. "See you in the morning, lass." The door clicked shut behind me.

I stood on the other side of the door, reeling, blinking into the shadows of the spider-filled servant hall. My necklace glowed weakly in the dim light. What in the sunny lands was that? Returning to my room, I sat at my bureau, staring at my reflection and wondering what kind of beauty mark could cause the steady chef to stumble.

Chapter Three

Father First

Later that evening, the tea platter shook under my grasp as I turned the corner toward the herbalist's room. The stories I told the lords weren't a complete lie. My father was researching ways to cure the queen. But he was also decidedly unwell...and nearly as volatile as the Shade himself.

The teacup vibrated noisily against the metal kettle. Taking a calming breath, I reminded myself that I had been here before, had borne up under his displeasure before, and that it would be okay. I'd drawn my hair forward with loops of curls and braids, hiding the beauty mark as Chef had instructed, but I ached to rub at it again. I shifted the remnants of the herbs the washers had readied from my search that day. They looked truly pathetic.

Rallying my courage, I stepped into the room. The candles had burned to the bases, all but a few snuffed out in their own wax. I pulled a fresh one out of my apron pocket before resting it on the tray as well. His snoring preceded him. The potion-making glassware lay scattered around him as he slumped in his seat, his cheek smeared on the table, with a puddle of drool seeping off the edge and onto the floor. The liquid swirled with the amber drops that fell from the bottle, tilted in his hand. A white stellate scar spread spindly legs across his wrist just past the cuff of his shirt—evidence of his cursed bond and his attempts to destroy it.

My cheek pulled back in disgust at the scene. The savior of the queen, the healer of the wounded, passed out and drooling on the floor, saturated in despair and alcohol. He had power because of his magic and his skill with herbs. Even though lately, I had been the one making a lot of the potions for the queen. I had been the one to clean up his messes and hide the truth from the others. But I pressed my eyes shut and shoved the bitterness down. This was my father. He loved me, and I loved him. I would help him as I always did. I would be helpful, quiet, nice. Setting the tray down, I tidied the table before him, shifting his glasses away to be a bit more out of reach. Then I stepped back.

"Father," I called from a few feet away. I had learned not to approach immediately. "Father." A bit louder. He didn't stir. I bit my lip, pulled the tips of my hair, and stepped behind him. Reaching forward, I placed a hand on his shoulder. "Father, it's me, Aelia."

He roared to a drunken awareness, swinging and flinging his arms as his glazed and unfocused eyes darted about the room. I was not far enough back. A hand flew back into my stomach, knocking me into the table behind me. I tripped over my skirts and fell to the ground. Gasping, I tucked myself under the table like the coward I was. Tears filled my bottom lids as I gulped for breath, my arms holding my stomach. Long moments later, the muscles released, and I could inhale fully, albeit shakily.

Hostile, bloodshot eyes suddenly appeared before me. He had crouched so his round face hovered mere inches above my own. His acidic breath exhaled remnants of the mead he favored. Glancing down, he grasped my wrist and, with a push of his loamer earth magic to heave the stones beneath me, pulled me out from under the table. I scrambled to my feet, keeping my eyes on the shifting floor—his magic was as drunk as he was—and gave a slight curtsy.

"What is the meaning of this?" he slurred. "Why are you here?"

"I'm sorry I startled you, Father. I brought you your evening tea."

He frowned at the tray on the far side of the room as he slumped into his chair with a putrid sigh. "Did you design to bring it to me cold? Get it here, girl!"

I briefly curtsied again and slipped around the tables. Setting the tray in front of him, I gathered his three sugars and cream and passed him the cup and saucer. "Here, Father." Disdainfully, he took the tea and dropped more amber liquid from the bottle into the cup. As if he needed more.

His red-rimmed eyes peered over the rest of the tray. He grasped the remnants of the herbs I'd gathered, rolling them between his thumb and forefinger. "What is this? What stagnate hollow did you drag this out of? Is this supposed to help me? Help Her Majesty?"

"I...I'm sorry, Father, it was...that is, I had more, but the storm—"

"Excuses! She is dying, and you don't even care."

My heart beat heavily in my chest. "I'm sorry."

"Not as sorry as the queen will be from her grave! Or her husband from the throne! I am constantly protecting you. All I ask in return is a bit of help and care. And you do this!" Father picked up the metal kettle faster than I could duck and threw it. The kettle went wide and hit the wall behind me. Hot water flew about the room, some seeping quickly through the thin linen of my back. I cried out despite my best efforts to stifle the reaction. He was too far gone to be reasoned with. I had to go.

"You know we need more." He threw the tray next, though his stumble sent it wide as I crawled toward the door. It clattered to the floor. "Get back out there! And find more white thieves too. Don't return unless you have them and the racerbristle. Am I clear?" I scrambled up, grabbing the tray and the metal kettle, and turned to rush out. I felt the rumble of his loamer magic a second before the ground shuddered beneath me, destabilizing a table and knocking a potion bottle to the floor.

"Clean that up! And get this last potion to Her Majesty. She could die tomorrow because of your laziness." He gestured to the half-filled vial by the door, the purple liquid sloshing in the latent vibrations as it stood in the cabinet on the wall.

"Yes, Father." I hustled to grab the broom and finished in a moment, snatching up the potion and tea items as I slipped out of the room. As I left, I could hear him muttering and grumbling as he cradled the portrait of Mother he'd knocked over with his rumbling. I left him rubbing at his wrist and nursing his broken heart.

It was a small mercy that Chef was not in the kitchen when I returned the tray; she would have undoubtedly looked at me with pity. Even without magic, she could always see right through me. I clung to my mantras and my apathy like a shield when I dealt with him, but her big, sad eyes would undo it all.

Hardly breathing, lest my breaths break into uneven sobs, I barged into my room, pressed the door shut, and settled before my little mirror. A single tear betrayed me, falling with a pat upon the table. I smeared the tear with my thumb, frowning and trying to hide the evidence of my weakness.

That hadn't been as bad as some visits. My blue eyes shimmered as another wave of tears threatened, the water making my eyes appear more cerulean than sky. It could have been worse. He was right, of course; the herbs were burned, and the queen was sick. I should have found a gentler way to wake him. I should have searched harder for the herbs. I should have cleaned my skin better. I failed so many of those who mattered to me today. I vowed to work harder tomorrow.

I closed my eyes, unable to stop the escape of two more drops.

"He loves me. He loves me. He is my father. I love him. I am here to help him. It is my purpose as a daughter. As a servant of the crown." A breath seeped out between my teeth, slow and agonal. The mantras weren't helping tonight. "He loves me. He is just grieving. He misses Mother. He...has a lot of pain from the severed soulbond. He would never hurt me. He loves me."

My ears were ringing as I rose to cool my face in fresh water. I just wanted to be helpful. I just wanted—well, it didn't matter what I wanted. My head throbbed; my throat tightened with emotions I refused to feel. Shaking my head to shed them completely, I reviewed my appearance in the mirror. I was Able Aelia, here to serve. Patting the potion in my pocket, I headed toward Her Majesty's quarters.

I carried the precious cargo down the dark servants' passages, popping out just before the royal suites. A guard watched as I passed, and another opened the queen's doors so I could enter. The hallways for the nobles were almost as bright as noonday with the luz lamps that lined the walls. Unlike the prince's audacious golden rooms and the king's royal navy rooms, the queen's rooms were a soft ivory laced with sage green, blush rose, and wispy gossamer fabrics. The room was lit by gobs of luz, and pans of healing oils dispersed pungent odors into the air. But despite our best efforts, the room still stank of illness. My eyes immediately prickled again. I blinked furiously before I moved past the drawing room into her bedchambers.

The nurse sat in the corner, twisting fibers onto a spindle, her eyes glazed and distant. A seer from the temple rocked back and forth on the balcony, muttering, chanting, and throwing some watery substance off the ledge in a prayer for the land to heal our monarch. She glanced back at me, and a shiver wormed its way down my spine. I smiled and curtsied rather than revealing my discomfort at her penetrating black gaze.

"I see a change coming," the seer whispered.

"Aelia?" The queen's soft voice whispered through the curtains of her four-poster bed and pulled straight the silken sheets. My smile bloomed into a genuine one—somehow, she always knew it was me.

"Yes, Your Majesty." Coming beside her, I pulled the potion out with a little wave. "I have your medicine."

The queen was pale, her cheeks sunken in, and her mouth dry and waxen. She was set up among a thousand pillows, making her diminutive frame appear even smaller, dwarfed by the comfort that propped her upright.

Her knobby hands reached for mine. "Ah, sweet girl, *you* are my medicine." A cough wracked her, and the nurse rushed to dab at the trickle of blood that spat onto her lip. "You are good for me." Her dry lips split into a grin. "Now tell me of the castle."

And so I did. This was our near-daily routine these days. Before she got so sick, Leon and I used to play hide and seek in her rooms with some servant boy, to the queen's great delight. She started having me over for tea in her rooms for my birthdays when I turned eight, even though she didn't always feel well. Queen Gemaline was more than a monarch to me. She was like the mother I had lost so long ago. As I grew up, she grew weaker, unable even to be wheeled out to the sitting rooms, so I brought the tea and potions to her instead. I would tell her about the kitchen gossip, the weather in the lowlands, and the herbs I'd found that day. We would argue over which pastry was Chef's best and predict which servants would be married next.

She asked me about the Mastersons. Her happiness that yet another couple found their match was something I was unwilling to steal away with my negativity. The queen often reached for my hands, earning a tut from the nurse and a scowl from the seer.

When I was ten, the queen had told them all off, claiming that she must know the inner life of the castle to rule well when she recovered. Now, they mostly let us be. I was harmless entertainment for the ailing monarch.

I told her about the wolf and my clumsy meeting with the forester. Her laugh was airy and weak, but my heart was pleased to ease her suffering, even for a moment. She retold one of her favorite tales about Leon, but I never minded. It was when they had gone to the coast, found my father's herbal shop, and wooed him to the kingdom of Nuren with a job.

"So Leon leaped off the tree and landed on his bottom in the shallow water!" The queen chuckled. "Poor boy was so put out that his splash was not the epic explosion he had planned. He ran out to me, sopping wet and mud dripping everywhere as he rushed into my arms. Oh, we were filthy! I dare say as filthy as you were!"

I laughed with her. My stomach ached from where Father had been startled, and I rubbed it idly. The queen must have sensed my shift of mood.

"You alright, dear?"

Traitorous tears threatened to line my lids, but I waved them off. "Of course I am, Your Majesty."

"Lying does not become you."

My smile wavered. I gave her one truth. "I miss my mother."

Her hand squeezed mine. It would have been weak if not for the force of her gaze. "Mothers are precious, aren't they? To us mothers, our children are even more precious."

I nodded, then cleared my throat. "Which is why we must restore you to the prince." Thunder rumbled, and the late evening sunlight from the balcony doors darkened too soon.

"The storms are worsening." The queen watched the collision of fire and black clouds, her face lined with sadness and worry.

"The Shade is fighting harder than ever. The prince and king lead the nation with light and hope." I rattled off the common mantra, though it felt odd not to call him the king regent in front of the queen. She'd been sick for so long, and he had led us all that time, so most of us saw him as the king.

She glanced at me with a raised brow. "Certainly, the prince battles on."

I peered at her odd expression. "If only the Shade would stop, then the land wouldn't be poisoned by the rain, the prince wouldn't have to use his fire, and the ground wouldn't dry out from their demonstrations of power. The herbs you need wouldn't be so hard to find. The people wouldn't struggle to keep their gardens growing."

The queen's thumb played along my knuckles. "Sometimes we fight things that don't need fighting. Sometimes, we fear to fight the battles we must. Sometimes we end up fighting ourselves. But that inner worth is so precious, Aelia. So worth protecting." She sighed. "Discernment is rare but more precious than luz."

I thought of my father. We fought, but he was my father, and our relationship was important. I ignored a squiggly feeling in my gut.

She continued. "What we must not do, Aelia dear, is lose sight of the light. We mustn't lose sight of ourselves, of what matters, or of the truth." Her green eyes brightened as she tried to sit up, locked with mine. "We must not forget to love, but we must also remember that love isn't always enough."

I laughed awkwardly and scratched at my dress. "Love is important."

"Love is most important," she said as she leaned back into her pillows. "But sometimes people confuse something else for love. Don't get mixed up."

"Yes, Your Majesty."

"I think it's time you go." The seer's crusty voice whipped through the room. "The queen is tired and talking in circles."

Her Majesty faintly rolled her eyes before she squeezed my hand again. "See you tomorrow after the ball?"

I curtsied after I rose. "Of course."

Slipping back to my room, a wayward tear slipped out. I loved the queen. I ached for her healing. I glared at the black oil that coated my dress and towels, which were still soaking in the tub. If only the Shade would stop killing her. He was suffocating the land with his black magic and dark violence.

I had seen the shadows in her room the day she fell ill. The king had workers building the tall tower for the new light to go. There had been a thunderstorm, and I was clinging to Chef's apron in fear. I remembered how the dinner looked funny, and the plates were not as full that week. Leon and I were running through the halls after each other, dodging between the statues and the knights who acted like statues beside the royal suites. We heard the king's loud bellow and rushed to the open door. Behind it, a swirl of shadows flowed from the queen's bed toward the window, where the king shouted. The queen had fainted on the floor and had looked as pale as death. Only after running to her and seeing her chest rise did I take a breath myself.

I was only seven, but the images stayed before me as if they had happened yesterday. Since then, my father had raced to modify his tonics to cure the queen, but he only found supportive potions, never the one that would save her. Even with my recent suggestions of new herbs, nothing had been curative.

I finished cleaning my clothes and wiping the bathtub of its blackened filth, heaving the towels into the basket to be added to the general laundry in the morning. I didn't need servants, but they would have been helpful today. I was tired. Soul-dried, marrow-cracking, heart-aching tired.

Surely, hope could return in the morning. Leaving the blinds open to let in the ever-present light from the tower, I settled into my bed, clutched my flickering necklace, and buried myself in my scratchy sheets.

Chapter Four

Racerbristles

The nightmares woke me before dawn. Again, I was a child, looking up through a dark tunnel at the screaming seagulls. Shuddering, I tried to brush off the memory and replace it with one of my mother's touch. I wondered these days how much of her was memory and how much was a fantasy I had created.

I counted it lucky to wake up so early. I could leave to find a new racerbristle bush and return in time for the cursed bonding ball. I meandered to my door and picked up the note tucked under it: the seer's daily predictions. Today, the storms would be moderate and possibly light. The sun would be bright. Shoes should be put on the left, then right, to receive full blessings. The washers should moisten their skin with oil, and the inferni should meditate this afternoon for twenty minutes to restore their full flames. Blessings upon the bonding couple. Noted. I threw the missive away.

Dressing quickly, I snatched a clean woven basket and eyed my wool cloak before grabbing that too. It was a hot day, but maybe the cloak would protect my finds from whatever magical maelstroms fell today. I hoped to be out of the storms' reach as I journeyed farther south.

Peeking through my doorframe, I saw that no noble yet stirred. Only cindermaids were whisking about in the halls with me. Distant granddaughters of lesser nobles, they used their smidgen of infernus magic to light the fireplaces of the acknowledged, magical, and useful nobles. They were well-dressed servants, but nothing more. Our relationship was strained as I had less magic but more access to the events and tables of the nobility. I tried not to let their harsh gazes cut me as I slipped past them in the servants' passage.

Beyond the covered gardens, I crept through the village, turning around the winding stone streets until I was in the rolling hills between Nuren and the flat coastlands. The castle stood in the palm of the easternmost peak, the fingers of a bald rocky peak rising behind it. The city was framed by massive walls that hugged the houses to the castle. But hundreds of villagers made their homes outside the city limits. The middle mountain was shorter but boasted a regal white temple—home of the seers—with an arduous and holy narrow road to the top. To the west, the far mountain peak cut off into a cliff, with flattened mesa, slashed deep valleys that cut through red rocks. Somewhere on that mountain, past the pines, deep in the canyons, the Shade boiled and brewed his chaos to suffocate the light and destroy our kingdom. He was monstrous and evil, and everything the prince wasn't. Light from the tower filled the whole region, wavering recently but always a beacon of hope for all the people.

We had lived here since I was seven. The king had first summoned Father to act as an herbalist in the land and then given him a long-term contract to cure the sickly queen. Father, a tinkerer and herbal enthusiast, had been renowned in our last village for his unique and powerful creations. When Mother had died earlier that winter, he readily agreed to a change of scenery. He was too broken to stay where every building and person reminded him of his bondmate.

What fools would bind themselves and allow themselves to be broken into unsalvageable pieces later? The Mastersons, apparently.

The bonding ball was as much a wedding ceremony, as it was a ritual magical binding of souls. Two independent people smooshed together into one clump of misery. I would never choose to take that risk. I saw how it had broken Father. I would never break like him.

I tapped on my sunny necklace beneath my dress. Mother had bought this for my seventh birthday—the year my magic should have shown up. But she died before giving it to me. Father gave it in her stead, but it always seemed too painful for him to look upon. It had glowed since the moment I put it on, but every year, it seemed to dim more and more. Perhaps the magic charm was waning. Fitting, really, for a magicless woman to have a magicless necklace.

It was rare that noble bloodlines resulted in complete duds, thus, my confusing state of noble daughter/servant/almost-herbal apprentice/over-educated errand-running girl. When the mask was on, I was a noble lady at the king's table. When it was off, I was scrubbing potatoes in the kitchen with the washer girls. Anything to make up for my deficiencies.

I felt the heat from a burst of flame at my back, roaring back at a burst of shadowy clouds, and swallowed down my envy of Leon's magic. He was the strongest infernus. Wind, water, fire, earth: all were valued gifts of the kingdom. The most magical led us—as they should—and the weakest supported them in whatever ways they could.

And then there was me. The weakest of all. Which is why I struggled to be useful and helpful. To not dishonor Father further, nor Leon or King Harold.

As long as I could please them, I could be happy where I was planted, no matter what the others said. Maybe I could learn enough to research beside Father, find a cure for the queen, and establish myself as worthwhile and worth keeping around. Or maybe Chef would recognize skill and recommend me as a head housekeeper of a noble family.

Helpful. Endlessly helpful. Able Aelia. I shoved a smile on my face. I would choose to be happy. Father loved me. Leon was my friend. I could use my hands. I could use my mind. It would be fine. I squeezed my eyes shut for a moment. I would be fine.

I turned my head toward a sudden squawk as a bird startled at my arrival. I was far away from the castle now, and a cool wind from the coast made me pull my cloak tight. I needed to focus—it was time to help the queen.

The journey was longer than I would have liked before I turned off the main wide road and headed over a creek and up a rise to the inner curve of the eastern mountain. The ground was not cracked here, and fresh green shoots burst through the soil. The light from the castle was like a mirror reflection in the sunlight, but it was barely visible. The trees became denser, and the soil a bit more rocky.

I searched in the shadowed coves of the hills until I found a most glorious sight: a tight bush with bright yellow flowers that glimmered in the morning light. It had six petals with orange stamen and smelled like vanilla—a racerbristle bush.

I snapped off most of the flowers and collected the lot, trimming a small portion of the root like Father had taught me, along with a single stem of the leaves and bark. The whole plant was useful and could be toxic like any medicine if mismeasured into the potion. I skipped to the creek to rinse the sticky resin from my fingertips and bounced down the path again. The day had undoubtedly improved. I could now easily find the rest of the herbs we needed. I marked the location with the bald peak and the creek that flowed from the castle so I could return next week for more of the bush without stressing it.

The sun beat against my neck, reminding me of each minute I'd been out here—much longer than I intended. I tugged the cloak from my neck; it was a terrible idea to wear it in this heat, and now it was in the way. I'd found white thieves behind the oaks and was in the midst of digging up the bulbs when a deer bounded past me. Crashing through the brush, it landed with a clatter. The antlers nearly caught on the nearby branches before it sprinted past and disappeared. Then the baying began. Three dogs and five horsemen wove between the trees toward me. Each of the riders held a bow with an arrow strung.

I threw up my hands and fell back against the tree as one cocked arrow turned my way.

"Where did it go?" the man demanded. My shaky hand pointed, though why they asked instead of following the echo of their dogs was beyond me. Four horses took off down the animal path. My basket lay overturned at my feet. Wincing, I lifted it and heaved out a breath of relief. The plants were undamaged if a bit dusty.

I placed them back into the basket, but when I returned to my trowel, the last rider strode up beside me.

"Aelia?"

I froze. I would know that voice anywhere. I brushed off my dirty hands on my woolen cloak, pulled it over my cotton garb, and ducked into a curtsy. "Your Highness."

"We're alone." Leon smiled, his dimple in view.

"Leon." I corrected myself, but still tucked into the curtsy for one more moment.

His riding outfit was cream with red and orange piping, and his horse was as white as his clothing. His blond hair contrasted with the coal of his eyes, and he was all the things that made up masculine beauty. The sharp cut of his chin and dimpled cheek had charmed the whole land, me included, at one point. His expression slowly shifted to confusion. His weighted gaze drifted slowly from my worn boots to my knees, undoubtedly stained from kneeling, to my unkempt hair that had unraveled from the day's work. If I was unlucky, which I often was, I likely had dirt on my face too. So pretty.

"What are you doing in my hunt, dressed as you are?" His face glinted with mirth.

"I apologize, Leon. I was gathering herbs for your mother. I didn't realize you and your men were hunting here today. It's my mistake."

He turned behind him, looking at the castle tower in the distance, chuckling. "You've come a long way."

"Yes. The conditions were not quite right by the castle. So I needed to journey farther."

"On your own?"

"Always, Leon."

"You could always ask me to come with you. Aren't you afraid?"

I glanced up at him at his question. "No. You keep the kingdom safe. The animals pay me no mind, and the bears run from my singing."

"That bad of a singer, huh?" He grinned, the pearly whites of his teeth radiant against his deeply tanned skin.

"Perhaps. I like to think they just want to be left alone like most of us." I smiled back warmly, wondering if he would linger or return to the hunt. "I mean, not that I want to be away from you. After all." I stopped my sputtering.

He was gorgeous, but as usual, my nerves twittered in my gut. As a woman of the court, especially since we'd caused mischief around the castle together as twelve-year-olds, it would be a lie to say I'd never wondered if I could catch his eye, make him love me, and become queen. Magic or no magic, true love could overcome the obstacles between us. He could undo the law stating that the magicless could not lead. And he was handsome, so very handsome. The thought made me smile more genuinely. If only my future subjects could see their filthy future queen now.

The tone of the dogs changed as if they had turned back toward us. A whistle pierced the forest, quieting the hounds and bringing my attention back to the present. The prince straightened. He reached for my basket. "It is quite the journey back up. Unfortunately, I cannot take you with me, but may I assist with your load? I could return it faster to the healer."

"Oh, well, yes." I ducked and gathered five more of the exposed white thieves' bulbs before handing the lot to the prince. "Thank you, Leon, but you don't have to help."

"It's my pleasure to help a lady, especially one so lovely as yourself. The seers told me it would be a bright day today. Your hair nearly glitters from the sunlight through the trees."

And if I wasn't sunburned already, my cheeks were undoubtedly red. "Th-thank you, Leon." I dipped into a curtsy as the other men returned, their horses clomping and circling the prince with narrowed and suspicious gazes thrown at me. Now that I was not in front of an arrow, I recognized some of the party with some of the noble lords, the village leaders on the plains, and Lord Masterson. I kept my head low, aching to disappear back up to the castle, as I watched Leon return to his stiff role of the prince. The haughty tilt of the nobles' noses seemed exaggerated from where I stood. I smiled and turned to escape their attention.

Before me, my friend Leon shifted by icy degrees into Prince Leon, His Royal Highness. "My good sirs, you remember Lady Aelia."

I froze as the group stared. A few sucked in sharp breaths. They hadn't recognized me until then. I closed my eyes to gather myself before applying my trademark smile. Then I turned back to them.

Each met my gaze, yet no one smiled except the prince. "My lords." I curtsied again and gestured desperately to the great wilderness. "Don't let me keep you from your next great hunt!" My pitchy laughter was painful even to my ears. "Good luck out there." I dipped. "Your Highness."

But the men were no longer looking at me. They all stared at the ground, suddenly amused. My foot grew uncomfortably hot, and an unpleasant odor filled the air. I looked down to see one of the dogs actively peeing on my boot.

Chuckles murmured through the group as I squealed, backpedaled, and slipped in the loose dirt, falling on my backside. The dog, having already finished, kicked some dirt behind him. At me. My shoe and the edge of my gown dripped the vile liquid. And a few of the lords were laughing.

The prince whistled, and the dog ran off. His expression was conflicted, his gaze flicking between the lords, but as he looked toward me, he attempted a soft grin. "It seems that he likes you."

My smile was more challenging to pin in place this time. I rose and brushed myself off. "If His Highness says so. I must be heading home. Thank you again, my lords, Le—Your Highness." I curtsied. "Goodbye." My hand covered my forehead, the heat of my skin no longer only from the sun, as I bustled off the hillside and dashed behind the thick cotton brush.

Out of sight, I dropped my head into both hands, willing the jeering of the lords to fade even a little from memory. My toes squelched within my boot. Boots whose leather I hadn't recently polished, apparently, or sealed from water or...other liquids. My rear was sore from the hard landing. The right side of my skirt, now wet, hung heavily. And the odor worsened as it baked in the noontime sun. Despair knocked at my heart, but I shoved it away.

I had to focus on what had gone well. I had found what I needed, the prince would bring the basket up for me, and my father would be pleased. The queen could feel better. And I could restore my reputation with the lords by degrees somehow. Tonight was the blasted ball, after all. I could earn their admiration with my grace, presence, and ethereal beauty. If anyone deigned to dance with me, I could impress them with my confident steps. Nothing, not even the awkwardness of that meeting, could deflate me. We finally had what we needed for Queen Gemaline's potion.

Chapter Five

The Ball

My pace was frantic by the time I made it back to the castle. The main road led uphill, and time undoubtedly slowed as I pushed myself up the endless ascent despite my burning thighs. The luz tower was a north star for direction but taunted me as it hardly seemed to get closer. Thank the sun and stars that Leon had taken the herbs, or they would have wilted the way I was in the beating sun. Now, I just needed to find him.

I raced to the prince's rooms first, in case he had expected me to grab them, only to be turned away by a sneering guard who informed me that the prince was already at the ball for last-minute preparations. I then swept through my room, finding it also without a basket. Reluctantly, I dragged myself down the hall toward my father's workspace to see if it had been left there. I braced for his displeasure. I now knew where the herbs grew, so I could go again—maybe tomorrow, if needed—but if Leon had forgotten them or lost them...no, he wouldn't let me down. He couldn't have...

Stepping slowly toward the corridor, I heard the clear, sober voice of my father. He sounded pleased. I rushed around the corner.

"And you found these on your hunt?" he asked.

"Yes, Lord Remsha. We were chasing this glorious buck," Leon answered. My brows furrowed.

"How fortuitous, you saw them and gathered them," Father replied. "The seven stars were shining on you today." The prince lifted a finger as if to speak again, I hoped to clarify. By now, I stood in the hall, stunned by the prince's words. My father waved me toward them. As I approached, I saw my father's pleased face crumple into one of embarrassment as he took in my filthy state. He searched about us as if looking for some closet to shove me into, but the prince chose that moment to turn.

Father laughed awkwardly. "Your Highness, you must forgive her appearance. She's either been tossed in a dust storm or had less luck and more work searching for these herbs than you did!"

The prince smiled and shrugged an apologetic shoulder at me.

My breaths were coming too fast, and I fought back my indignation at Leon not correcting my father. "But of course, Father, I was searching. I—" I glanced at the prince, who raised a brow. "I-I'm so glad the herbs for our great queen were recovered today." My tone sharpened. "The prince leads the nation with light and hope."

Prince Leon's smile looked a bit sheepish. "Indeed. Well, the ball awaits. I hope to see the fair lady there?"

Father patted the prince's shoulder—too intimately for his rank—as they both turned down the hall. "She'll be there. I have a surprise for her, and therefore, for you. We'll turn her around in no time." The prince's gaze was fixed on my father's hand, which now rested on his forearm. Father retracted it and rubbed his hands together awkwardly. The prince clicked his heels with a terse nod to Father and then me, before he headed toward the ballroom.

My father's smile lingered until the prince was out of earshot before turning to me. "What am I to do with you, child? You look...poor. We cannot have that. And what is on your boot? Why is there a leaf in your hair? It couldn't be a racerbristle, but it's similar. Did you roll around in the forest? Come. Come with me." Tucking my hand into his elbow, my father escorted me through the servants' passages to my room, avoiding the common, bustling hallways and judgmental looks of the nobles.

He shut the door and grasped my shoulders, brushing my cheek with his thumb. "I was the worst of fathers, the worst of men to you last night. I'm so ashamed. Could you ever in that big heart of yours imagine a way to forgive me?"

"But of—"

"No, no. Don't answer yet. Just look!" With a flourish, he threw open my wardrobe. A silver ballgown hung to the floor, white gloves were draped over the hanger, and sparkling white shoes sat beside the dress. "Look, my honeystar, it even matches your hair! The seers said I could find something on the market street, and it was such a good deal at the store. It was the last of its kind in stock, but I knew my daughter had to have it. Can you forgive me now, my sweet girl?"

I squeezed his hand, my smile fixed like flint as I took it all in. It did match my hair. So well. Too well. I would look like a wraith, a ghost, better suited for hanging from the ceiling as the chandelier than mixing among the nobility. But his face was so earnest. He had even apologized. He loved me.

"Of course, Father. It's okay. Thank you for this dress."

My father grinned at me, obviously pleased with himself. "Now hurry, girl. The ball starts soon, and you cannot be late!" He gave one last grimace at my appearance before sweeping out of the room.

I turned back to the dress from last season, tugging softly at the square neckline, wondering if Father even realized the style was now a broad scoop. But it was too late to fix. The dress I had planned to wear was nowhere to be found, and I was out of time. It was nearly too late to bathe.

I felt happy he got it for me. I was certain I could feel happy.

The bath wasn't able to restore my aching muscles, but it served its purpose to clean me up. I tried to create a swooping hairstyle to cover the dark swirl on my neck that still had an upward-rising twist. Fashionable enough, and no one would see it. The hairstyle was also not in fashion. Nothing about me would be, but at least no one else could see my new beauty mark.

The dress was exactly as bad as I'd expected. The only mercy was that my pink-hued, sunburned cheeks added some color to my wraithlike appearance. Even my blue eyes seemed bleached out in all the shades of silver and white. I reached for my mother's necklace and placed it just below the notch of my sternum. Maybe I could draw attention to that, and no one would notice the dress. As white as I was, perhaps I could blend in with the curtains…or the tablecloths. An image of myself lying across the royal tables as the nobles set their wine glasses and plates upon me made me laugh. I would be the lumpiest of tables.

A knock at the door pulled me back to the present. Double-checking that my hair covered the mark, I glided to my father in my new, pinching shoes. His darker olive skin tones, earth-brown eyes, and black hair with just a hint of gray were all suited for silver, and his matching suit appeared much more flattering on him than my attire was on me.

"What a vision," he breathed. "You are ethereal. I shall have to buy you more dresses just like this!" He pulled me toward him in a tight hug. "Come, my dear. Let me continue to make it up to you at the bonding ball."

I tried to smile. "Thank you, Father, it is a generous gift."

His eyes drifted to the necklace, and his cheek jerked. Instinctively, he rubbed at the scar on his hand. His Adam's apple bobbed.

I watched him rub his thumb over the rolling skin. "Was it worth it, Father? The bond?" He glanced down and, noticing his habit, shoved his hands into his pockets. "You paid such a cost."

"Your mother was everything good and light." He cleared his throat, the dark shadows of memories vanishing from his eyes. "But now we must focus on someone else's happiness. Not just on our own sorrows. Enough with insipid questions."

He turned and offered me his elbow, leading us out to the main hall and up the grand staircase. The walls contained more luz lamps than usual and beamed with light, making the room seem brighter than daylight. A steady stream of visitors crossed the ornate marble floor toward the ballroom, all dressed in their finest. I noted that several of the more popular, and therefore more powerful, young ladies were adorned with feathers in their hair—another new trend. I'd need to collect some the next time I was out.

At the ballroom, the caller announced us, and Father walked in with a proud tilt to his shoulders. The men bowed to each other, and the women curtsied, but behind fluttering fans, smiles soured to snickers as their eyes flicked over me. Several seers meandered, blessing the guests with a greeting as they passed like specters.

"My dear, go mingle. I need to catch up with Lord Brynett." Father motioned toward the group of young men and women at the front of the ballroom near the archway where the Mastersons would be bound and wed.

The noblemen and women milled around each other like wasps flitting around carrion before the massive windows that displayed the glorious sunset. The Mastersons were the center of it all, laughing and beaming at each other in a true demonstration of infatuated obsession.

It was the fifth bonding ceremony of the season. These balls, added between the usual holidays, were a social dance I knew well. I would eat and smile, and occasionally, some foreign lord would ask me to dance before he was taught better by the others. We would watch the happy couple be sprayed with river water dripping from razewa branches as they decided to be trapped together forever. Then, I would leave and pretend my loneliness was a welcome state. So, as usual, when my father turned, distracted, I headed to the back wall by the banquet table.

The elderly ladies gathered there were too polite to be rude to my face; some were even quite cordial. Lady Brynett dipped her head, and I returned a shallow curtsy. The lady was one of the queen's main attendants, and I often saw her tending to the queen when I came with the potions. King Harold turned around the corner beside us and caught her up in conversation, so after I greeted him, I twisted away and sipped on a glass of something too sweet.

A door along the wall opened behind me, and Chef struggled to get through while carrying a large tray. I moved to help, but her glare froze me in place. Heaving it onto the table, she finished arranging the desserts. She murmured, "Are you an apparition? Or here to match the calla lilies?"

I took a fake drink, my lips hidden by the glass as I replied, "A gift from my father."

Chef looked me up and down again before moving a breadbasket to the left. "He's better with herbs than with fashion."

A genuine smile split my face but lost some of its brightness as I responded. "He felt he needed to apologize. He...tries."

Chef snorted with very little grace. "Seems to me that he could not do things that hurt you in the first place." I glanced at her, shocked, but she had already turned toward the kitchen.

The Mastersons were near, edging closer to the king. How did I end up so close to the main throng of people?

"He bumped my arm at the market," Lady Marva said. "That's when the first mark appeared."

Lord Masterson's eyes were honeyed and fixed sweetly upon her face. "Even before the mark, I knew that you were the most perfect woman in the whole realm for me." The courtiers twittered and fanned their faces as they whispered back and forth.

"I knew you were handsome, but you convinced me with your bravery fighting against those horrible spyrings from the mining tunnels. The Shade has no shame using such evil to attack us."

I glanced up at this, having not heard about the attack from the giant spider-like monsters of the deep. Luz was mined from the mountain the castle sat upon, and occasional monsters were gossiped about by the workers. But I'd never heard of an attack on the surface.

"There, there, Lady Marva," King Harold set his hand upon Lord Masterson's shoulder. "Let's not dwell on unpleasant things during the moment we've gathered to celebrate your bonding."

She curtsied. "Of course, Your M—Highness. The prince and king lead the nation with light and hope." The gathering around us murmured the words back in response. King Harold smiled as brightly as the sconces behind him, and he nodded magnanimously, preening under all the adoration of his people.

I'd been slinking away from the gathering of people when a male voice said loudly, "My lady, watch out! A dog!"

My body lurched at the memory of the odor and warmth. Unwilling to be peed on yet again, I leaped to the side with a yelp and swirled to search the floor around me. But there was no dog. This was a ball—of course, there was no dog. Heat billowed up my cheeks and sweat gathered at the base of my neck. Three of the lords from this morning's hunt now stood between me and the king's posse, cross-armed, with halfcocked smirks that belied no friendly tones. Leon had been approaching his father's side and turned with a frown but made no move to correct or deflect their behavior.

I curtsied a goodbye to the lords before I bumped into Lady Nora, an unbonded betrothed of one of the lords behind me. "Leaving so soon?" she asked.

"I heard her father couldn't afford anything else. I saw it too—the late Lady Ernst's dress." A woman whispered loudly while leaning in toward Lady Nora. "Yellow from a dog might actually do that sallow dress a great service."

I stumbled back a pace and moved away, placing myself more in the center of the room. "My lady, could I have this dance?" A man I barely recognized approached me. Relief flooded through me, and I smiled. Anything to get away from—

His gaze fell to the hem of my dress. "On second thought, can you smell that?" His eyes gleamed with cruelty. "I'll pass." My jaw fell slack.

The group had gathered and muttered just loudly enough for me to hear it.

"I saw her in the kitchen."

"Did you see that filth on her neck at the dinner table? Did she roll with the pigs?"

"He said she was digging in the dirt. I bet there is some still under her nails."

"How can she be noble? I mean, *really?*"

Words like arrows assaulted me from every corner. The snickers increased from every side. Their eyes on me, fingers pointed, noble fangs bared. Their fans lashed sharply, beautifully hiding sharper words. Leon looked torn, but his father set a hard hand on his shoulder. The prince stiffened, his face resetting to flint like his father's. At their unwelcome expressions, my spine straightened. The king glanced toward the doorway, his message clear. It was time for me to go and spare him any further embarrassment.

Racing toward the escape, I iced over my heart, holding back the tears and refusing to worsen what was already a terrible moment. It had been better when I was ignored. It had been better when no one had noticed me at all. Why today did they say aloud what they had once only murmured in private? It was likely a long time coming, but none of the lords had ever seen me in this state before. I had brought shame to the king and to Leon. I had also shamed my father, who made no move away from his companions to follow me out of the ballroom.

No footman moved to open the doors for me as I approached. Nearly falling upon the handles, a smoky whisp slipped through the crack, but I paid it no mind. Wrenching open both doors, a wall of thick black smoke billowed in, curling and racing through the threshold. A figure stepped forward through the haze, and I found myself face-to-face with Death himself.

Behind him, the boiling cloud of shadow filled the hallway. It reached forward, wrapping around the base of my dress, then creeping into the ballroom like a cauldron full of spiders had been poured out. It moved with intelligence, sliding, grasping, and climbing as it transformed my escape route into a blackened pit. The nobles in the room drew back from the shadow's touch, but I was already surrounded. It clung to my gown, and its cool touch slipped past my ankles like grasses at the bottom of a lake. From within the cloud, a man emerged. He was clothed in black, with a long black jacket, black gloves, and a silken black cravat. The details were lost behind the obscuring smoke, but the Shade's bright green eyes were fixed on me.

I was trapped. Ensorcelled. Paralyzed. The weight of his presence filled my mind and surged through my body until I was frozen like stone. My skin prickled. Hot. Electric. Ice that burned. But I didn't feel the sting of shame as I had moments before, but fear. Mortal terror gripped me. A wayward tear trickled down my cheek. As his gaze followed the tear's slow progress, whatever power he had over me lessened a fraction, and I could breathe again. His eyes flicked back up to mine, and his brow furrowed.

The sounds of panic and backpedaling behind me suddenly halted. The entire room held its breath, terrified but morbidly curious to see what he would do with me.

So I did what any lady would do in a moment of panic when faced with terrifying courtly egos.

I curtsied.

Chapter Six

The Shade

I dipped low and full of grace, hardly even trembling as I curtsied in the face of the nightmare before me. Moments became hours and seconds years. I willed him to pass and did not rise. But as he silently walked to stand before me, the shadows flickered and coiled even higher, now about my arms and waist. My wide dress shifted as his legs pressed close enough to move the ruffles and hoops back. The shadows swept up my shoulder, playing with the ends of my hair.

Behind me, a collective gasp hissed through the room, and his thumb caught the tear that wavered on my jaw. Startled, I glanced up to his face. His brows pinched, and his eyes stormed. Anger and hatred and violence and murder all swirled within them. I should have felt more afraid. I should have trembled in terror. But his touch exuded comfort, and his caress was a relief. My chin lifted into his touch on its own.

Subtly, he pulled me up with a pressure beneath my jaw. I rose, but he didn't release me. A spark ignited and shot from my neck to my chest, hot and sudden, and I stepped back with a gasp. Afraid he would perceive it as an insult, I dipped again quickly, then pulled myself to the side to allow him to pass.

This was the Shade, the one responsible for the oily storms that plagued us. The poisoner of the queen. The root of the drought in our lands. He was evil incarnate, a menace, a monster and darkness and curses in human form.

I felt his gaze on me like the burn from the sun, though I kept my eyes on the ground. He turned. The shadows swirled about him like a vortex, and he raised one gloved hand. Then he snapped.

From behind him, the shadows carried three men suspended in their black embrace, dressed in plain clothes, battered and bruised, dripping and bleeding, along the ballroom corridor until they were thrown to the floor in the middle of the room. The prince stepped forward, a hand hesitantly reaching for the bloody men before he turned in a fury to the Shade.

"What is the meaning of this?" he barked.

The shadows darkened and writhed like dogs at the end of a leash. The Shade leaned back on his heel, his voice rumbling like a distant thunder. "I came to return your property. I found them on mine."

A flame lit in the prince's palm. "You have made a mistake coming here, murdering good guards." From behind the prince, a group of armored men swept behind him, arms up, gusts ready. The galers prepared to battle.

But the Shade simply chuckled. The sound vibrated through my core. From the prickling of my scalp to the tingling of my toes, I felt every word of his husky, low voice. "It is not I who is mistaken." Dark green eyes flicked to mine and back. "Do not mistake this warning as mercy."

"Now!" the prince shouted. Flames curled from the prince's palm, and magicked wind blew it toward the Shade. Nobles and ladies screamed as they tucked into the corners behind the tables and pillars and each other.

Time slowed. A ball of flame, hot and angry, boiled in the air as it barreled toward the Shade. I was off to the side, but not far enough. The consuming fire decimated a table, burst the linens into flame, and destroyed the flowers as they burned before me. Ash held the stem and the petals in suspension for a moment before it crumbled into dust. The writhing heat coiled, churning closer like cream swirling in hot water. Beautifully. Horribly. My life would end in fire. I saw the prince's expression as he realized I stood too close to the flame. At least he looked adequately conflicted that I was about to be killed at his hand.

Then I was yanked away, a pressure squeezing around my waist as I fell backward, my face to the ceiling. My vision went black. Strange. I'd expected to see light from the flames as the fire killed me. But something caught my head before it hit the floor, and warmth curled behind me. My hands grasped fabric. A collar. Death wasn't painful at all. I realized a moment later...Death breathed.

I ducked my chin to meet the brightest eyes, like spring leaves not yet darkened by the sun, studying my face. Gone was the murderous glint of his expression. Instead, the gaze of the Shade held...something else. I inhaled, expecting Death to smell like peat, but he smelled of pine and forests and evenings in fall and midnight in winter. He held me backward, like the end of a dangerous dance. His eyes seared my skin as they regarded me, and his thumb tilted my chin as he took in the mark on my neck with a furrowed brow. He brushed it softly. My skin prickled in goosebumps as that shock raced through my system again.

Above us, the shadows behind his head lightened and swirled, backlit as the fire raged above it all, passing us by. The shadows danced and flickered like smoke in a sunset. The roar of the flame was muted in our dark cocoon. The shadows were a misty window to the inferno around us.

"Beautiful," I whispered, before I realized I had said that out loud. Wide-eyed, I glanced down at the Shade, who only raised his brow. The flames stopped, and everything went dark again. His palm brushed my cheek, I felt stone behind my head, and all at once, the smoke swirled and disappeared.

I was lying on the warm stone floor. Above me, tapestries and curtains crackled with fire, and dark gray smoke drifted hazily through the room from the charred walls and doors. My once-silver gown was rumpled but not stained, though the hem closest to the room's center was singed. I was unharmed, uninjured. But the guards by the entrance hadn't made it. Despite being farther from the Shade and hiding behind a column, both the columns and the men were charred beyond recognition. I scrambled away, trembling. My back hit the wall.

"He's gone! What a coward!" the prince began, his regal voice back in place. "Forgive the rude interruption, my honored guests and our bonding pair. Let us take the ceremony to the gardens." He clapped twice, and the room emptied with loud chatter as everyone escaped through the back doors. His voice lowered as he spoke to a washer on his way out behind the crowd. "Clean this up. The next bonding ball is in a week. Get the unfortunate lady to a healer." Prince Leon cast a worried look at me, our eyes connecting for a moment, before he turned his back and spoke to a seer. He said something else, but the sounds were warbling.

A face crouched before me. Chef.

She gathered my hands in hers and lifted me from the ground to unsteady feet. Her lips were moving, but the sounds were mushy. Despite my lack of response, she tucked me beside her and swept me down the servant's hall. Then I was in the bath, her gentle hands washing me. Still in a daze, I was taken to my bed. Chef's palm pressed against my cheek, tender as always when she was treating me for one wound or another. Her eyes widened as she looked at my jaw. She pulled my hair forward and patted it twice.

Then I fell once again into darkness, but at least this darkness was sleep.

Chapter Seven

Hide Yourself

B irds chirped merrily from my window as bright sunshine landed on my pillow. My eyes were crusted and aching, and dried tear tracks lined my cheeks. I brushed the evidence away hastily. Surely, last night wasn't real.

"You're awake."

I sat up with a start. "L—My prince." I dipped my head, unable to curtsy, and tried to smile as I raked my fingers through my knotted hair. "I apologize, I didn't know to expect... I didn't know you were here."

Leon leaned back in my dressing chair, arms crossed and his face deeply lined with concern. "You gave us quite a scare, Aelia."

"I'm sorry."

I startled when the king pushed off the wall he had been leaning against behind me. His arms were crossed, the harsh flat line of his lips underscoring the irritation of his eyes. "Quite."

Prince Leon continued. "I felt horrible having to attack that monster with you so near. My very chest was split in agony with the weight of the crown."

"But he had to take him out. You understand, don't you?" King Harold asked. His presence filled the room, powerful and merciless.

"Yes, I-I understand." My mind rushed through the events of the evening with a thunderclap of emotions—the Shade, the fire...the guards. "I'm so sorry I was...in the way. The guards, did any of them...?"

"All dead," Prince Leon said.

My gaze fell to my hands. "I'm sorry."

The prince unfurled his arms and leaned forward. "As am I." He studied my face, and my hands twitched to cover it. "How are you alive?"

"What?"

His dark amber eyes stared hard into mine. "What did he say to you? Why did my guards die, while you survived?"

I furrowed my brow. "I'm certain I don't know, Your Highness. He said nothing."

The king took one further step closer. "You can't expect us to believe that. You colluded with the Shade and brought him to my doorstep! You"—he sputtered—"you *curtsied* to the monster!"

An icy grip seized my chest. "I coll—Your Majesty and Your Highness, I would never. I've been dedicated to the crown and you and the queen and our people for my entire life! You have sheltered us, given us a home—"

"Your status is such, though, that anyone could understand why you might reach for power not your own." King Harold frowned. "You could have made a dark pact in a desperate grab for evil magic."

My jaw dropped indignantly. "I could *not*. Not ever. I aim to help and be a gift to everyone I meet. I would never hurt the crown or you in this way."

Prince Leon studied me before he sat back, all tension gone from his shoulders. He scratched at his chin. "Very well. I had to be sure." King Harold seemed less satisfied with my answer.

I let out a long breath. "Of course, Your Highness. I...I understand."

"I'm also sorry on behalf of the other young people of the court. I know they hurt you yesterday," the prince added.

Unexpected angry tears sprang up against my will. I tried to laugh them away with a quick wipe of a finger under my lid. "I'm sure I would have done the same in their shoes."

His gaze captured mine. "I'm not sure that's true, Aelia. I think you may be too sweet for such low humor." He smiled, his dimple warming up his face in the expression I knew best. He was my friend, as much as a prince could be anyway. The king crossed his arms. I pulled my hair around my shoulders in discomfort at the silence, and the prince's gaze dropped to my neck. His eyes narrowed at the mark.

"Chef says it's only a mole. I cannot remove it." The prince's expression flickered with something I couldn't name, but his dimple was gone. Any warmth remaining in the room fled with it.

Huffing out through his nose, he sat back. "I'm certain she is right." He crossed his arms again. "I must return to see the progress of the repairs."

Relief filled me. "Alright. Thank you for checking on me."

He stood and took me in again. "You are my responsibility as much as anyone in the kingdom. We must care for our own."

"Speaking of which," King Harold held up his hand to pause Leon's exit. "The castle is in an uproar. The ballroom was destroyed. The guards are searching for whatever weakness allowed that scoundrel entrance. The whole world is now eyeing the other as a conspirator." The king's black eyes pierced like a sliver. "Lay low, Aelia. Better to rest from the burns that he no doubt gave you, the reason you must always stay in your room to recover."

I frowned. "But Your Highness, I feel—"

"Terrible burns. Horrible. Only saved because you hid behind the monster who shielded himself and accidentally protected you." He glared at me meaningfully. "Remember: Prosperity requires sacrifice."

I was to lie? My lips pinched in confusion. "Y-Yes, Your Highness."

Leon and King Harold exited into a group of soldiers, their tromping steps echoing as they made their way from my chambers.

The door in the back of the room that accessed the servant's passage opened, and Chef bustled in with a tray full of steaming soup, tea, and cookies. Setting it on my lap, she sat on the bed beside me. "Gave me a fright, you did. I plan to live to see my grandchildren, child, and you go getting wrapped up in that demon-spawn shadow-mongering night-licker."

I had yet to hear her curse like this. "Chef!"

"It's only the truth. That demon shouldn't be allowed to breathe or live or poison our air with his presence. It was a good thing you were so near to him. His shadows must have doused you both when the prince threw his flames. Though, how the prince could... Well, never mind. You hadn't a burn on you! It seems a shame he escaped, however." She stirred the soup and held out the spoon for me.

I jerked my head down. "A shame," I agreed as I sipped her offering. My mind conjured those bright green eyes, piercing and searching. My scalp still felt the pressure of his hands as he gently held me above the ground.

"Your mark has another line today, this one on the bottom. A swirl with two arms has started."

My eyes widened. "What does it mean? Am I sick? Should we cut it off?"

Chef's face flooded with compassion. "These kinds of things are not cured by a simple procedure, as you might know." It was nearly black, entirely too dark to be a bond mark. It had to be just a scabbing from the acid rain. I ignored the squiggle in my gut.

My father chose that moment to burst into the room. Chef stood, and the cutlery clattered against the bowl.

"My child, are you alright?" He stumbled to my bedside, clasped my hands, and leaned too close, his fermented breath burning my nostrils. "I was worried you wouldn't wake from the shock of the experience."

"I'm not convinced I'm awake yet." I rubbed my forehead, still dazed from my encounter with the prince and king. "I'm apparently terribly burned and bound to my room for the time being." At my father's examination of my very unburned features, I continued. "As ordered by the king."

"The prince and king lead our nation with light and hope," Father muttered.

I stifled a grimace. "Even so."

He patted my head before pacing in front of my bed as Chef dutifully fed me breakfast. "Fortunately, the racerbristles the prince found were of such high quality that they have improved the queen's energy. But we'll need a few more soon since I've needed to dose her higher and higher. You'll have to ask him where he found them." I swallowed the truth before it could escape. Let Leon have his moment. "You must have taught him well how to collect everything—he did a very nice job."

The room darkened as a shadow storm swept before the sun. A screaming whistle of wind ripped through the air. I shuddered as memories of the fireball in the ballroom screamed through my mind. My gaze remained fixed outside.

"The battles will last longer and be fiercer now," Father said, his back to me as he regarded the battle. "The crown must save face. Some of the king's most talented soldiers died last night because of that creature of death!"

Heat from the outside maelstrom wafted into the room. "If they continue to grow bigger and hotter, then they will destroy all the racerbristles entirely," I said quietly.

"True words, my daughter. True words." He pulled a flask from his jacket pocket, taking a long drink. "If only you could go gather more today."

Chef frowned at him before minutely shaking her head. But only the prince and I knew where the bush was found. My sense of duty twisted within me. "The king and prince..."

"Only want you to avoid being seen. Surely you could be subtle and go unnoticed, daughter. You would do it for me. You could do it for Queen Gemaline."

My stomach knotted before my concerns collapsed to silence in the face of his desperate expression. "Yes, Father. I could certainly get the rest from that bush, but then I'd need to find another source."

Father swept to my side, holding both of my cheeks in his palm. "Dearest, that would be wonderful. Since you aren't expected to be at court during your convalescence, you could search even longer and save the queen!" He nodded vigorously. "You could take the back passages with Chef—yes, and hide from the other servants." My father dragged my cloak and tossed it on my bed. "Wear this." Chef glared at him. "To protect yourself, of course."

I finished my porridge. "I can certainly do so, Father."

"Good girl. Go now."

My eyes widened with fear as I looked out the window. Tiny fire-balls which ignited oily bites of shadow rained over the courtyard. Hot, blazing winds ripped through the trees, taking even the hardiest leaf with them. "I must wait for the storm to pass."

"If you wait, the queen could worsen. She could die."

I blinked several times, the responsibility of caring for Her Majesty squeezing any breath from me. "I...I suppose I could go now."

"That's the spirit." He smiled. "Always a good helper. Always my good girl." And my father swept out of the room.

The clang of a ripped-open door brought my attention back outside to the servant who struggled against the wind to shut it again. Billowy shadows turned the midday sky as black as night—black except for the light from the fires. A washer poured water on a sill to extinguish a small flame.

"You don't have to do this, you know," Chef muttered. "He could go himself, the lazy buzzard."

"I know where the bush is, actually. Besides, he's older than me and must concoct the potions, Chef. It's only right." I rubbed my face again and took a final sip from the tea. "Thank you for bringing this. I feel better already." I sat stiffly before the mirror and brushed my hair, distinctly ignoring the dark circles under my red-rimmed eyes. I looked a bit like a skeleton.

Chef approached behind me, and our gazes met in the reflection. "He was right about one thing, though. Make yourself scarce. The nobles were tolerable before, but if they find you, they may be dreadful now. People are muttering about you, my dear. Don't let them catch you unawares."

Icy water dripped down my spine, and goosebumps pricked my arms. "I have nothing to hide. But I'll be careful. Thank you, Chef."

"The Shade saved you, my girl."

"The Shade saved himself, like the king said." I stood, picked up my basket and cloak, and kissed her wrinkled cheek.

She kissed me back and murmured. "Someday, I want you to say no. I know it won't be today. But when you realize the true cost of never saying no, I hope to the seven stars you take your courage and say it firmly."

I paused, her words uncomfortable and unwanted. "Thank you for breakfast. You are the best of all things."

She smiled sadly at me and gently placed her palm on my cheek. Her touch was a comfort in the storm. "Don't forget a second light. Go quickly. I'll have dinner ready upon your return." Chef gathered the tray and bowls, her movements too heavy for the indifferent expression she wore, and with a squeeze on my shoulder, she silently led me down the servant corridor.

Chapter Eight

Prosperity Requires Sacrifice

T he battle storm raged every day that week and late into the nights. After the first day, when I'd taken everything I could from the racerbristle without killing it outright, I began searching farther and farther as my father requested an increased supply. He looked so haggard and stressed, I felt compelled to help him even more than usual. My cloak was becoming embarrassingly holey since the small oily fireballs struck it each time I journeyed from the covered awnings of the streets in the city center. The heat and wind had desiccated everything for miles. The Shade would kill us all, and the prince might be helping him.

I continued to do as my king had asked and hid from everyone. Leon had checked on me a few times and had even sent the healer to help keep up appearances. Thankfully, Chef was there to be sure the healer came in the mornings or evenings when I was actually there. He spent his time snacking on the tray that Chef kept stocked for me and ignored the burns on my shoulders from the acid rain.

I was about to slip down into the servants' hall yet again when the front door to my bedroom opened, and Leon let himself in. He quietly set the lock before turning and searching for me when he discovered I wasn't in bed. Frowning, I returned and sat upon the edge of the mattress. Leon pulled up the chair, regarded my damaged cloak, and sat heavily. I frowned at his gaunt face, deep worry lines, and the pale, yellow tone of his skin. He moved stiffly, much less graceful than I'd ever seen him. His dimple was nowhere to be found; his gaze distant and fixed on something out the window. A few of the other inferni must be working, as billows of fire still shot out from the tower windows.

"Are you okay, Leon?"

His gaze flicked to me for only a moment before settling again in the distance. "There is never enough time to recover my strength. Fighting the Shade takes all of my energy. Father continues to demand more. He is so desperate to please the nobles that he's bleeding me dry." He rubbed his eyes with his palms. "But as he also says, 'Prosperity requires sacrifice.'"

"Has the Shade…" I swallowed, my mind conjuring the wisps of black smoke and strong hands. "Has he returned to the castle?"

The prince slowly dragged his gaze to my face with a hostility I'd never seen before. "Wouldn't you know?"

Shaking my head vigorously, I leaned forward. "I wouldn't. I never met the Shade before that moment and hope to never meet him again." I shuddered. "The ordeal was so"—green eyes flashed before me—"troubling." I sucked in a breath. "You know me, Leon. You know I wouldn't hurt you in that way."

His lips pulled up as he crossed one leg over the other. "Not in that way."

Though he merely repeated my words, they sounded full of other meaning. "My prince?"

Sucking in a breath through his nose, he stood abruptly. "I need your help, Aelia."

"Yes, anything, my prince. Name it, and I will do it." I stood up as well. "I've been searching at my father's request—"

"I know." He sliced his hand through the air, cutting off my words. "But we need to do something different—something big—to stop these endless battles. They are weakening our city and me. The nobles are unhappy. Father is furious. The seers brought us an old prophecy. Perhaps it's time to see if we can trigger it."

"The seers?" My mind raced through all the books I'd read. Which prophecy was he referring to? "When was it seen?"

"The day you arrived," the prince said with a stern look. He watched me as if to read my thoughts as he spoke.

"The ruin of kingdoms from the weak ones come,

but bind, entwine, and tie them some.

As day from night, the brightness fights,

A sacrifice will make it right. "

"Hmm. The brightness fights." I gestured to the window and smiled brightly. "You seem to be doing a good job of that already. The fire lights up everything, and the luz glows stronger than ever." My attempt to lighten the mood fell flat. Leon's brow worked as he seemed to mull over my words. Clearing my throat, I asked, "How have I never heard that prophecy?"

"The king has kept this one in his chambers. We thought it referred to the peasants. But now..." He shook his head as he pulled out a list from his jacket. "We need you to grab these herbs for the ceremony. We think there's a way we can appease nature's forces, rejuvenate our land, and even push out the Shade. But I need more power, I need more fire, and then we can end him for good. My father demands I—I mean *we*—end this now."

I set my hand on his forearm, and he covered it with his. His dimple returned for the briefest moment. "I would do anything, Leon."

Tapping his finger on the list. "The seers require these things by tonight. At dusk."

I glanced down at the many items. "My father has many of these dried."

"They must be fresh."

Huffing out a breath, I shook off the fatigue that weighed my limbs as I turned for the door. I regarded his worn face and untucked hair. He put up a hand to stop me. "I am sorry, Aelia."

Poor Leon. He needed rest and hope himself. "As the king wishes. I'm always happy to help a friend. I'll return before tea."

Leon's face flashed with some emotion before a soft smile returned. "You are the very best of friends, Aelia. Thank you."

After searching all day, I procured everything on the prince's list. I proudly set to cleaning and preparing them for the evening ceremony.

My father worked beside me, chopping and boiling and measuring what we needed—the list of ingredients and the instructions for the potion between us. His jaw clenched regularly, as his fingers began to shake. I turned to reach for another bowl when he grasped my hand, his eyes wild and wide. His mouth opened and shut several times before he clenched his fist, closed his eyes, and hugged me.

I stood stock still for a moment before returning the hug. He patted my head. "There's a good girl. Always helpful." Then he released me and returned to chopping, taking a swig from a wine glass in between. Perhaps that would help his shaking.

We gathered the supplies and headed down the stairs and up the center hill. The temple stood at the top, the home and ceremonial center of the region's seers. Besides meting out daily prophecies, they sometimes acted as judges, mediating disputes, resolving conflicts, and assisting with peacemaking. Of course, they were present at the bonding ceremonies too. Besides those who attended the balls, tended to the queen, or left their daily reports throughout the castle, I hadn't interacted much with them. I'd never had a need, especially since I would never be bonding.

A few soldiers were posted outside the temple entrance. Within the threshold, Prince Leon and King Harold stood alongside three seers. Twenty guards gathered around them, lining the walls inside the main room. The clouds over the sun darkened the world with a sickly light. Most faces were dulled by the flickering light of the large pyre in the center of the room. As we entered, Lord Brynett passed me the lead rope of a black and white goat. I frowned but didn't question it as we made our way to the center cauldron that was held above the flames. Already boiling and billowing, the bitter smoke seared my nostrils and eyes.

The king stood to the side, and I smiled at him as I always did, curtsying with grace before him and his son. The king turned to sit in a tall-backed chair. Behind the seers, a carved stand held a massive leather-bound book. The king's gaze pierced me, freezing me in place before he shifted his attention to my father.

"All the supplies are here?"

"They are," my father answered. "Fresh as requested, as well as the potion. I wasn't sure about certain specifics since I wasn't given the final instructions, but we gathered everything on the list."

The seers surged forward and grabbed the bowls from us. The eldest seer, the leader, her head topped with an ornate, decorative hat, reached for the potion we had just finished. The seven seers circled the cauldron and set down the bowls. At some unseen signal, they grasped hands and began to dance slowly around the cauldron chanting in an ancient tongue. One by one—in various pauses of the chanting—a seer would take a bowl, lift it toward the dim light of the setting sun, then pour it into the liquid.

The bluebuds made the smoke glitter with a crackling cascade of sparks. The willow exuded a smell that reminded me of the riverside eddies. One seer tossed in bark from the razewa tree, and the cauldron ceased boiling for ten long seconds before erupting in bubbles and grumbling like thunder. Each substance produced a unique result.

Finally, they poured in the potion. After the plume of purple smoke had cleared, the head seer dipped a ladle into the brew, poured a small portion of the liquid into a bowl, and approached me.

The seers chanted together:

> "The ruin of kingdoms from weak ones come,
> but bind, entwine, and tie them some.
> As day from night, the brightness fights,
> A sacrifice will make things right.
> Lest the deep reject the vile ones
> that slink beneath and this way run.
> The stars and sun turn black as pitch,
> and light must fight to cure that which
> has doomed us all to dark decay,
> Still, love must reign and find a way."

I frowned. A handful of guards had clustered closer at my back. A rumble from the boiling pot vibrated through the room. One seer painted a symbol on the goat's forehead. Then she turned to me with the brush in her hand.

I stepped back, my voice wavering as tension gripped my stomach. "F-Father? My prince? Your Highness?"

"It's only a bit of paint, my dear," the king grumbled. "Let them paint you."

"Yes, Your Highness." My mouth turned dry as ash. But I held still as the cool paint splashed upon my forehead.

"Prosperity requires sacrifice," the head seer announced to the quiet room. "The weak must be removed, like chaff from the wheat. The weakest among us has weakened us as well." I blinked and stared at my prince. His fist pulsed, and he nearly vibrated where he stood. His father clamped down his wrist as if to still him. "The ruin of kingdoms comes, but light must find a way to save us from the dark decay. To stop the evil, to stop the death." She smiled at me benevolently. "Your sacrifice will save us all."

Father shifted back and forth on his feet, rubbing at the scar on his wrist. What sacrifice was she talking about?

The seer crooned. "The prince and king lead the nation with light and hope. A sacrifice is needed to make things right. I shall take a hair now."

I looked at the prince, who nodded slowly. He bit his lip, his eyes a bit wild as they flashed between me, the seer and the king. He shifted his weight.

"Y-Yes."

The old woman approached again and chanted as she plucked one hair from me and another from the goat and tossed them both into the vat of boiling liquid. The potion hissed; a cloud of smoke flashed brightly before it dissipated, leaving green blind spots in my vision.

The seer canted her head toward the prince. "It is time to ask."

Stepping up to the cauldron, the prince closed his eyes and dropped a piece of paper into the cauldron, speaking the words written on it aloud. "How can the battles with the Shade be stopped?"

The room brightened suddenly as a narrow beam of light surged from the center of the boiling water and straight to the rune on my forehead. The silence in the room was only broken by the bubbling liquid. The light vanished.

"Who can save us all?" He tossed another paper into the water. Again, the light beamed toward my head. I stepped to the side, but it followed me still.

Leon wrote the final question out on the stand before he said aloud, "And how will she save us?" When he tossed the paper into the cauldron, it boiled over and turned a dark, deep red.

The seer stuck her finger into the potion, then brought the liquid to her mouth. "With a bond. From the color, it appears to be a bond of blood, Your Highness."

Blood bond? There were only soulbonds. What dark magic was this? I froze as the prince took one step toward me; his face looked happier than before. "With your blood, Aelia, you can save us all. It won't be much, Aelia. A quick prick would be enough."

"It would require it all, Your Highness," the seer corrected.

My heart stopped beating, and the prince stopped moving, his face contorting to horror. The room fell to harsh murmurs and the shuffling of guards.

"Surely not." My father cast his arm before me, his elbow nudging me backward. The white scar on his arm glinted beneath his cuff. "Can't we transfer the sacrifice to the goat?"

Tilting her head side to side, the seer tossed one more question into the cauldron, and a black beam pierced the goat, who fell to the ground instantly. Dead. The cauldron boiled higher, and shards of light shot chaotically around the room.

"The sacrifice was not accepted," she said.

My mouth was agape, and I had to return my eyes from the goat to the prince. "I-I can't, my prince, my-my king. Why would you... How could you ask this of me?"

The king stood, the power of his presence filling the room as he paced toward me and guards pressed in behind me. "You always said you would serve the crown. Serve the kingdom. Serve the queen. Now is the time for you to save us all. You can stop the fighting. You can save her life. The end of the fighting would mean healing for Her Majesty. You could protect us all."

My hands quivered as I clasped them to my chest to still them. He was right. I always helped. I served. I obeyed. I was able and capable and wanted to do everything I could for those around me. But...this. To die? My breaths quickened. I looked at my father, but he was stricken, frozen. Then his shaking hand reached for his flask.

"Prince Leon, tell her." The king gestured toward me.

My prince, my friend, stared hard at the monarch, his mouth opening and shutting several times before he straightened his spine and took my hand. His voice was harsh and laden with guilt, but it didn't stop his determined tone. "I'm sorry, Aelia. I—" he glanced again at his father, who shook his head. The prince swallowed, then straightened his shoulders. Any compassion that was once there became stilted and frozen as he spoke with a kingly air. "We will make your death quick and painless. The people will celebrate this day in your name. You will be their savior." His voice broke. "And Mother will live."

Was this where our friendship had led us? I searched his face and the seers' faces behind him. Was this how my years of service would be repaid? My heart raced as I stepped back. Could I do this? Was I willing to give my life to save my kingdom? To obey the king? To help the prince? To save the queen I so dearly loved? My gaze fell on the goat.

For the first time that I could remember, I shook my head. "No."

Then, ripping my hand from Leon's grasp, I ran.

Chapter Nine

Nowhere Else To Go

"Stop her!" the king bellowed as I bolted to the exit, smearing the rune on my forehead before they could use it like they did on the goat—if that were possible. The guards collapsed over me at once; one grasped at my wrist, but I wrenched it away. Ducking past another, I tripped and crawled toward the door. The prince dove and pulled on my ankle.

"Leon!" The king yelled.

"Please, Aelia." The prince yanked me back toward the center of the room.

A surge of fury rose within me, hot and caustic. "Get OFF!" I kicked and landed a blow on his face. When his grip loosened, I scrambled past the others, tripping one man until I reached the threshold. My skirts wrapped around my legs, and I raised them as far as I dared. The men ran to the prince's side.

"Leave me. Go get her!" Prince Leon's shout was muffled as he held his bleeding nose. "Just keep her alive!"

A knife flew past and grazed my forearm, slicing through the thin fabric. I cried out and tried to cover it with my other hand, but then my skirts tangled as wind magic came from behind me swept around my feet. The guards seemed out of practice at chasing human targets, so their magic was chaotic, and their efforts didn't slow me at all. Abandoning the hold on my arm, I swept up the fabric again. A guard at the door threw a whip of water that soaked my clothes, but I twisted and lost my balance, falling down the side of the hill. My descent rent me from the water's grasp. The grasses were tall near the bottom, slowing me enough to pick myself up and sprint again. A zip warned me just before an arrow pierced the tree beside me, and I lurched to the side—so much for not killing me.

I reached the deciduous forest, the razewa trees still tall and re-gal...and well known to me. I spent more time here than anywhere in the castle, and I knew I could lose my pursuers. Their longer steps approached, but I knew my way through. The wind was useless here, and there was very little water for the washers to attack me with. For once, I was thankful for the dry earth.

The clouds swirled and darkened above me, and the world went eerily dark. The canopy darkened the forest floor the rest of the way. I felt the heat of the prince's flame as he formed a fireball for light. I nearly tripped over the root of the hemty tree but caught myself just in time.

If the cries behind me were any indication, the men had run into each of the forest's traps, and were now hindered by the roots, tripped up by the deep cracks of the earth, or held by the arms of the naked trees. My relief was short-lived—I had nowhere to run. I had no friends or allies outside the castle. I couldn't ask Chef to put her life at risk to help me. The queen wasn't strong enough to protect me. The castle was no longer safe. I had avoided the villagers—most nobles did—and knew no one who would be willing to stand against the king.

It was too far to escape down the mountains, too far to run to the coast to my homeland, too far to any adjacent village. I needed to hide. I needed to stop the bleeding. Dizziness struck me as I regarded the red streaking my arm and forced me to steady myself on the bark of a pine tree.

A wayward fireball landed beside me in an explosion of sparks. I fell, recoiling from the heat. How could my life end like this? Pushing back to my feet, sweat and furious tears dripped down my face. I had done everything they had ever asked. I had followed every rule, agreed to every task. But this was too far. Too much.

I started to run again when an arrow plunged into the side of my thigh. Shrieking, I grabbed the tip and tried to rip it the rest of the way through, but it caught in the fabric of my skirt, and I couldn't remove the shaft. I screamed again in my final attempt, but the men were closing in. I wouldn't give them what they wanted. The forest shifted as I limped. I no longer passed the dead patches of aspens and razewa and hempty, but blackened silhouettes of tall pines that pierced the sky. The ground below me was rising again. The mountainside belched pillars of shadow and smoke. Deep, dark ravines cut through the mountain face, and gravel shifted beneath my feet.

I crossed the boundary into the Shade's land, pausing, gasping, with my hands wrapped around my torso. My palm was slick with blood, and my shoe began to fill with it as well. Every step was agony as my clothes pulled on the arrow. The men behind me slowed only a little, but with a rally cry, they also pushed onto the Shade's land. There was nowhere to hide and plan my next move. There was no time, if even the threat of being so near the Shade wouldn't slow them down. I had never come this far for herbs and wasn't sure where to go next. The sounds were more distant—they were regrouping, I guessed, rather than giving up. I slowed only a little, exhausted from the long flight. I limped to a dry riverbed, its edges quickly rising to tall cliff walls that blocked out the sky. A clamoring like metal hammers echoed up the canyon. Cave entrances and massive caverns appeared on the sides as I dragged myself down the sandy path.

Panting, I stopped and fell forward with my hands on my knees. My body ached, my side split with pain from the exertion, and my head swam from the shock. Blood left a footprint on the cracked earth from the wound on my thigh. There was no escape. Tears dripped down my cheeks. A shout from the ravine drove me to run again.

The cliffs turned ashy, then black as night. Silver veins of mica glittered against obsidian stones. I passed one statue carved into the wall. Beyond this was a carved column. Then, as I turned the corner, a massive fence of metal and stone arched in front of an enormous black castle, built into the walls of the mountain itself. The large door gaped black like the maw of a dragon. My head tilted upward to follow the spires, which were lost to dark clouds that hung low on the cliff face.

My heart froze as I took in the hazy smoke that drifted in the front garden and the glaring stone monsters on the turrets. Any light from the sickly sun was absorbed by the darkness of the stone. High metallic screeches echoed from within. The hair on my neck stood on end.

"There she is!" The sounds from the men sharpened. The bays of bloodhounds crooned to the night. A plume of fire and wind surged through, scorching the rocky outcrop of trees to my right, knocking me off my feet, and scalding my hand. The fire that reached the fence collided with a billowing cloud of shadow, which laced the edge of the fencing like a magical wall.

My hand seared in pain as blood continued to drip from the tip of my elbow. My thigh burned in anguish, but the rest of my leg was cooling to ice. My heart twisted in my chest. My prince had just burned me. My king would sacrifice me. And my father, yet again, had abandoned me.

My mind recalled green eyes and menacing magic. The only person the prince feared. I was a dead woman anyway. Exhaustion leeched power from my body, but that last scrap of my will to live wouldn't just lie down if there was any chance, even an unlikely one, at the end of the path.

Struggling forward, I reached for the large handle, but the gate swung open on its own. I clumsily dragged down the path and up the stairs with the last of my strength, then collapsed against the door. I pounded weakly on the wood with my fist. "Please. Please let me in." The barking dogs and shouting men approached from behind, so I hit the door harder. I was hanging on only by a fraying thread.

At last, the door opened, and I was engulfed in billows of smoke. I fell to my hip and gazed up into the impassive and terrifying face of the Shade. His dark brows furrowed as he took in my haggard appearance and the arrow protruding from the folds of my dress. His eyes flashed up to mine.

"You." The word was a threat and a question and an accusation wrapped in one.

Terror seized my chest. "I'm sorry...I-I had nowhere else to go. The prince..."

Behind me, the clamor of voices grew closer, and the Shade flipped his gaze to the gate. His teeth clacked as his jaw clenched visibly. He stepped over the threshold and stood with his hands tucked into his pockets. Then he relaxed back on one heel and glared disdainfully, as if the prince had interrupted teatime and not threatened him with an army at his home. As the prince hesitated, the Shade lifted a single eyebrow.

My head was heavy, but I needed to see what was happening, so I lifted it with what little strength I had left. Beyond the gate, the prince took a slow step forward. He held out his hand, palm up, and called loudly over the shadowy storm. "Give me the girl."

The Shade blinked slowly before casting a quick glance down at me. A grumbling growl preceded a single word. "No."

"She is none of your concern. She's a criminal to the crown, and she's trespassing. Just give her back so I can deal with her."

The Shade furrowed his eyebrows. "A criminal? This bloodless waif?" The Shade stepped toward me and crouched, placing a thumb on my chin. He slowly turned my head side to side as if attempting to solve a riddle. "What is your crime?"

My thoughts were muddled and costly. My eyelids drifted downward against my will. Clearing my throat, I managed to say, "My crime... My crime is...not dying."

A pool of blood seeped around his shoes and dragged heavily through my clothes. Distantly, I thought that it looked like too much blood loss for someone to survive. Shivering, I smiled at the Shade. "Well...not dying before...when they asked me to." I laid my head on the stone, and his eyes fixed on the swirl on my neck. My words sounded garbled. "I think I'm dying now, though. He should be pleased."

The prince stepped into the courtyard, and without looking, the Shade threw out a wave of shadow down the path, buffeting him and his men backward.

The Shade studied me, our eyes locked as I focused on him alone. He murmured, "Do you want to live?"

I blinked and huffed a desperate laugh. "I'm cold." My good arm moved weakly across my middle. "I don't want to be cold."

His voice rumbled again, annoyed and growly. "Just say yes."

"Yes?"

A smirk pulled his lips to the side as he sliced a small X across his palm with a small dagger and tucked the hand beside my neck. His palm connected beside my jaw where the mark was, and I felt a frisson of an electric shock. Black and purple light burst from the connection.

Bending down, the Shade whispered. "I'm going to kiss you now."

My eyes flew wide, and his lips descended even as he pulled me up to him. Lights like fireworks burst above us as the shadows whipped about like smoke in the wind. His lips were hot and sweet. Death smelled like the pine forests in winter. He ended it before I was ready. There were surely worse ways to die.

His breath tickled as he whispered, "And now you are mine." The frisson of emotion that raced through my spine was not fear, though it was embarrassing to admit that. The Shade pulled back, lifted me into his arms, and turned back to the prince. "Begone, princeling."

"But-but she is my ward, servant to my crown!"

"No longer." The Shade smiled, a wicked sort of thing. "I have claimed her. Now. Go."

A burst of black wind from the manor swept past us and filled the courtyard with impenetrable smoke. The prince and his men shouted something, but I couldn't see through it. The crook of the Shade's arm shifted my head, and I turned my face into the warm, smooth fabric of his shoulder.

"Rest," the Shade murmured. "You will not die now."

I didn't believe him; the cold had seeped into my core. But speaking required energy that had bled out onto his stoop. I should probably clean that up.

The Shade turned to enter his home. Shivering, I sighed in a strange sort of peace as sleep dragged me under. My heart slowed its rhythm, and the mortal fear tugging in my belly halted as our gazes connected. Possessing, studying, disapproving. Green and ethereal. His eyes were bottomless. His face was as sculpted as his mansion. He was like marble. Blackness clouded around the edges of my vision.

At least staring Death in the face was a beautiful way to go.

Chapter Ten

Introductions

D arkness. Only darkness. My body felt weighed down as cool liquid poured over my cheek. Something large gripped my thigh, and it burned like ice pressed against my skin for too long. My arm was tugged and twisted. I curled my fist, but it felt so weak.

"What have you done?" a chirping voice asked.

A low grumble vibrated the very air. "What was required."

The small voice sharpened. "But how will we—"

"Our plans remain the same," the low voice replied. "Nothing has changed."

"You are a fool," the first voice muttered.

A deep hum was the only reply.

Nightmares wrestled within my mind, reviving the flight from the temple in vivid pictures. The prince of light. The hope of the whole nation. Except me. Awareness returned with a stab of pain. Betrayal sliced through me. Sucking air through my nose, I sat up, making a heavy blanket fall to my lap and tug against my waist. I blinked. My eyes were gritty and sore, and I rubbed them to clear my vision.

I was in a bed with black sheets and a fluffy, deep blue blanket. My burned hand, cut arm, and damaged leg were bandaged, but the pain was surprisingly mild. A fire burned on the far side of a large and otherwise dark room. I pulled my legs back to sit more comfortably, and my skin slid along the glorious silk. My hands dove beneath the blanket, and I nearly squealed with delight as the fabric glided over my fingertips. Silk like this was reserved for the royal family, while the rest of us used various qualities of cotton. My sheets at home were like corn husks comparatively. These sheets were impossibly black—as black as the Shade's magic.

Reality dawned slowly. Oh my. I was in the Shade's manor.

The stone floor around me stretched in panels of blue-gray slate, ending in deep blue, almost turquoise walls—like the last moment of twilight. Unlit wall sconces glittered in the firelight. The room had no windows. An arrow lay on the bedside table beneath a lamp.

"Like what you see?" a chirping voice asked from beside me.

I jumped and turned to see a tiny, upside-down face hanging from the bedside lamp, blinking back at me. My jaw dropped.

The bat fluttered its wings, shifting to wrapping them around its tiny body. *"I said, 'Do you like what you see?'"*

Air passed through my throat, but no sounds emerged. I coughed hoarsely, my throat raw and aching. My head dropped into my hands as I whispered, "I'm dead. A bat is talking to me. I must be dead."

The bat snorted a breathy, snotty sound. Was it...laughing at me? *"Lass, you are not dead. You should be, but your heart yet beats on this side of the moon. Despite my very excellent advice to the master, you still breathe."* It turned its head a bit to the side. *"And breathe so loudly. Who knew something so pretty could snore like that."*

"I do not!" My cheeks flushed. "I'm a lady. Ladies do not snore."

His claws loosened and tightened on the metal brace. *"If that's true, then I'm a crocodile."*

I smiled despite myself. "Nice teeth."

The bat's lips split into a wide grin, displaying tiny daggers for teeth with prominent canines. *"Why, thank you!"* The moment passed, and the bat's black eyes squinted. *"What is your name?"*

"Aelia." I swallowed, uncertain if talking bats also had names. "What's yours?"

"Jamison Harold Crocus Marcus Delaney the Third." The bat stretched out his arms widely—almost like a man flexing—before nestling back together. *"I'm supposed to tell the master when you awaken."*

Icy fear slid down my spine. "And then what?"

Jamison fluttered and flapped irregularly off the perch, then around the hall, before ducking through the tall, arched door. *"Breakfast, I presume."*

Breakfast. I blinked several times before shifting my legs off the glorious bed and onto the cold floor. The difference in temperature came as a shock. Beside me, the lamp flickered on with a whoosh, revealing plush slippers tucked along the bedside. Slipping my toes inside, I grabbed the fluffy violet robe that hung outside a nearby armoire. I hugged myself, nestling into the cozy fabric.

"The master will see you now." Jamison chirped, now dangling from the doorway threshold.

"See me." My eyes widened. "I had hoped...that is... Could I take breakfast in here?"

"Ha," the bat scoffed. *"No. In no uncertain terms. Come now."*

"But I'm not dressed." I pulled down the black nightdress that fell to mid-calf, exposing the lower half of my legs. "I need to change."

"Humans and their garments." Jamison rolled his black eyes. *"Do you see me in a huff about my fur? No. Come as you are. Or else I shall fetch the master, and he won't be pleased at all."*

I shivered at the threat. "Okay. As I am. Right." I tried to brush my fingers through my hair, but it was so tangled and chaotic that I only succeeded in removing a small leaf that lingered from my recent flight. I stepped gingerly, waiting for the moment my injuries would waylay me, but it never came. I felt well. Healthier than I'd felt in a long time—especially considering the attack of the Shade and all my treks over the last couple weeks, not to mention my flight from the temple. My lungs expanded fully without a cough. My body seemed healed, and I wasn't fatigued in the slightest. How in the seven stars could that be?

Despite the massive torches that lit the walls, the hallway was long and dark. The floor was full of natural shadows but remained remarkably spotless. No spiderwebs arched the corners, and the wall sconces gleamed. The Shade seemed a clean villain, at least. Doorways took off under tall archways on either side, but still, no windows. I shuddered in the darkness and paced closer toward the lamps on the walls, gripping my barely shining necklace.

My slippers shuffled, the echo expanding down the cavernous halls around us. Jamison chirped intermittently as he flitted about, taking the lead. Black spiked masks lined the walls, their deep and vacant eyes watching my every step. Several hallways diverged from the main one, but the bat continued straight ahead until the pitch of the echoes changed, and we entered a massive dining hall.

A long table with ten seats on each side sat alone, dwarfed by the room. The ceiling was carved with coffered stone and sparsely lit with chandeliers. The table was black walnut stained black, with matching black high-backed chairs.

At the head of the table sat the Shade. A raven glared from the corner of his chair, his beak clacking in a menacing croak. Shadows billowed on the tile around him, shifting, watching. My legs seized with terror, and I froze in the doorway. My heart raced as fast as the wings of my batty escort as he flew to a lamp along the wall.

The Shade's irises were shadowed in black before flickering back to green. He extended his hand toward me, and I flinched. His eyes narrowed as he gestured to the chair near him. "Won't you sit?" A thick arm of smoke reached toward me, wrapped around the legs of the chair, and pulled it back for me. The shadow rose and patted twice upon the cushion.

A thousand retorts filled my brain at once; my throat was dry and sticky. Instead, I politely shook my head and dipped into a wobbly curtsy.

The edge of his lips turned upward. "Are you not hungry?" My gaze latched upon those lips as tingles burst on my own at the intrusive memory. He had kissed me. I had kissed the enemy. I hadn't planned on being so desperate while dying.

"Well?"

I shook my head again. "Not particularly, my lord." I dipped into another curtsy. Surely that's what one must do to survive this encounter, right? Be polite to Death. Though, at this rate, I would curtsy myself to an early grave. Against my will, my stomach gurgled loudly, nearly echoing off the cold stones of the dining room.

The Shade lifted a brow. "Sit anyway."

"Yes, alright."

Something shoved me from behind, a fuzzy warmth that pushed me toward the seat. Fear seized my leg muscles, and I stumbled. A growl rumbled from the large black wolf that had nudged me, and he stalked past me toward the Shade. Spinning once, the wolf lay with his head on his paws, his orange gaze piercing mine.

Scurrying now, I collapsed into the chair. The shadow scooched it in for me, and I desperately coaxed my diaphragm to breathe normally.

"Eat." The Shade's voice rumbled.

I glanced down at the covered tray and reached for the metal handle when a white owl on silent wings flashed before me, grasped the loop, and lifted the top of the platter. The owl then flitted over to a side table and set down the metal cover before returning to its resting spot.

That's when I noticed the eyes—so many eyes. Under the side table, a dozen black glittering eyes peered out from six gray fuzzy creatures with naked tails and pointy teeth. A basket beside them held a few fat rat-like creatures who wiggled their noses at me, their backs covered in spikes. A flap drew my attention to the ceiling where fifty bats of various sizes hung upside down, some as big as my thumb, others larger than my arm, all unblinkingly watching me. An armored creature—like a groundhog with a tail but covered with dragon-scale plates—lumbered down the edge of the wall, standing up on its hind legs with its clawed hands together. It licked its maw with satisfaction as it blinked at me. Crows inhabited various coat stands around the room, along with a few more owls, and the ugliest bird I had ever seen, with a wide beak and a flattened head. A smaller version peaked between the feathers of its belly.

What in all the world was happening here? The evil Shade collects...what? Animal sacrifices?

"Eat," the Shade said again, making me jump. I reached my shaky hand toward a fork in obedience. My plate was covered with what looked like eggs scrambled with unrecognizable vegetables. My nostrils flared. It smelled...good.

"It is good," he muttered. "Made with eggplant, onion, diced potato, and tomatoes." He stabbed his fork into the mixture and took a bite. "The finest of the nightshades."

I blanched again. "Nightshade?" The poisonous plant my father used in tiny pieces as medicine? I'd only ever eaten potato; the other names were foreign to me.

"These aren't poisoned, Dayspring. Just eat."

I was about to ask about the name when Jamison interrupted. *"She really is a coward, my lord."* Jamison's tinny voice scratched my nerves. *"Look how pale she is. Her bravery, if she had any, no doubt left with the blood loss."*

"I've always been pale." I clamped my lips shut. Why was I defending myself to a bat?

"Have you always been a coward? A blooming pansy?" The bat stretched a taut wing around himself.

I scowled at him as I stabbed my fork into the soft...eggplant? "I am not a flower."

The food, to my chagrin, was delicious. I finished the plate before I realized how unladylike and quickly I'd eaten. Glancing up with flushed cheeks, I found the Shade merely watched me, a slight tug on the corner of his lips. Amusement? Contempt? It was hard to say.

"Th-thank you, my lord. I will help clean this up." I stood quickly and reached for the plates. But as I did, my full stomach gurgled again.

"Is she dying now?" Jamison asked, with an ornery sort of glee.

The Shade's lips split into a full grin. "Afraid not, my little chiroptera."

"I'm fine. Sorry to make such a racket." I straightened up, grabbing the plate again. "Just point me in the direction of the kitchens, and I'll start washing."

"The racoons will do it." The Shade gestured toward the collection of the fuzzy, striped creatures in the corner. "They're excellent at it."

I picked up a glass, then glancing at a fork, snatched it up too. "But—"

"Dayspring..." His voice rumbled, a storm threatening lightning, and I startled. I set the plates down with a clatter.

I reached for a napkin, pulling it between my fingers as I searched the room. "I could...dust something?" But the room was spotless. My eyes roved over the table, landing on the rolls. "Or bake. Or..."

"You will do no such thing."

"But then, what will I do here?" A thousand terrible things rushed into my mind. The Shade was evil and killed people and...

"Rest."

My mouth popped open. His gaze seized the very breath in my chest, and his voice dropped to a tone that reverberated deep in my belly. "Rest, Dayspring. Jamison will take you back to your room."

The bat sneered in a distinct look of contempt. *"As the lord commands."* He flapped unevenly past my head. *"Come, you waifish thing. Let's not get you lost in the caverns. The blind worms are hungry these days."* He flew into the corridor, and I heard him mutter. *"On second thought..."*

I scurried to catch up with him, my hand tracing along the wall for something solid and steady. I turned at the last moment to look back at my captor. The Shade rubbed his chest with a furrowed brow. At a battish screech, I turned and stumbled through the threshold after Jamison.

My breaths came faster from the exertion but freer now that I was away from the Shade. And his eyes. And the potent power he exuded throughout the room. The bat took a few turns, then entered the room where I had started this escapade. My room? I sighed and collapsed onto the bed.

The bat took his position on the lamp beside me. His eyes narrowed. *"You really are a fragile thing."*

As fatigue swept through my confused state, I had to agree. But I'd worked hard all these years. "Only some days. You'll see. I'm very helpful. And I'm nice."

"Ew. Don't be nice."

Sleep dragged at my eyelids as I stared at his tiny fuzzy face. "What a funny thing to say."

"Nice is not nice. Nice is lies."

I frowned at the absurdity and wondered why his lips didn't move. And then I fell asleep.

Chapter Eleven

Bathtime

My eyes peeked open to the darkened room before me. The bat hung from a lamp, and the manor held its breath in baited silence. Jamison had wrapped himself fully in his stretched wings, and he didn't stir as I sat up. My body felt rejuvenated, and no dizziness assaulted me as I stood. I cracked open the far doors of the room, pleased to find the toilet. Beyond another doorway, a drip, drip of water drew me closer. A massive room, even larger than the castle's drawing rooms, was filled with steam. I could hardly see the walls on the other side. The room was lined with a walkway that circled a massive belowground basin of roiling water. The smell was thick with a pungent earthy odor and a slight hint of eggs—a hot spring. Glancing around quickly, I snicked the door shut, disrobed in a frenzy, and slid into the hot water.

In all my days at the castle, even with the inferni heating water and the washers pushing water through plumbing in all the nobles' quarters, I had never experienced such luxury as this. This bath could seat the king's whole table, and the water was so hot, my soul boiled in pleasure. The room was filled with thick, happy clouds that wafted the perfumed oil I'd found lined up on the edge. The water was so opaque with minerals and fragrances that I could hardly see my hand an inch below the surface. All of it worked to clear my mind and cushion my heart.

Oh, my heart. The ache renewed its beating pulse behind my ribs. My mind ruminated on all that had passed. I had run from my prince and my father to the very person the court had accused me of colluding with. But they were the ones who had wanted to sacrifice me—not the Shade. I shook my head. A bead of water flicked from my chin. I couldn't have said yes to that—no one could have—but what if it actually was the only way to save the queen and our kingdom? My stomach solidified in dread. What if my refusal killed her and I have doomed us all? Was my life worth more than everyone else's?

The hot coal of indignant resistance within my chest that had ignited in the temple burned hotter. Who had determined that I was the prophesied sacrifice anyway? A cauldron? A set of isolated, wrinkled crones with fancy words? I had never doubted the seers before, but I had to in the face of my near demise. My chest grew hotter as I thought of my father. The one who had led me to the temple, who did so very little as the prince brought me to my death. Was my life so meaningless to him?

I clicked my nails along the edge of the bath. And then, I had raced to Death's doorstep. I sucked in a slow breath. I wasn't dead yet.

Cold prickles ran down my body, which erupted in goosebumps despite the heat of the water. What was I going to do now? Was I a prisoner? Was I trapped here? What would I do with my time? Sleep and bathe and...? I could run back to my homeland. I could escape if he would but supply me. Or I could steal what I needed and leave when he was sleeping. But the manor was filled with animals, it seemed. Could I even run without detection?

Perhaps I would explore then. Find the exits. Make plans. I owed him nothing. I scrunched my nose. Well, nothing except my life and my health and my protection. Air hissed between my teeth. Then I would help him for a time. Clean the manor, care for...Jamison? Or something. Pay him back a little. Then run.

My plan set, I pushed up on the seat, about to emerge when the steam shifted and green eyes latched onto mine from the other side of the pool.

Squawking, I careened backward, caterwauling and dipping under the water like a deranged cat. I squeezed my arms around my chest and stayed low as I emerged. The rippling surface would have to obscure the rest of me.

The Shade rose slowly, water dripping off his very naked, very cut physique to his waist which—thankfully—was under the cloudy water. And he moved toward me. Water dripped down the curves of his chest and the leather bracelet on his left arm. His skin was tanned, unblemished, unmarked by a bond mark. Mercifully, he sat again, the water up to his shoulders, giving my eyes a chance to unlatch and regard something more appropriate like his face—his smirking, amused, teasing face. His eyes searched mine as the green flickered with a flush of black.

"Why do you hide?" The Shade's voice rumbled through the room, echoing around me.

I blinked slowly. "I-I am naked."

He furrowed his brow. "Jamison doesn't care."

A frantic laugh escaped before I could curtail it. "It's not Jamison I'm hiding from."

He idly searched about the empty room. Then raised a brow. "There is no one else."

I gestured wildly at him, flicking water between us. "There is you!" My voice squeaked at the end, sounding shriller than I intended. "You are here!"

"But I do not care what you wear or don't wear in the bath. That seems like a personal decision." The Shade's eyes glinted as mischief played across his lips. "I could leave now." As he rose to stand, the water lowered.

My face was now as hot as the sun, and I flipped my back to him, hiding my eyes behind my hand. "No. No!" I cleared my throat. "That is. I do not presume to tell your...his...the Shade what he is to do or not to do. But, sir, if you are asking me, *please* remain as you are!"

A low chuckle rumbled behind me. "As you wish."

"And perhaps, I also wish..." I swallowed. "Would you turn, sir, that I might cover myself? Or move to the other side of the room? Please?"

A slow "hmm" was all I had as assent. I looked behind me, confirming that his back was indeed to me, before dashing out of the water and grabbing one of the robes that hung on the wall. Tying it with nervous force, I double-checked that the important bits were covered. Despite the robe being too large, my calves, once again, lay exposed. I could hear my father's berating from here.

"Would your father be so startled to see you so clothed?" the Shade asked. He stood behind me in his own robe and casually slung the belt about his waist, his chest still visible and gleaming in the lamplight.

My mouth gaped; I didn't think I had said that aloud. "My father would be convinced I was ruining the family's reputation by the clothing, the company, and the room, sir." My eyes widened. "Not that you're not excellent company, it's just that—I mean to say that—it's my legs, sir. They're exposed! And you, you are here!"

The Shade took his time evaluating my legs. I could feel his gaze sweep every curve, dip, and sway of my ankles. My hands clutched the robe at my neck and belly tighter. Nerves flip-flopped in my gut.

"They look like sufficient ankles. They helped you run here, didn't they? Does your father not approve of ankles?" *Sufficient*? He continued, his eyes glittering, "And why wouldn't your ankles be exposed in the common steam room? The hot spring is large enough for the whole manor. My bedroom is just there." He indicated a far door on the other side of a tiled wall. In my haste, I hadn't thought...hadn't considered...a public bathing room?

I couldn't bear any further scrutiny. "Excuse me, sir." I dipped hastily into the roughest, shallowest curtsy of my life and rushed into my room, being careful not to touch him. Jamison only stirred long enough to open one eye before nestling back into his wings. I swept to the wardrobe, opened both doors, and ducked in as far as I could to hide my body. Oh, my sun and stars, what was happening?

Peeking around to be sure the Shade hadn't entered my room, I slipped into a silken black dress, the length fully covering my ankles though its style was a few decades old. The *V*-shaped neckline was a bit low, but it was very well made. I tugged the shoulders back and pulled on the sides of the *V*, but they wouldn't stay together. It was fine. I was fine. It highlighted my necklace nicely; its swirls above and below the glowing gem lined up well with the deeper neckline. Plus, I tried to reassure myself that the exposure of skin was apparently nothing to someone like the Shade.

"It's not nothing." A murmur came from behind me. I flipped around, and he stood but three paces away, this time fully clothed in a long black tunic with an artful silver hem that swirled and slashed at the bottom and the sleeves.

"You-you need to wear bells." My face heated again. "You startled me."

"Apparently." He took in my appearance. The smoke that hovered around him swirled for a moment before settling again. "Good, you're dressed. Let's go." He turned on a heel and strode to the door; this time, his heels clacked and clattered as shoes should. "Ding-a-ling, Dayspring. Ding-a-ling"

I peered at him, wondering briefly if he was stomping on purpose. And was that supposed to be a bell sound? A low chuckle echoed into the hall.

Slipping into some shoes, again, the right fit—should I be grateful or terrified?—I bustled after him. The silk slipped past my legs in luxury, but I feared they showed more than they should without all the layers I was used to wearing. Shaking off the thought, I caught up to him and stayed two paces behind him.

"Where are we going?" I asked as he turned down a hall I hadn't seen before.

"A tour."

Chapter Twelve

A Tour

The Shade remained silent as he turned down three different corridors.

"Could you"—I skipped to catch up again—"please, tour a bit slower, sir?" And don't tours usually come with words of instruction?

"Words are excessive. Watch. Learn. Keep up." He stopped suddenly, and I nearly careened into him. "And why are you behind me?"

"I'm sorry. You are faster than me."

His green eyes flashed with black, and he gestured beside him. "Come here."

My hand lifted my gown as I approached. He nodded once and stepped away; I followed just a step behind. He glanced at me again. "No." Grasping my shoulders, he pulled me forward. His hands felt hot through the thin fabric. "Walk here. At my side."

"But—"

He raised a black brow as he pursed his lips. That new rebellious coal in my chest wondered if I should push the issue, but when trying to survive Death, I surrendered. "Very well."

We took off together. As I was no longer racing, I suspected he had slowed. He threw out a hand intermittently, indicating doors but providing only the briefest description as we went along. We passed many guest rooms and the servants' quarters. We went around another corner before I dared to speak again. "What... what shall I call you, sir?"

The Shade paused, staring straight ahead in thought for a moment. "The Shade is adequate."

I was pleased he didn't say Master. The stairs ascended in rocky steps that were worn down in the center. The next ceiling was not quite as high—perhaps only nine feet. Small windows on the left let in some light as the rooms jutted off to the right.

"Here is the armory. The second kitchen is where a lot of bread is baked. The western wing. The chicken coop."

"I'm sorry?" I'd stopped before a door that had been cut in half. The Shade strode to my side, his shadows sweeping aside my skirts as his shoulder brushed mine again.

"Chickens, Dayspring." Opening the top of the door, I could see twenty black chickens milling around a stony room, the floor covered in straw. When he opened the lower door, chickens ran toward us, murmuring and clucking. Their combs, waddles, legs, and eyes were all black, but their black feathers shimmered in a rainbow of color under the lights. A shadow slipped between us, entered a drawer, and pulled out some seeds and mealworms for the excited chickens.

I blinked once, twice, and slowly turned to regard the Shade. The menace of hope and light had...chickens? Probably for blood sacrifices.

The Shade snorted, then scratched at the light stubble on his cheek as he turned his face toward the hall.

Eyeing the room once more, I turned. "Sir, would you like me to care for the chickens?"

He raised an eyebrow. "Why would you do this?"

"As a servant of the Shade." I curtsied briefly. "I'm happy to do what needs to be done." I pulled the fine dress out to examine it. "Though this outfit would be soiled, so I'll need a more casual outfit."

A rumble burbled. Was he...laughing at me?

"Come, Dayspring. You will not be a chicken tender."

I bustled behind him as he took off with long strides, light opaque shadows streaming behind him. "A maid then? I could clean."

"No."

"A...a chef? I've baked before at the..." Don't mention the prince, don't mention the prince. "I mean, before."

"No. Speaking of him, why did the prince want you dead?" He turned so suddenly, I almost ran into him, but his shadows caught me and held me upright. My heart ached at his question.

"Well, the seers told him a prophecy."

"Which prophecy?"

I shrugged, studying a very interesting crack between the stones on the floor and picking at the fabric near my thigh. "Something about how my powerlessness was going to ruin everything, and as things turn black as pitch, someone has to be sacrificed." I rubbed the place where the arrow had pierced my flesh, the images of the previous night flashing through my mind. Images of those I thought I could count on for protection, friendship, or moral leadership. All had failed me. I could see my father's stricken face but frozen body, my king's apathetic but hungry observance, the prince's deadly request. His mild regret didn't make up for the betrayal—demanding my life to save his. Well, his, the kingdom's, and the queen's. Guilt surged along with anger. "I was the only way the queen would live. The goat was not an adequate sacrifice, they said. My father..." The words stuck in my throat, forming a ball of pain that swelled and ached, and I fell silent.

The Shade mercifully moved on. "I've heard this prophecy. It's a convenient one."

I turned my eyes to him, frowning. How could he have heard it?

He merely shrugged and walked on. "It was passed around many years ago." He turned back with a smile. "Who else is as black as pitch and has doomed the land to death and decay?"

I vaguely remembered those words. "I mean, you are the Shade. Your magic is very black."

"Ah, yes. Black magic, black heart."

"Sir! I didn't say th—"

He abruptly turned to head up yet another stairway, cutting me off. This one landed us in a large sitting room with a plate of rolls, pastries, and a teapot. He sat heavily in the chair, and his shadows pulled up a chair for me. Windows on two sides of the room let in the early morning light. Had I slept a whole day? I turned my face toward the sun like a flower—the manor had been very dark.

We were so high. I approached the window to see that we were hundreds of feet up though not quite at the top of the cliff. Birds flitted around, free and weightless, entering and exiting holes on the adjacent cliffside.

"The problem with prophecies is that one can always pick out the tasty bits and discard the rest, Dayspring." He picked up a roll and pulled it apart. "For example, I am an excellent villain that the good prince of fire and light can battle against."

"You do seem to send a lot of black storm clouds."

The Shade took a bite of his roll. He had a penetrating gaze and raised brow as he considered my words. "So it would seem." He passed me a pastry. "Tell me about this father of yours."

My throat threatened to close again, but somehow, it was easier to talk about up here. "My father is an herbalist. He makes the queen's potions to help her feel better, give her strength." The Shade remained quiet, watching me, and I rushed to fill the empty space. "He brought us here after my mother died. We had lived in Aswan."

"By the ocean?" he asked. I nodded. "That must have been quite the journey."

"It was. Mother had just died. He burned his bond mark right before we left, and it festered some as we traveled. We barely made it with the small trading caravan because he became so ill. I was six, almost seven, but I remember how worried I was for him. It was such a long trip—not one I would make again easily."

My feet and back had ached, and my father's bandages stank as he changed them nightly. Despite the common healing potions, his arm had been swollen and dripping and red the whole trip.

"And your arrival at the castle? Was it a warm welcome?"

I laughed once. "I mean, it was fine at first. I was often passed off to the prince's tutors as I had no mother. But later, I was tossed to the servants when my magic never surfaced."

"You had no friends?"

"I thought Leon was...once. There was also a servant boy we liked to run through the gardens with—he was a bit older—but he disappeared after a few months, and I never saw him again."

"What do you like to do now?" he asked abruptly. When he stood, his shadows tilted my chair, nearly dumping me out of it. We left the room, turning down a long hall with one side full of windows. My breath froze in my throat as I looked out at the steep expanse. "Dayspring." He murmured, ripping my attention back to him. I hurried beside him again.

"I'm sorry. I...uh. I like to do whatever pleases the Shade."

He rolled his eyes—rolled them. I hadn't rolled my eyes since I was nine. "What pleases me is to know what you enjoy."

My mind whirred through what I usually did—collecting herbs, making powders and potions and poultices with father, helping Chef in the kitchen, washing dishes, helping Her Majesty with some task or other. "I enjoy being helpful. The world is better when people help others. And I love to help the queen."

He halted again. "But what do you enjoy for you?"

My mouth opened and shut like a fish without air.

He huffed out a large breath. "That is a problem."

An impolite scoff slipped from my throat. "And what do you enjoy?"

Green eyes flicked to mine, ran down my person, and then gazed out the window. "I enjoy a great many things."

I crossed my arms, ignoring the shiver his gaze had caused, and considered everything I knew of him. Like fighting Prince Leon? Like drowning our world in shadow? Like poisoning our queen? Like—

The Shade scoffed. "Like gardening, Dayspring."

At a sudden right turn, I almost had to shut my eyes from the bright light of an enormous solarium. The walls soared above me as unrefined glass covered every surface. The light drifted down through three levels of a room rivaling the castle ballroom's floorspace. The air was heavy and humid, and mist sprayed into the room at intervals. Colorful birds flitted about the trees, and an armored groundhog with plates in rows waddled past a spiky plant and scratched about the loamy soil on the edge of a hard rock path.

"Armadillo," the Shade supplied. "And those are parrots." He indicated the flying rainbows above us.

"Hmm," I grunted intelligently. "Why does that armadillo look different than the one in the dining room?"

"That was a pangolin."

My brain was buzzing in wonder. I meandered down the narrow path, skirting through the purple ferns and large solar hastas, beyond the arching trees and dripping long leaves of the mother willow.

Another turn led to tables holding thick, healthy herbs such as white thieves and purple dranger, pericott, rainboss mushroom, and…there was so much. The Shade followed at a distance, judging his work with a hard eye. He dispensed a dead flower here and trimmed a failing leaf there, but I was entranced by the living world around me. We climbed the steps, his shadows drifting behind him, to a level with countless flowers of all types, blooms I had no names for. I touched a petal here and there. We turned a corner, and he indicated the sign that warned of poisonous plants. I withdrew my hand. Then, at the top of the next level, my heart stuttered. I recognized that vanilla scent. The room was full of racerbristles.

Racerbristles.

There were easily a hundred bushes in this very space. My fingertips ached, and I touched one, then another. My heart rate raced, and my breathing came in pants. All the wasted hours and days, all the storms I'd endured and burns I had suffered searching for this infernal plant. And they were right here! I whirled upon the Shade who was studying me, shadows in his eyes.

"Racerbristles," I spat. "So many racerbristles." Gesturing to one side, my pitch rose, despite any attempt to maintain control. "Sir, this many could save the queen!"

The Shade huffed. "Racerbristles alone would not compl—"

The coal in my chest ignited. "They would help her heal. They would restore her!"

He shook his head. "Racerbristle is not the cure the queen needs."

I pointed a finger at him. "*Your* shadows—" He took a step toward me, and the room darkened as bursts of shadow flew from him and curled around us. Death and danger and power stopped my very breath. He towered above me, the shadows closing in like a whirling cocoon.

His green eyes flashed as he raised a brow. "What of them?"

I panted, but this time, I felt fear. I was a fool. A hopeless, feckless fool. "Th-they are lovely." Another surge thickened them and plunged us into blackness. The only remaining light came from the necklace at my chest, which glowed with yellow warmth. I clung to it.

"Liar. What of them?" He stepped into my space, and I backed up a step. The table pressed into my back. A single shadow reached from his side to caress my cheek. My hand trembled at my utter helplessness. His shadow ducked lower and raised my chin, forcing my gaze to meet his. "Speak the truth, Dayspring."

The words were whispered, treasonous, and harsh. "Your—the shadows are killing her."

"Finally, a truth you believe." He withdrew his shadows by degrees. "But belief, Dayspring, even if fervently held, is not the same as the truth."

Outrage twisted my stomach. Of course, it was the truth. I had seen the queen's frail body. I had mixed a thousand potions for her. I had been burned by the acid rain from the shadow storms as I trod the sick earth looking for the herbs she needed to live.

"The truth is you killed those three soldiers! You've killed before, so why not the queen of your enemies?" I gasped at my own words. His sharp glare froze me to my core, and I shuddered. Stupid, stupid girl. "I'm sorry." I curtsied and waited for the death I had once escaped.

The Shade turned his back to me as the shadows at his feet churned like angry clouds. "Those men deserved it."

The shadows dissipated, and the room stirred, silent but not suffocating. A bird chirped at the top of a tree, silhouetted by the white, sunlit window. It was trapped just as I was. Quietly, I asked, "Sir, why did you bring me here?"

The muscles in his jaw feathered as the shadows coiled and twisted around him. He extended one hand to the plants around us. "Keep them alive."

The Shade paced from the room. The shadows swept behind him, falling and rolling down the steps. I was alone. And somehow, I was emptier for it.

Chapter Thirteen

The Solarium

"**K**eep them alive?" I murmured. "With all of these, he could keep the queen alive." I paced with heavy steps to grab an apron and the shears that hung beside it. "He could send a fraction of these to her and still have too many plants." Selfish, jealous monster. I tried not to take out my blossoming frustration on the plants around me and focused on my new job. At least I wasn't idle. At least it wasn't dark.

As I trimmed, watered, and repotted small saplings, the blood rushing in my ears slowed its throbbing rhythm as the surrounding sounds caressed me, warm and familiar—birds chirped, insects buzzed, leaves clattered. When I closed my eyes, I was almost back in the forest, below the castle, away from the barren battleground. The Shade's solarium was a world of its own.

A woman muttered something behind me, and I whirled to see who approached. But the room was empty.

"*...climbing all the way along, just—Klay, no, not there.*"

There were only racerbristles. There was no one there. I was losing my mind.

The woman's voice spoke again. "*You're a dear. Over here, please.*" A young voice whined, "*But Moooooom.*"

A bush shook and rustled. Stepping closer, I pulled the branch away with a trembling hand. A black and white spotted creature was digging at the base, and three miniature creatures scuttled between the stalks. They froze, their black shiny eyes fixing on mine.

A baby lifted a single paw. "*Mom, should we run?*"

"*Don't move. Let's see if it goes away,*" the mother's voice cautioned.

I frowned. Their mouths didn't move. Our stare down continued.

A baby's tail twitched; this one's voice was higher. "*I have an itch!*"

"*Freeze, Lolo.*"

I cleared my throat. "Um. Hello."

Terrified, the three babies squeaked and rushed to hide under their mother. She bared her teeth and lifted a black-and-white tail, turning her rump toward me.

"*Hold together, dears. I shall spray her, and then we shall run.*"

Wait, spray? I took a step back. "I mean you no harm. I'm..." What am I doing talking to more animals? "I'm Aelia. The Shade brought me here."

"*She smells nice.*" The high voice...said. But the sound didn't come through my ears.

"*She has white hair like us.*"

"*Do you think she's a skunk too?*"

A sharp chirp. "*She's a human,*" the mother scolded.

Skunks. Okay. I shook my head. "I'm sorry. I'm not a skunk." Six tiny eyes peeked from under the mother. One teetered out and bumbled toward me. He squinted an eye. We studied each other for a moment before I leaned forward. "Hi."

"*Hi.*"

Frowning, I crouched. The mouth of the skunk definitely did not move as it spoke.

"How is it I can hear you?"

The baby turned back to its mother, who answered, *"The Shade understands us. Why shouldn't you?"*

Huh. Perhaps the magic of the manor?

"If you would excuse us, we're already up too late," the mother continued. *"We need to finish up our work and get to bed. If you'd like, you can trim that side for the spent blossoms."* Her nose twitched. *"Come, Lolo, Klay, Jarlz. Go snuggle in."*

"Yes, Mama." Two trundled after her.

Jarlz, the one closest to me, stayed a moment longer and bared his tiny teeth. *"I'll be watching you."*

I bowed seriously but couldn't prevent a smile as he rushed after his mother. Perhaps the Shade was evil, the manor frightening, and the magic unusual, but these little babies were joy in a black-and-white package.

I stood up and turned slowly, taking in the room thick with healthy plants. I hadn't seen plants like these...maybe ever, certainly, not this many so close together. The racerbristles at the castle were small, spindly, and anemic, the green was more yellow, and the leaves on each branch were infrequent. Here, the plants not only grew larger but also sprouted dense, healthy branches and plump, dark green leaves. The flowers were such a bright yellow they rivaled the sunlight through the windowpanes. The flowers burst with six broad petals and orange stamens, wafting the vanilla scent through the entire room.

In this solarium, temperature controlled and protected, the racerbristles were shielded from the rapid temperature changes and even the castle's heat. Surely, he had to know the queen was sick. Did he truly not know that the racerbristles could help her? But if he knew, how could he be so merciless toward the queen? How could he turn his back on his leaders? Guilt twisted in my chest. Wasn't this what I had also done—abandon my queen and my kingdom?

It was too painful to consider. Brushing my hands free of this painful thought, I started to trim off the dead flowers where the mother skunk had indicated.

Snip. Dead flower.

Snip. I should have died.

Snip. The queen was dying, and I wasn't there to save her.

Snip. Perhaps the Shade should be the one dy—No, I refused to think such horrible things and make myself just like *them*.

I froze, whirling in the mire of emotion as a single tear dripped down my cheek. I had no mother. I had cared for the queen and thought she cared for me as well. How could I abandon her? Was my life worth more than hers? Did I do what was right and good for anyone but myself? My father was inconsistent at best, and...and heavy-handed at worst. He had become increasingly unreliable, volatile, and distant since we'd arrived in this land. Chef was a friend, certainly, but my hours spent beside the queen, chatting and storytelling, wrapped her around my heart tighter than the vines along the windowsills. I would have said I would lay down my life for hers, but when it came down to it, I failed. I was not the helpful, selfless person I thought I was.

I moved to another table, and my toe clipped on something that made the sound of clinking glass. Ducking, I found a box with a large pot, several glass potion jars, a stirrer, a hot clay plate, and a mortar and pestle.

Perhaps...perhaps I would make some potions on my own and convince the Shade to bring them to the queen. Perhaps he just didn't realize the treasure he had in this room and how it could save her. Making the potions was the least I could do for now. I could only hope it would be enough.

I tucked the box back under the table. Either convince him...or sneak out and bring them to her myself. Maybe I could still help her. Sneaking around the Shade would be the second boldest thing I'd ever done in my life, but I couldn't abandon the queen. Not when I was able to help. With a sigh of relief, my guilt somewhat assuaged, I returned to my work.

Hours passed, and the day grew hot as the sun beat through the windows and evaporated the pools that ran through the gardens. Between the misting humidity and labor, sweat beaded on my brow. The third floor was so massive that I had only finished trimming a third of it before a sound clattered through the walls—like fingernails clicking on the table or hail clacking a staccato rhythm on stone, the sounds were rapid, frenzied, and growing louder. I turned as the strange clicks slowed. They were coming from the inner corner.

I stepped closer, wondering if the skunks had awoken, but when I moved the fronds of an enormous arcing fern tree, eight red eyes, set in a twisted, writhing, armored face, glared back at me. The creature stepped forward on six legs, each twice as long as its body and ending in whip-like feet. Two more legs angled around its twitching mandible with red-spiked pinchers that pulled invisible things toward its toothed maw. Too many legs rattled forward, and a thorned knee knocked aside a racerbristle pot, smashing it to the ground. The deformed spider's body was much larger than a forest coyote.

A spyring.

It jumped. One moment it was six feet away on the table; the next, it was right before me. I staggered back, nearly tripping over my dress. More noise came from above, and I dragged my eyes up to a gaping hole in the corner of the wall. Dozens of pairs of eyes glowed in the darkness. I was going to die.

"Mama, what was that?" a small voice asked behind me. I dared a glance at the small skunk that bumbled out from under the branches near the pool. *"Mama, I'm thirsty."* The little one—Jarlz, I thought—sat on his haunches and blinked blearily around him, his tiny paws rubbing his cheek as he stared unseeingly ahead. The monster spider spotted the baby and turned in its direction with a slow tap tap tap of its legs. The pincers snapped twice, and it crouched backward like the tightening of the rope of a trebuchet.

A hissing voice whispered, *"Hungry."*

Oh no.

I flipped around and dove just as the spider leaped for the baby skunk. But I was closer. My hands clutched the tiny, warm body of the baby skunk, and I dashed toward the stairs. The monster slammed into the table and stumbled under the falling plants. My spine prickled as it released a discordant wail, sounding somewhere between a woman screaming and a goat dying, accompanied by a burst from the others. The glass jar beside me broke from the sound. The other spyrings flooded into the room, their clatters becoming a roar as they rushed toward us.

"Hungry. Hungry. Hungry." Again, the voices. Again, they were inside my mind.

Get down. Get out. Get down. Find help.

The narrow stairway gave us only a slight lead as the spiders rushed down en masse, almost too large to fit their legs, each fighting the next for solid footing on the stairs and railings. They funneled behind us. The ones that got through clambered up onto the walls and windows.

"Mama!" Jarlz cried.

"I got you. I got you!" I grabbed the pot of a plant I didn't recognize, which was labeled as poisonous, and threw it at the closest spider. It hit the monster's head, broke, and knocked the spyring to the ground. The pot did more damage than any toxin from the plant. I grabbed a nearby rainboss mushroom pot and threw that instead. Violet gore splattered as the bulbous mushroom ruptured over three spiders, who collapsed in a soul-ripping wail. Their legs writhed, and the whiplike ends took out another couple of spiders as they lashed a bout.

The others' chants continued, "*Hungry. Hungry. Hungry.*"

I sprinted down the second stairwell and onto the main floor. Spiders spilled behind us—so many that it seemed the walls and the floors were shifting like water rather than solid stone.

"SHADE!" I yelled, wondering if he was even awake. I ducked and squatted on the ground as a spyring jumped and flew at my head, the skunky bundle squeaked as I tucked him closer against my chest. Rising, I looked behind me again as we turned the last corner before reaching the doors. Grabbing a handle, I lunged forward and ran headfirst into a hard chest. The smell of pine and the cool sensation of enwrapping shadows swept past my legs. I collapsed into him, pressing my cheek to his warm shirt. "Oh, thank the stars."

His arm wrapped around me, and I tucked the baby skunk between us. His growl rumbled like thunder and vibrated through his chest before his right hand flashed forward. "Now."

I peeked under his black billowing sleeve as creatures of the night tore into the room. Five wolves, several raccoons, owls, big-beaked birds, and bats whipped past us. The screams of the spiders became pitiful wails as twitching legs were removed from bulbous bodies, shadows guided by the Shade's subtle hand movements speared right through them, and the wolves bit a pincher and spikes clean off. The smaller bats dropped bulbous potions on the creatures as they flew above. The hissing green steam killed them more quickly than my mushroom had. Great black arms of magic whipped around, protecting the animals from leaping spyrings, rending the monsters in pieces, and even blowing up portions of the stairwell. The Shade tucked me behind him as he ascended. I tiptoed around the carnage, mindful not to slip on monster gore. Racoons, once cute, now screeched around the room, taking down spiders twice their size in a rabid frenzy.

The cacophony lasted for several minutes before everything went silent. The Shade was breathing harder, likely from expending so much magic. I huddled against his back, held tight by a broad shadow, and I felt...safe, a feeling I should *not* be feeling with someone like him. I pushed a hand against him, definitely not noticing the strong cords of muscle on his back, and he loosened his shadow's hold to allow me to step away.

The aftermath of the battle was chaotic. One raccoon washed what must have been a spyring leg in a pool before happily crunching through it, and the other animals sat back on their haunches, cleaning themselves. The bats swirled around the ceiling while others hung from it, waving their wings with self-satisfied grins.

"Is it safe yet?" the small skunk in my hands asked.

"Yes," the Shade and I said at once. He smirked as he glanced at me.

"So I can go home now?" Jarlz asked.

I pursed my lips. "Should I...get a basket and gather his family?" I scratched the little one's chin. Worry made my voice wobble. "I didn't see them as I ran."

The Shade pulled his hand from my back, leaving the place cold, and tightened his cravat as he addressed the animals. "Clear the room of this filth." They all swung into motion, pulling the remains down the hall and through another door. *"Then go back to sleep."* My brows furrowed, and I took another step away. The Shade didn't speak that last bit aloud.

He inhaled slowly, then swept past me into the greenhouse. He paused for only a moment before his shadows took off around the room, righting pots, sweeping the steaming slop from the spiders, placing it in a large glass container, and moving the bodies toward the door.

"The mushrooms were a good thought." His voice startled me, as quiet as it was.

I pulled the end of my hair forward and tugged it. "It was the only thing I thought might work at the time. It just didn't work as fast as I'd hoped."

"We use the same component in the potions the bats used, just dried and reconstituted with brynlan paste."

My mouth formed an *O*. "Clever. The acid would help it penetrate more quickly."

"And through shells and exoskeletons and armor."

Curiosity bloomed in my chest. "Why did the spyrings attack you? Aren't they yours?" We moved up the stairs, his shadows a constant moving force. One pressed against my middle, guiding me to the side as another shadow righted an overturned potted tree and moved it back into place. Then the shadow arm repositioned me so we could climb the final stairs.

"The manor is plagued here and there by various beasts," the Shade said finally. "More come with each moon-cycle. These slipped through. But the spyrings are not mine. They are usually independent and don't work well with other creatures." He studied the mess of racerbristles. "I've never seen them coordinated before."

Did that mean he had tried to befriend them? A frisson of fear raced through me, and I shuddered at the thought of breakfast with a spyring. The wolves were enough for me.

Glancing around the room of the beautiful racerbristles, I worried my lip. "I'm so sorry," I started. "I can fix this and pick it up."

The Shade's eyebrow tucked up into the hair that had fallen forward. Without breaking eye contact, his shadows swept the room and put it to rights. One even dragged a new pot over and swept the dirt back around the bush.

I cleared my throat. "Okay, well then, I will just...return the boy." I ducked around the Shade and his overwhelming presence and went to the table. "Mama Skunk?"

"Mama Mae? You can come out now," the Shade called as well.

A bush shook, and the mother skunk rushed forward. *"Dark One! Have you seen my—"* Her voice cut off in a high-pitched, worried squeak.

The young kit in my arms started writhing, and I set him down quickly before I dropped him. *"Mama!"*

The two reunited with more purring and chattering until the two other babies also arrived, their questions almost indecipherable. *"Where did you go?"* *"Did you die?"* *"What were you thinking?"* *"Hide-Spray-Live, as I've always told you."*

I smiled. A flush of relief flooded me, followed by a feeling of warm contentment. I was wrapped in his piney scent as he stepped up behind me.

"Let's see to this weakness of my defenses, Dayspring. Where did you first see the creatures?"

All warmth fled as I strode with false bravado to where I'd first seen the spyrings. The shadows shifted the plants, the table, and finally the fern tree aside, revealing the cavern entrance. On the distant wall of the tunnel, eggs and spiderwebs clung to the opening of a hole in the room. Dust and rocks filled the floor.

"I see." He took a cloth from his pocket, wrapping it around a stone and igniting it with a match. Then he threw the whole lot down the sloping tunnel, surrounded by waves of shadow. The light diminished as the distance grew...and grew. The tunnel was enormous. The Shade's frown deepened. He brought a hand forward and swept the eggs and rocks that had fallen into the room back into the tunnel. With a slash of his palm before him, the shadows formed a grate-like barrier at the entrance.

"This will be annoying to clear."

"You think there are more down there?"

He turned, his shoulders low. "There are always more." He strode past the skunk family and gestured for me to follow. "Come, let's rest. It's been quite a day."

Chapter Fourteen

Under the Mountain

I skipped after the Shade, unwilling to be left behind in the green-house. Spyring pieces quickly piled up along the corridor as the animals worked together to drag the remnants down the hall. I turned away from the carnage with a shudder. The Shade swept with unnatural grace down the stairs and across the tile. The shadows bounced after him like bubbles down a stream. I couldn't tell if the smooth motion was his natural bearing or an illusion from the shadows that swirled about his feet. His leather shoes were silent. Perhaps the shadows dampened that as well. Even my silk dress and soft slippers made more sound than him, which, after years of court training, felt decidedly unfeminine. I willed my legs to step more smoothly, but it took so much effort that it slowed me down.

It was hopeless. He was magic. I quit and caught up just behind the Shade. "Will there be another attack?"

"Hmm?" He slowed and looked back at me. "Oh. Not from the spyrings. Not today, at least, and not from there. But moonlight knows, they show up when they want to."

"Where do they come from?" I asked as he led us down the hall and back to the central kitchen.

Grabbing a piece of bread and a slice of cheese from a tray, he turned and leaned back against the counter. "Below." He offered me the oily bread, which I took hesitantly.

"Down the mountain?"

Tapping his fingers on another roll, he answered, "Under it."

"Under the mountain?" I blinked. "Did you build your house on their nest?"

He raised a brow. "When I made my home, there were no monsters but me and mine."

"Hmm." I bit into the oily bread, the mixed-in cheese and herbs were warm and gooey, wholly distracting me for a moment. I missed Chef. Looking outside at the late afternoon sun, I asked, "So where do the monsters come from, really?"

He hummed in a noncommittal way. "The king's mines scrape at the center of the earth. He found more than just luz ore. The monsters of the deep are swarming and irritable."

"The prince has only one mine. We are rich in luz. The castle is full of it. The tower light shines brightly."

"The prince has a great many secrets that he doesn't share with the populace." The Shade filled a glass of water and set it before me; I felt a spark when our hands touched. "Or with nobles' daughters."

"I was an herbalist apprentice. Surely, I would have heard something about this since we add various ores and minerals to the plants we gather."

The Shade shook his head. "Not even then."

I felt unmoored and rattled off a pathetic chorus. "The prince and king lead the nation with light and hope." My voice deadened as I recalled the prince's eyes, begging for my sacrifice.

The Shade came toward me—one step, then two—crowding me back against the island counter. "Yes," he spat out. "Your arrival was certainly full of light." His nostrils flared, and the shadows flickered around him, darkness swirling within his irises. "And you were bleeding from all the hope he gave you." The mark on my neck flared with heat, and I touched it with one hand, wrapping the other hand across my waist protectively.

I shook my head, though I wasn't sure what I disagreed with. My eyes prickled at the rebuke. The prince had once been my friend. He had visited me. He had cared for me. He had betrayed me.

The Shade scratched at his leather bracelet. "He betrayed us all."

My heart ached suddenly with a stabbing pain. The Shade glanced down before stepping back, rubbing a button of his shirt. "The prince is searching for things that the mountain cannot give. And he grows desperate. Rather, the king regent grows desperate."

I grabbed his glass and cleaned it in the sink, willing my hands to stop shaking. He might be less desperate if the Shade didn't fight him constantly.

The Shade's quiet scoff caused me to turn. "The prince fights himself and cannot clean up the messes he makes. He fears to fight the battles he must. And so the mountain itself turns against him." Grabbing the glass from my hand, he took the rag as well. "You do not need to clean."

"I need to do something. I'm here to help. You saved my life, so let me repay you."

"The greenhouse will not be enough?"

"Perhaps I can do laundry."

"The creatures have things well in hand."

I tapped a toe, wondering if I should risk asking. "Then...I can help make those potion bombs."

He tilted his head. "Perhaps." His eyes squinted, peering between thick black lashes. "But what if you did nothing?"

"If I do nothing, then I am nothing." I parroted as I tried to smile. "My father called me Able Aelia."

His jaw muscles feathered as he glared at me, his slow gaze judging, measuring as it perused my person. I felt more naked now than I had in the bath.

"That's stupid." My mouth popped open in offense and outrage, but he held up a hand to stop me. "*You* are not stupid. But that phrase, *that* is stupid." He paced back to add a log to the fireplace. "It implies that to rest is not valuable, that it's nothing. But that would mean that the sick and disabled are nothing. That the elderly are nothing." He eyed me. "That the queen is nothing."

I squeaked in outrage. "Of course, she is something!" Defense for my queen rose within me. "Just because they cannot do something extravagant right now doesn't mean they are worth nothing."

"But this same logic doesn't apply to you?"

My mouth opened and shut, but no brilliant counterargument surfaced.

"Let me ask you something else. If I asked you to scrub the toilets—you would say…"

I felt relief. "Yes. I would be honored to serve the Shade."

"And if I asked you to care for the wolves."

I hesitated a bit longer. "I'd say yes and hope they don't eat me."

He chuckled darkly, and I wondered if they might accidentally eat me. "And if I asked you to flap your arms and squawk like a dragonling, you'd say…"

I bit my lip, my cheeks heating at the image. "If it would please the Shade, I'd say yes."

The Shade mumbled something under his breath and stepped away, toward the threshold of the room, before stopping again, agitated. His shadows enveloped me. His piney scent filled my lungs.

His presence flooded out all thought. His murmured voice, low and quiet, sent vibrations through my heart. "I'm grateful, at least, that when you finally ran—despite this idiotic saying and the training of your youth—you showed discernment. You showed everyone you are worth something, worth more than some sacrifice determined by an old crone. That you don't have to please the world to earn your place. That saying no is the first step to a full and joyful yes. None of those things I just asked of you would bring you fulfillment. Nothing you have ever shared with me has been what Aelia wants or needs or hopes for. That's a problem."

The Shade stepped out, unnaturally smooth again, but as he turned the corner, a slight limp became evident on his left side. I hardly noticed it in my emotional turmoil. I was outraged at the audacity. I was offended that he thought I was a doormat. But deep within, I was horrified because I suspected he was right.

If I truly believed my own words, that I was a tool for the crown, an able servant willing to do anything for my prince, then I would have died that day. I would have willingly stepped forward with the love of my kingdom in my eyes, placing my head on that platter enthusiastically. Instead, I stepped back. And I had run. I had said no. And I hadn't returned.

I threw the rag I had been wringing by the wash basin and stalked down the hall. Daytime animals scurried along the walls. Rats, crows, and an enormous spotted cat sunbathed on a windowsill, but I passed them all in a huff.

Of course, I was worth something. I believed that. I was excellent at finding herbs. I made excellent potions for the queen. I could bake with the best. I—I was still listing things I could do. Alright, reframing. I was worth something because...I was nice and looked out for the needs of others.

A whisper came unbidden within me. *"But what about your own needs?"*

I laughed awkwardly under my breath. The question shouldn't have been funny, but it was. What needs? What did I really need? Food, bed, clothes?

The whisper corrected the list. *"Affection, love, safety."*

My eyes pricked with tears again. A tiny seed in my heart sent a tendril of a root—fragile but present. Maybe I wanted more than I'd been given. I felt ungrateful, a traitor to my upbringing, my kingdom, and my father.

Again, a deep whisper—so deep it rumbled in my bones—spoke. *"Betray yourself, and you lose everything. First, be true to yourself."* I turned to look for the Shade, but he was nowhere nearby. Perhaps my inner voice now sounded like him. It spoke again, *"You must love yourself first, before you can overflow to others."*

I paused, then wondered to the voice, *"And do you love yourself?"*

A grumbling sigh filled my mind and chest. *"Some days are easier than others, Dayspring."*

I knew it. I could hear his thoughts. More frighteningly, he could hear mine.

Awareness that wasn't my own brightened within me. *"I will never betray you."*

"You already have," I muttered. "My mind is my own, and you're in it."

The Shade chuckled from wherever he was hiding. *"Your mind became mine the moment we kissed. I will safeguard it. I will treasure it. I will respect it and stay silent if you wish. But you came to me, and now, you are mine."*

Crying out in frustration, I stormed into my room and shut and locked the door, willing the door and the distance to spare me his intrusion.

I was no one's. I was not property. My mind could not be owned. But keeping my thoughts away from my heart was more challenging than I expected. Deep down, a quiet part of me reveled in the sensation of being wanted. When the Shade said *mine,* I didn't feel owned or betrayed. It had felt...like I'd returned home. Like my mother's kiss on my cheek. Her hand sweeping my hair from my eyes or behind my ear. Her lullabies. The safety of the hearth after dinner. Chef's sweet embrace. The pressure of the queen's hand on mine.

Safety. Warmth. Being wanted. None of these things were like the Shade—the dark, malicious, sinister, evil...

"*Vile,*" he supplied.

Yes, vile Shade. I changed into night clothes and shoved myself into bed. Perhaps the Shade couldn't follow me into dreams. Perhaps I wanted him to. Perhaps I should stop thinking about him.

As I drifted off, I heard him again, amusement thick in his voice. *"Just rest, Aelia. We will practice. And meanwhile, until you find your footing, I will keep you safe."*

And again, like an idiot, I believed him.

Chapter Fifteen

Storms Rumble

"*Madame, if you would come with me.*" The chirping sound preceded a slap of wings hitting my face. "*Madame, please, wake up.*"

I blinked hard. The room was dark and my eyes were gritty. I had not slept very long. Before me, Jamison Harold Crocus Marcus Delaney the Third dive-bombed me again. I waved him back and sat up. "I'm awake. I'm awake." Thunder shook the walls of my room, dust slipped between the cracks of the ceiling and fell in waves, and I startled out of the bed.

"*Come now, we must go deeper into the manor.*"

"What's happening?"

He fluttered to the doorway. "*This way, Madame.*"

I grabbed a black silken robe and followed him into the hall. A menagerie of animals—those of the day and of the night—filled the halls as they traveled down the stairs to the lower levels. "Jamison, what is going on?" I asked as we entered the fray of the creatures running down the stairwell.

"*The prince, Madame. He has returned.*"

I stopped in my tracks, earning several angry hisses and squawks from the animals that suddenly had to detour around me.

"He's here?"

The bat rolled in the air and flew to my face, baring his tiny teeth. *"Nearby. He wouldn't fight so close to the master."*

"Where is the Shade?"

"Protecting us, of course." His eyes bounced to the ceiling.

I tilted my chin up the stairwell, biting my thumb as I considered his words. "Fighting and storming, you mean."

"I said what I mean, Madame. Now come with me!" He grasped a bit of my hair with his feet, but I brushed him aside and turned around, racing up the stairwell while dodging the animals running down. I had to see what was happening. The prince was here. Was he here for me? I was still angry at him...but what if he came to apologize? He wouldn't be able to get close enough to apologize if this madman of a shadow monster didn't stop battering the prince and his soldiers with his magic.

Inexplicable pain flared up within my chest and left leg. I paused for a moment, then continued to run. Jamison screeched irritably behind me, his grumpy murmurs constant in my mind. I glanced out a window to see bursts of shadow coming from above. Passing the third floor, I climbed the stairs leading to the tower and pushed open the door. The room was small; its furniture dark and sparse. A stand with a water pitcher and glasses stood beside a tall chair in the center. Four enormous windows opened in each direction, and the Shade sat facing the eastern opening. The floor billowed with smoke, and I stepped uneasily. My eyes told me that the floor was moving, but my shoes landed securely on the wood planks.

Pain dragged at my arms as the shadows outside the tower whipped forward, battering back a blazing ball of fire that erupted from the other side of the canyon. The Shade was panting, his hands moving before him, twisting and ripping the air with curled fingers. Shadows poured from him and through the windows. His magic further blackened the dark early morning sky.

I peered over his shoulder. On the other side of the canyon, the prince and seven galers moved in formation, sending fire from the prince's palm billowing toward the castle. One flame surged at the tower and nearly licked it before the Shade stood and pushed both palms downward toward the floor. The night fell upon the flame and doused it, knocking back three of the galers. Even the prince stumbled.

The Shade collapsed back into the chair, one hand shakily held before him, holding a wall of shadow before us. He turned an icy glare over his shoulder, his voice lower and more dangerous than I had ever heard it before. "What are you doing here?"

"I..." What was I doing? Stopping him? Helping him? Waiting to hear Leon's apology? "I don't know."

The Shade scoffed, and his other hand swept across, thwarting another attack. "Your lover returns."

A grimace escaped before I could school it. "He's not my lover."

"He's intent on rescuing you."

Raising a brow, I stepped beside him. "Do I need rescuing?"

He chuckled darkly as he shoved his body forward, sending a burst of black energy at the men.

"What does Leon want?"

"The prince hasn't said yet. He's more of an 'attack now, consider the consequences later' type, wouldn't you agree?"

I didn't want to admit that I did agree. "What if he's here to apologize? To make things right?" I backpedaled at the Shade's look of skepticism. "Or not."

The two enemies sent more volleys between them as the sky rippled in black thunder. Acid rain pelted down, obscuring the view.

My belly clenched uneasily at the show of power. "Could you kill them?"

His green eyes flashed to mine, then ahead again. "Yes."

"Will you kill them?" My heart clenched as I waited.

"No." His thought echoed in my mind. *"Not today."*

"Why not?"

With a roar, he stood again. A surge of shadow and power rushed through the room and burst out all four windows as he whirled toward me. "Because I am not a monster! I am not the creature you think I am! I am not evil, nor am I Death." I scurried backward through the whirling shadows, but he pursued me. My shoulders hit the stone walls, and he towered over me. The mark on my neck throbbed and burned.

The Shade put a hand by my head, still breathing heavily, and a bead of sweat trickled down his temple. "I am not a monster...I am just a man."

"But your magic is killing the queen," I whispered.

He hissed and whipped a hand toward the east...toward the prince. "His magic burns the land. His greed poisons the earth." He turned and pointed two fingers toward the sky, cutting them downward and dousing a thin blast of flame the prince was forming. "Him and that usurping king regent, Aelia. The leaders that somehow you still venerate!"

"He's my...our...prince."

"Are you so blinded by your upbringing and rote venerations of the king? You were not always this way. You were always bright and kind. Not this fake nice garbage. *Think,* Aelia. Think." He scoffed. "Being in that castle ruined you." He stumbled back to the chair and sat heavily, resting his elbows on his knees. Pain blossomed again in my gut and my left leg...pain that I didn't think was mine. "He doesn't deserve your attention or your respect. He showed you who he was. He demonstrated that his father dictates all his actions, even over your supposed friendship. Cut him off at the root, Aelia. He showed you his fruit—it's poison."

I opened my mouth to retort in defense of our friendship when Leon called out from afar.

"I'm coming for you, Aelia!" he shouted. My soul twisted, filled with dread, tempted by hope that he might be truly sorry. He continued, "I will save you from this nightmare and welcome you back into my grace! We can still save the queen! We can still save our nation!" I walked toward the window to get a better view. The prince and his galers were backing away. "I forgive you for running away!"

I froze and shut my mouth with a clack of teeth. He forgives *me*? There was no apology, no acknowledgment of wrongdoing, no plea to the years we had spent together. Disappointment and embarrassment burned hot on my cheeks. All the hope that I had for Leon to realize what he'd done and come for me burned to ash. My eyes prickled, and I begged the tears to remain in place. I refused to turn at the low rumble of the Shade's voice as he approached to stand beside me.

"Forgiveness. What a perversion of the word." The Shade scoffed. He outstretched one palm before him, ready to fight back, until the men drifted out of sight. Then he slumped his shoulders and dropped his hand. Shadows swirled slowly on the floor as they withdrew from outside. Distantly, the bright light of the castle tower shone, but despite the settling of the Shade's magic, the sky still rumbled with darkness. Thick black clouds belched toward the castle—clouds the Shade wasn't making.

"Those aren't yours?" I asked quietly, gesturing to the acid-dripping sky.

"No."

"But...where do they come from?"

"The mines, Madame, obviously," Jamison chided. *"The work in the mines makes the clouds. Sometimes, within the tunnels, fire magic sets something ablaze within the earth. They let it burn through since there is no real way to stop the burning even with all the washers of the kingdom. The metal workers also produce smoke by smelting the ore of the mountains. The smoke is toxic, and the rain drops it on the mountains. The prince manufactures the battles himself. It's easier to blame the Master than take responsibility."*

I blinked in horror. The Shade plodded back and sat heavily in his chair. I felt a wave of fatigue.

"But the queen suffers because the land is sick, and I couldn't find or grow more racerbristles."

"It's always harder on those with more power and sensitivity." Jamison, who had perched high in the rafters, fluttered over to grab the water flask and brought it to the Shade.

"Thank you," the Shade said to our minds.

After taking a deep drink, he turned to me. "What is the queen's magic, Aelia?"

"She's a..." I pursed my lips. "Well, of course, she's got...um..." Why couldn't I remember what the queen's magic was? In all the years since I moved to the castle, she'd never been well enough to use it.

The Shade rubbed his forehead, dabbing the sweat with a handkerchief and leaning his head back against the sooty wood of the chair. While his eyes were closed, I studied him. A dark shadow of day-old stubble defined every sharp corner of his jaw, and thick black lashes rested on angular cheekbones. His black hair was longer on top and the most unkempt I'd ever seen it, as if his fingers had repeatedly run through it.

What would it feel like if I did that? I clenched my fist to refocus. I followed the line of his temple and was startled to find his bright green eyes on mine. A wry eyebrow rose, and my cheeks flushed.

He closed his eyes again with an amused huff. "She's a loamer."

It took me a moment to recall who he was talking about. "The queen has earth magic? Like my father?"

The Shade grunted. "Even so. When did you come to the castle again?"

"I was just about to turn seven."

The Shade nodded. "And how did you find the gardens?"

"They were enormous. They took up much of the castle grounds, like they had once been grand, but they were unkept and dry."

"Exactly."

Exactly? My mind was sluggish, and the confusion was frustrating. "Exactly what? My father is a fair loamer, but he—well, he isn't well, but he isn't dying." Earth magic was uncommon but not that rare in the world. Just...rare here.

"Well, he's surrounded by potions, isn't he?" Jamison hissed the accusation, and I immediately rallied in defense of my father before I started to wonder if it could possibly be true. My father wouldn't steal from Her Majesty, would he?

The Shade pushed himself up out of the chair with effort and spoke to Jamison. "Please inform the others they can return to bed if they'd like. Or if they prefer, they can stay and rest below. It's been an adventurous week."

"As you wish." Jamison eyed me suspiciously before ducking out the door.

"Can't you just tell them with your mind?" I asked, unable to keep a tinge of sauciness out of my tone. He was so invasive in mine, already.

He chuckled darkly. "Of course, I can."

"So why didn't you?"

He struggled toward the door and limped down the stairs, holding tightly to the banister. "For one, I'm tired." It was probably my bleeding heart because I swore my legs ached with his.

I skittered after him, the tower suddenly darker without him. "And for two?"

"The only thoughts I am interested in right now are yours."

I froze wide-eyed; his chuckle echoed through the stairwell. "Come on, Aelia. Let's see what the cats dragged in for breakfast."

As we entered the kitchen, an extremely fluffy, spotted, enormous gray cat was—in fact—dragging a small deer onto the large wooden kitchen island. The Shade scratched the cat's ears and whispered something I couldn't hear. As he reached for a knife, a screeching, human-sounding yowl came from behind us.

"Put that down right now, young man, before the wind pushes you over and you cut off your own hand!"

I whirled to the door. An ancient man bustled past me, his knobby finger pointing at the Shade as his thick, wiry eyebrows partially covered his black eyes. The man's head barely rose to the Shade's chest. "You know better than to push me—me, in my decrepit state, just a toe away from the edge of the grave!"

I froze in place. One: because a human being I didn't know lived here was standing before me. And two: the way he was scolding the Shade—scourge that he was—was liable to get us killed.

But the Shade just *laughed*. He set the knife down, and the older man beamed in a self-satisfied way. In a speed that shouldn't have been possible for an elder, he began to masterfully prepare the meat.

The Shade's eyes glimmered with amusement and he settled himself onto a stool as I stood gawking.

As the older man worked, he glanced up and waved his knife as sharply as he did his finger between us. "Well, son, you gonna introduce me to the fine woman, or do I need to do it myself?"

"Uncle, meet Aelia. Aelia, meet my Uncle Koll. Entertainer, animal tamer, and—"

"The only reason you can cook at all."

The Shade's grin grew. "Not untrue."

The Shade can cook?

"Not today, he can't," Uncle Koll muttered. "Not when he is partially b—"

"Uncle." The Shade glared at him.

"—that is, beat down from exerting all of his magic," Uncle Koll finished. I frowned, tilting my head as my gaze flicked between them.

"Sit. Both of you."

I shouldn't have felt so frightened by someone half my weight, but something about the flint in his gaze and the butcher knife in his hand had me sitting immediately. The Shade rested his elbows beside me before he reached into a cabinet underneath and grabbed a small bottle. It was a lovely, familiar pink hue. He passed it to Uncle Koll, who took a quick drink.

"Ray, the berries!" Uncle Koll shouted.

Ray, a large fluffy, something—*"Honey badger,"* the Shade said inside my mind—rude but helpful—bustled out of what must have been a pantry, dragging a basket behind him. He pushed it up to the Shade, who grasped the handle and set it before us. I reached forward for the cutting board and knife to help with the preparation, but before I could reach either, a spatula tapped on my hand.

"Ah-ah. My kitchen now." Uncle Koll turned and poured cubes of venison into a boiling soup pot. "I got this. But Lady Aelia, won't you be so kind as to tell us about yourself."

The words started slowly, but as Uncle Koll bustled around, chopping the herbs, I was reminded so much of Chef that my shoulders relaxed, and the words fell more easily. I spoke of her, of the staff, of my father, of the potions.

"You seem close to Chef." Uncle Koll commented idly as he minced garlic.

"I am. I...was." I squirmed in my chair. "When she came to the castle and saw me... floundering, she kind of took me under her wing. Though she wasn't a lady, she taught me what I needed to know so as not to embarrass the king... king regent...at his table. My father could only teach so much."

Uncle Koll dumped some vegetables into the pot. "And were you close to your mother?"

"My mother and I were two peas in a pod. When she died, my father almost did too, cursed by their soulbond." The men shared a look. "I remember flashes from when we were together. Happy moments, until she got sick."

"It's not fair when a life ends too soon." Uncle Koll's words caught in my throat, so I just nodded my agreement. "My Lydia and I were bonded." He pulled out his arm, and around his elbow, a band of leaves and swirls wrapped like a light brown tattoo. I frowned at it, uncomfortable with his frank vulnerability. "She was a gift from the heavens, my other half. When she left this world, I wondered if she took the best part of me."

I grimaced. "You must have been devastated."

His sigh was heavy as he stirred the ladle. "I was for a time. And certainly, moments are just as painful as before, but they trigger less and less often as your heart expands, time passes, and new love enters." He ruffled the Shade's hair. "My next love was for a black-haired waifish boy who got in more mischief than he could handle."

"Don't you regret the bond?" I clamped my lips shut, regretting the words immediately. Who was I, and where did this unfiltered speech come from? "I mean. I'm sorry. That was rude."

Uncle Koll smiled sadly, rubbing at his chest. "It certainly still hurts, at times. My heart will always have an ache for my Lydia. But all this grief is just love unshared. All the love that I have for her is now reflected in that memory—in the pain, certainly—but even more in the joyful memories of what was. This grief is a gift—the knowledge that she was here, and she mattered, and I loved her. I live every day trying to raise this young man in the way she would expect, and I work very hard to make her proud."

"But you'll never find that kind of love again…"

"Ha. Poppycock. I mean, perhaps the stars will only match me with Lydia, but you know as well as I how sometimes after a loss, a new bond can be formed. Not every marriage is a bond-match. Take the king and queen, for example, a love match, even if they weren't bonded. Somehow the magic knows what we need. What I had with Lydia is special, but if the stars give me another love—bonded or not—that will be a gift as well. Love is not a piece of bread you cut smaller and smaller pieces from. It's a living, growing thing that expands and changes as we grow and live our lives. There's enough love in the world to expand to cover us all."

I didn't realize a tear had beaded on my lid until it dropped to my cheek. I hastily wiped it away with a pretend cough. How could this be? My mother died, and my father spared very little love for me after and would certainly never remarry. His whole existence was her, and as a result, he had become a shell of a human, sustained by his drink and his proud work.

But—my conscience sharply reminded me—of course, Queen Gemaline had nearly adopted me, even in her sick state. She had welcomed me in, combed my hair, listened to my rantings and ravings and smiled at me with such warmth. "I can perhaps see what you mean. The queen certainly demonstrated extraordinary kindness to me when we moved in. I do not presume to say she loved me, but I certainly began to love her. She already had a whole family and a whole people to love, but she let me in and cared for me as much as she could."

Both men stopped moving when I mentioned the queen.

The Shade picked up a bread crumb and dropped it onto his plate. "And how is she?" His voice was low, and its huskiness made my brows pull together.

"I'm worried for her." A tightness crawled up my throat, squeezing my chest. "I search and struggle to find what she needs for the potions, but it doesn't seem as effective as it once was. She used to be able to walk the halls or attend the balls and sit with the king, but lately..." I shrugged. "It doesn't help that I can't find enough racerbristles." My eyes slid to the Shade, and I couldn't stop the heat from their glare. He could save her.

The Shade flicked the bread across the room. "And who is bringing her racerbristles now?"

Guilt blossomed beside the anger in my chest. I didn't feel guilty, but he should. I blinked a few times to clear the weird sensation. "Likely a servant. Leon knew where a bush was." I shifted uncomfortably in my seat at the memory. "I'm sure someone has brought them."

"Maybe we should make a deposit," he murmured.

I fully turned in my seat. "A deposit?"

The Shade nodded as he started in on the fruit and Uncle Koll dropped off a plate of eggs and tomato. "You weren't wrong. I do have plenty of racerbristles."

I studied his face for treachery or mischief. What was he thinking? A siege? A chance to rob the castle, disguised in an act of kindness? Would he go so low to betray us all?

Uncle Koll began to chop the vegetables aggressively, and I glanced up to see him smirking. The Shade growled, and the old man cut more normally.

The Shade's face was flint, so I continued, "It would certainly help. The land is cracked and baked and struggling."

The Shade reached for my hand, drawing it up to the table as our gazes linked. "Exactly." Exactly what? But his gaze held me captive as time slowed. My hand heated beneath his and the mark on my neck tingled and prickled like goosebumps. A deep ache burned in my chest. I squeezed back, mesmerized by the sensation of his skin on mine.

Jamison fluttered through the doorway and flew between us, breaking our eye contact and snapping me out of the moment as he reached the cabinet. *"All the animals are sorted and accounted for."*

"No losses?"

Jamison landed upside down near the hanging teacups. *"None, sir. Just some grumpier than others."*

Like you, I thought as I grabbed a strawberry.

"I'm not grumpy. I'm direct," Jamison chirped.

I froze, the berry halfway to my lips. "I didn't say that."

The bat fluffed his furry chest and stretched out a wing. *"You don't have to say anything. You think so loudly! We can all—"*

"Enough," the Shade interrupted, exhaustion dragging the word out and his shoulders down.

"But I didn't think them *at* anyone," I said.

Jamison said, *"You don't need to. You are throwing them around. You have no control."*

My eyes widened. "You can hear what I'm thinking all the time?"

"It's horrible." Jamison scrunched his fuzzy nose.

"And you too?" I pointed the strawberry between Uncle Koll and the Shade. "You've heard everything?" I couldn't believe it.

"Believe it or not, my lady, your thoughts are as clear to us as speech." Uncle Koll spoke quietly and not unkindly.

My thoughts whirled through the last hour—through the last five minutes. Through the Shade holding my hand.

Jamison chirped, *"Yes, everything."*

My face burned red as I leapt away and off the stool. "How do I stop them? It's...it's an *invasion!*" I set my hands on my head. "I don't want you in my head!"

The Shade's lips tipped up on the side, his self-satisfied smirk somehow still more alluring than irritating. How could he? And how could he not tell me?

"Think what you will, Dayspring, but it has helped me to determine if you were actually sent here to kill me or mine." The Shade returned to his meal and ignored my outraged squawk.

I tried to burn his handsome face with the fire in my glare. "And are you satisfied?"

His gaze darkened with a swirl of shadow as his eyes danced down my form. "Hardly." Jamison laughed in a sort of chortle, and the Shade grinned. "Even so, I can teach you to let out only the thoughts you wish."

Stepping to his side, I set my hand on his arm. "Please. Please, teach me. It's the castle, isn't it? The magic of the castle that helps me hear the thoughts and share my own?"

The Shade glanced at my neck before meeting my gaze. "It's something like that." He shrugged as Uncle Koll set out steaming bread and a vat of soft butter. "But Jamison is right. Well, you're right too. It's worth teaching you control. I'm sure the animals would like to keep their thoughts to themselves as well."

He passed me a torn piece of bread and drizzled a bit of honey on the top, licking his thumb after he replaced the spoon. "But first, Dayspring, let's make the queen her potion."

Chapter Sixteen

Potions

T he Shade and I walked into the first level of the solarium, surrounded by his plants and his ego and his shadows. My hands twisted around themselves as I paced to catch up.

"I am not my father."

He frowned. "I never said you were."

"I'm not a master potion maker. I don't have the magic to help you."

His fingers tapped on the wood of the banister of the stair as he considered me. I squirmed under his attention. "Are you a competent potion maker?"

"What?"

"Have your potions ever hurt anyone?"

My mouth dropped open as I stepped back. "Seven stars, no. I would never give something to anyone I wouldn't take myself."

The Shade turned and started again up the stairs. "Then you'll do."

I chased after him, my skirts swirling. "I want to help—really, I do—but I'm not the person you're looking for. Why can't we just take the ingredients to my father? He'll know what to do with them."

The Shade pulled to a halt. "What do you think your father is doing now without a daughter or the ingredients he needs to save the queen?"

Drinking. I winced at my own cruel thought. "I'm sure he is out finding more ingredients. He...values his position. He cares. He knows his place is to serve His Highness—I mean, Her Majesty."

His gaze latched onto mine. "Tell me honestly, if given the ingredients, can you produce the potion for the queen? Because that's all I need to know."

"But—"

"Aelia." His voice was ragged with exasperation.

My shoulders slumped. "I can."

He turned on his heel and headed back up the stairs toward the racerbristles. I followed behind him, the lingering shadows sometimes obscuring the edge of the step and making me slower. As soon as I had the thought, the shadows lifted and moved before him instead. I huffed a laugh and tried to catch up. Whatever I did, I couldn't look at the Shade's rear. That would really be—

The Shade had stopped, and I ran into him. His shadows caught me, though I felt his shoulders shaking with...was that laughter? He turned and grasped my upper arm to steady me.

"Alright, alright. As much as I enjoy listening to you, it seems only fair to teach you step one of thought blocking."

Heat soaked through my clothes under his palm. "Is that why I can't hear you?"

He nodded carefully. "I am very, very cautious to be sure I don't share my thoughts with you."

"Why not?"

He continued, completely ignoring my question. "The first thing to know about thought magic is that thoughts are like light. Thoughts zip through our minds like stars falling across a black sky." I blinked dully. "Or...like a lamp shining its light, casting its 'thoughts' about the room." His right-hand fingers tapped along the edge of my shoulder blade. Goosebumps erupted. "To block the light, you need to build a barricade, or a filter, around the lamp. Imagine building a wall of, oh, let's say shadow bricks, around your mind. And add a door."

As foolish as it sounded, I tried to do as he was describing. Black and swirly brick by shadowy brick, the walls formed. I pondered the door handle for a moment. I could choose the handle of my old room; it was round and bronze with a notch on the back half that my fingers had threaded a thousand times. Instead, I decided on the arching black iron handles of the manor.

"Don't forget the roof."

I hastily added a roof and a floor. I now had a lovely black box around a shining lamp. My cheeks heated; how was this anything more than an imagination game? "How do I know if it worked?"

His shoulder lifted, and his eyes glinted in amusement. "Probably think something."

My mind went blank, thoughtless, and empty. I scraped the bottom of the thought-barrel. *I have an itch on my back and my shoe is too...purple.* I tried not to grimace at the ridiculous statements, but he didn't flinch. "Did you hear that?" I asked.

He glanced up to the floor above us where the mother skunk was looking down at our interlude. "You blocked the thought." He smiled and turned back up the stairs. "Now, you can imagine walls around other minds too, to help prevent interloping if you don't want to hear it. The longer you are with m—within the castle, the stronger the magic will grow. You'll want to block out some voices here and there. But if you keep everything too tightly shut, you might not hear the animals when they speak to you."

I stepped forward, trying to imagine my own black box staying as I went about my business. I peered at the Shade…remembering how he was the Evil Dark Lord and all. With a grin, I followed the Shade up the stairs, happy to test his resolve and my blocking. *I like your Uncle. He was nice. I also like that he teases you.* I glanced up to be sure he was still moving. *I like your hands—they're warm. I thought the Shade's hands might be cold because you are Death. I wish I could trust you, but who could trust someone so handsome?* I glanced up to be sure he kept climbing. *I'd like to try out that kiss again sometime when I'm not dying.*

The Shade stubbed his toe on the step and hobbled to the next one. Shadows surrounded us until he reached to grab the broken pot shard before him. "Missed a piece. Tripped on it."

I squinted at him as he turned quickly and walked a little too stiffly. I glanced down at the mother skunk who had meandered under the tables.

"Did you hear anything?" I asked in my mind, opening a mental window in the box as I did.

She scratched at her nose. *"No, as I told him, I didn't hear a thing. Only from my children."* One bumbled out from under a racerbristle as she spoke. *"I'll go gather them up."* And she trotted away.

By the time I arrived at the top of the steps, the Shade was standing before a table that was set up near the racerbristles with shears in hand. "Begin. I'm curious how this compares to the potion recipes I've dabbled with in the last few years."

Oh, great, extra pressure. I hesitantly grabbed my own shears and tapped the handle on my palm. "Well, I'll need three leaves, one stem, and a twist of root from the racerbristles for every bottle." The Shade remained silent. "Twenty leaves of white thieves, three stamen from the auralius flower, two drops from adimantus mushrooms, and one cup of spring water."

"Anything else?"

"Fourteen bluebuds, five leaves of weatherwillow, and one thorn from the ice rose."

His eyebrow rose farther.

"And the root of the rototuber." I cleared my throat. "That's all."

His chuckle filled the space as his shadows danced.

"And..." Ice filled my veins.

He raised a wry eyebrow as if sensing my mood. "Yes, Dayspring?"

"I may have already started collecting some pieces."

With hot cheeks, I stepped over to the box of dried goods and crushed racerbristle ingredients I had collected that first morning before the spyrings attacked and set them on the table in front of me. I wished the space between us was bigger to hide me from his rage. Instead, I looked up and found amusement glinting in his eyes.

"We are going to need more hands." His shadow swept past me and down the stairs. Within minutes, the cries of able-bodied creatures echoed against the glass. The Shade's shadow pulled a much larger pot up the stairs, and others brought large mixing bowls and enormous spoons. "Shall we?"

I stepped to his side, his very presence thickening the air that pressed against my skin and filled my lungs. His shadows idly swirled at my ankles, causing my gown to shift like gentle eddies of a cool river. My skin prickled where I felt his gaze. Twenty animals sat or stood, their attention solely on me.

Snipping a stem off the bush beside me, I set it into the bowl with a hesitant smile. "We shall."

The animals burst into action. At first, the chaos of directing, collecting, and mashing the ingredients was almost overwhelming. But the racoons, ravens, skunks, squirrels, and crows were easily directed and brought the ingredients to me with a mere thought and brief image of my mind. The Shade filled in where my thoughts struggled, and soon, piles of the raw ingredients filled the tables around us.

The Shade rolled up his sleeves to reveal wholly ordinary and plain forearms that were definitely not corded with delicious muscles and that I was absolutely not watching as he worked. I was never distracted by his grin at the creatures' antics, or his patient gaze as he awaited my instruction. The day drifted by, my back ached, and my hands cramped, but we pressed on.

Around midday, Uncle Koll stopped by with a tray of food and tea that he placed on a nearby shelf. His eyes glittered as he took in the sight, then he returned to the kitchen. Sweat beaded on my temple, and a shadow swept past me to open the window. Below the table, shadows beat like waves, fanning the space. At least Death was a useful s ort.

Finally, twenty potions sat before us. The right pink hue. The right viscosity. The right odor. I beamed at the Shade. "These are by far the healthiest ingredients I have used in quite a while. Years maybe. Even the plants I've found recently were all incredibly dry."

"I've made the loamer potion before, but I never added the auralius stamen." He tilted his head in concession. "It's an excellent addition."

"The shelf life doubles with it. Father discovered it quite on accident. But it means the potion containers can be larger, and the doses will remain viable for much longer, so we can space out how often we make them." I bounced on my toes. "All of this can make a real difference!" I thought of the queen and how much this might help her, and with a happy squeal, I rushed forward, wrapping my arms around the Shade's waist.

Both of us froze. I coughed and moved to step back, but his arms swept around me and pulled me into his embrace as the shadows swept circles around us. The Shade smelled like forests and moss and dew on the meadow at dawn. My cheek buried deeper into his chest against my wishes. And then there were tears in my eyes. Wretched, wild tears that had no business being there. One fell on his sleeve.

"Oh, Dayspring." His chest vibrated against my cheek. "Your face is leaking."

I turned my nose into him. Muffled, I protested, "Is not."

His thumb caressed gentle circles against my shoulder. "But *why*, Dayspring. Why the tears? Aren't you happy?"

I was. I was happy that I could help the queen and have someone else's help—even if it was the Shade. But how would I confess that to my kingdom's greatest enemy?

"It's been a long time since I had a hug," I said instead, my cheeks flushing at the admission. "Chef sometimes hugs me, I guess, but not often, and not without leaving a cup of flour on me after."

The shadows buffeted my legs, and I glanced at his face. It was *angry*. The Shade's jaw muscles feathered as his eyes fixed on a distant point, the green and black swirling within them like violent storm clouds.

Fear slid down my spine, and I moved to skitter away. I knew anger. But he caught me again and brought his arm gently around my head to hold me tighter. "I'm sorry, Dayspring. I'm not angry at you."

I sniffed. "You're not?"

"I'm angry for you. On your behalf. Against those who should have..." He swallowed, and his hand drifted on my cheek, casting scattered thoughts through my mind. "*Kept you safe. Stayed their hand. Not your fault. Kill the ones that hurt you.*" Before the thoughts were pulled back again. He said aloud, "Should have hugged you." His fingers pulled through my hair softly. "Should have held you."

I let out a loud, ungraceful sob before pressing myself more tightly into him. I tried to wrap it all back again, safely secure behind a veneer of polite curtsies and braced smiles. The tears, however, continued to fall unbidden. Awkwardly, I half-laughed. "Your shirt is getting soaked."

"I'm very rich. I have another."

"Probably some snot."

"I live with animals. Namely, Uncle Koll."

I giggled and sighed, pressing deeper into his embrace. Closing my eyes, I felt the tears begin drying on my cheeks. Questions tugged at me, but I was unwilling to voice them and disrupt the moment of safety I had found. How was he so rich? How did he come to Nuren? And how did he so badly insult the prince that all blame now rested on him? But I held my peace and watched the shadows dance about the table.

"Did I hear someone say my name?" Uncle Koll clunked up the stairs with a cane, and I flew away from the Shade. I desperately wiped at my eyes before turning with a practiced smile.

The Shade offered him a chair, which Uncle Koll sank into heavily. He rubbed his knees and clasped the Shade's hand with an affectionately aggressive pat. "There's a good lad." His eyes landed on the table and widened.

"That is some fine work there." He tilted the potion back and forth. "It seems thicker than the ones you make for me."

My mouth popped open, recalling the potion from the kitchen earlier. "You need racerbristle potions?"

"Why do you think he has so many plants, my dear? My earth magic is not as strong, so the sickness of the earth doesn't make me quite as ill." He raised his cane to eye level. "But it's why I have this sun-cursed device I depend on so much." He looked between the two of them. "May I?" The Shade looked at me and waited.

"Of course you may." I pushed one toward the Shade who lifted it with a shadow to his uncle.

The first sip was loud and wet. "Well, hers tastes better than yours."

"Taste is not important for healing," the Shade muttered darkly.

"It is better for *adhering,* my boy. Sadly, I may be switching potion masters. But I will still take you up on your cheesecake skills." Uncle Koll smacked his lips. "What is it missing in this one that you have in yours though?"

"Burnt aspen," the Shade answered

I tilted my head. "Doesn't that interact with the rototuber?"

The Shade shook his head. "It acts as a binder, prolonging the effect of the potions. In my sleeping draught, it expanded the rest from four hours to eight."

I gaped at him. I had seen him use some potions during the spyring attack but had vastly underestimated how competent he was. He didn't need me at all. The thought stung.

"*Not true, Dayspring.*"

I blinked back tears, and Uncle Koll spoke again. "You know, that one time you added micahra, that one dust, to that...poison, I think. Didn't it actually heal the skin instead of burn it?"

"But micahra..." I started. We'd used it when we arrived here when my father had made a poultice for his arm wound. "I didn't think you could drink it."

"Maybe in smaller portions," the Shade rumbled.

I tapped my lips. "Maybe with lemonseed to augment the bones."

"Or perhaps the root of the kilterberry might help," the Shade added.

"Kilterberry?" I asked.

"The one with the stars for leaves."

"You would choose something with stars." I smiled. "But Father said that causes headaches."

"Only because it boosts the mind."

Uncle Koll chuckled loudly. "Alright you two, enough for this old man. All I know is that whatever you two concoct, I'll be happy to test it out." He stood without using the table. "This potion's a good one. My knee isn't quite so angry now." He walked more easily to the stairs. "My boy, if you would." The Shade's hand wavered ever so slightly as he reached out and created a shadow chair for his uncle. "So long for now." And with a wave, the shadows carried Uncle Koll back down the stairs.

I started tidying up the potions to be boxed up when I noticed the Shade take a small sip out of one. He set it down in the box as if to hide what he'd done. Then he turned and pushed in his chair. "Dayspring, tomorrow, I think we should figure out how to augment this potion."

I bit my lip and focused on the table.

"Spill it, Dayspring."

"What about cloudy mossweed?"

The Shade paused. "For what, exactly?"

"I just...I wonder if it could be heated and separated. The concentrate could maybe help with the fatigue."

"Do you think it would do more than the adimantus mushroom?"

"Yes, since that's really more of a nutrition supplement."

A swirl of shadow was the only sign of his consideration. "Maybe...maybe if we combine it with—"

"Bitterroot," we said together.

He smiled, and his eyes crinkled before they narrowed. "The trouble is, lately I've only seen the cloudy mossweed on the western cave walls. The ones on the cliffs near the castle were all killed off."

I deflated. "So it's too dangerous because of the spyrings?"

His lips peeled back in a smile that looked much like the wolf's. "Nothing is too dangerous for us, Dayspring."

"Then...we could go get some?"

Swirling out, the Shade descended the stairs. "Let's go tomorrow. Maybe some of the scary beasties will be sleeping the day away."

Tomorrow. The caves. I shuddered at the thought of the spyrings, but my fear was short-lived, replaced by the image of a potion that was better, stronger, and would help even more.

I couldn't give the prince what he wanted, but maybe I—maybe we could still help the queen.

I was afraid to wonder too hard about why the Shade would be willing to save his enemy. For a moment, I worried that he would try to poison her, but if Uncle Koll was our test subject, of course he'd be careful. I jolted at the realization that I trusted that relationship. I squeezed my eyes shut, trying to keep myself on guard and remember what I knew before I came here. The Shade was darkness, evil, vile...

"Tired, Dayspring. The Shade is tired. Let's go to bed." His steps seemed heavier as each struck the stone floor with a click. He swept a whirl of shadow around the room, dousing the lamps. I shuddered and stepped closer. I frowned in confusion at my own actions. If I really thought the Shade was vile, then why would I move closer to him just because I feared the dark? I really should be more careful of my thoughts.

"Sorry." My face flushed as my fingers slid to my necklace.

"Your thoughts were leaking."

"Sorry."

There was a pause as he slowed his steps. "I like knowing your thoughts." His eyes swirled with blackness as he regarded me, his gaze a weight that trickled across my skin.

A burst of nerves fluttered through my belly.

Fear, certainly. Those nerves must be fear.

Chapter Seventeen

Bitterroot Caverns

I awoke to the sound of Jamison fluttering about a new set of clothes. Not a silken dress this time, but instead thick linen trousers, a long-sleeved tunic, and a heavy wool cape were draped at the end of my bed. Two black boots with large buckles sat beneath them on the slate floor.

"If Her Royal Slumbering Almighty Highness could dress quickly, the Master is anxious to move out," the bat said with an annoyed tone.

Disrobing, I threw myself into the tunic before quickly shoving my bare legs into the pant legs.

"If His Royal Flappiness would deign to find me some breakfast, I would appreciate it."

"Fine."

"Fine!" I shoved my socked feet into the boots, realizing my grumpiness this morning bordered on petulant. "Why are you even helping me if you're going to be so...so..."

"Is it too early for the lady to make real sentences?"

"So *rude*, Jamison. I don't believe I've been rude to you."

"Your existence offends me."

"But why, Jamison?"

His tiny body flapped loudly before me, buffets of wind tickling my face. *"Because if it wasn't for you, my master—"*

"That's enough, Jamison. You may go meet the others in the foyer." The gentle growl did nothing to soften the words, as the Shade filled the threshold with his presence, surrounded by waves of shadow. With a final angry chirp, Jamison flew past the Shade's head and down the hall.

I twisted my hands awkwardly before dipping into a quick curtsy. "Good morning." I wrapped my arms around my middle. My legs felt very *visible,* despite the length of the tunic and the tall, thick boots.

"It is morning, but no morning is good." His green gaze slid from my eyes down to my boots and back. None of his shadows touched me, but my body responded as if to physical pressure. His eyes flicked back up to my burning face with a solid nod. "I wish to add the caveat that some things are good."

I swallowed past the dryness of my throat. "No sunrise hikes for the master of darkness?" He took four slow steps toward me—too close. I could smell his soap. His shadows, somewhat fewer today, coiled around us and tickled my knees. His fingers threaded down the tips of my white hair.

"Would you turn, Dayspring?"

I frowned and turned a bit to the left.

"All the way."

Heart hammering, I turned my back on our land's most dangerous predator. The man who murdered with darkness. The one who shadowed the very sun. My neck prickled into goosebumps as his fingers swept past.

And then the Shade...braided my hair. All words fled my mind.

"I'm a poor ladies' maid, I'm afraid. But you'll look put together enough for the cave creatures." His breath puffed hot against my cheek.

I nodded, my stomach too tight to speak much less breathe. With a quick tie, the hair was done, and the man stepped back to observe his work. "I'm out of practice." A seed of unease crept into me—a wave of uncertainty. He smelled like a forest on a snowy night.

I turned to find his face a mask. Quickly dragging my hair forward, I smiled. "You did well, sir." His unease lightened to pleasure.

"Let's see if the others are ready to depart, shall we?" He offered his elbow, and I took it with shaky hands. We swept from the room like a couple entering a ball.

When the silence grew heavy, I asked, "Who taught you?"

The Shade chuckled. "Well, it wasn't Uncle Koll, though his beard is certainly long enough." That pine scent wafted inside again but this time accompanied with deep pain. "It..." His forearm rippled under my hand as his hands fisted and released. His laugh sounded strained. "We all come from somewhere, Dayspring."

I hadn't really considered his origins. Monsters don't just appear out of nowhere. "A sister?" He shook his head. "Your mother." The Shade swallowed, and slowly nodded.

Tracing the braid with my fingertips, he watched as we paused in the hall. "Well, she'd be proud of you. The braid is very nice." Raw agony passed across his face and through my chest for only a moment before the classic side-smile reemerged.

"I am an amazing specimen, Dayspring. A gift to all mankind."

I smiled, and my heart lifted with a burgeoning happiness. I liked to see his smile too much.

Three wolves—including the gray one I'd met in the solarium—five bats, and a badger stood or hung at attention in the entryway.

The Shade paused and took in his unusual crew. "We get in, grab the moss, and get out. We do not go digging." He glanced at the badger. "We do not go sniffing about or fluttering into mischief." The irritated huffs and flaps of the animals displayed their displeasure. "Yet." The animals settled. "There is time for all this but today, while it is day, we need to get in and out without detection from man or beasty."

I gave him a hard side-eye and gestured to the crowd of animals. He cleared his throat. "The other wild, underground beasties." Walking to the table, he took a coil of rope and set it across my shoulders, then placed a lantern in my hand. "Dayspring, I know you're a wild hare, but no heroics today. Try to control your inner force of destruction, h mm?"

I'm certain my eyes glittered with the amusement I felt. His hand trailed down my arm and lingered on my fingertips. "Do stay close. I do not wish to see you harmed."

"Your world would be lifeless without me." I joked back, testing the waters.

His jovial expression darkened. "Truer words...Dayspring..."

He pulled the cloak around me, fastening it at my neck before he turned, donned his pack, and led the way outside toward the southern aspect of the manor. The manor was as black and tall and sharp-angled as I remembered from my flight here, but instead of menacing, the morning light made it look regal. The turrets gleamed as the sunlight struck them, and the black stone, likely laced with mica, glittered more than an enemy manor should. I smiled at the thought of the Shade wearing a sparkling outfit to match his obsidian home.

Across the expansive garden—before the canyon walls that angled back toward the valley—a cluster of arborvitae pines stood, their tops bent from the canyon winds. Behind them, built into the tall cliff walls, a small iron-bar doorway held back the menacing darkness.

Unlocking the door with a large key from around his neck, the Shade yanked against the rusting hinges, revealing the gaping maw of a cave. It was pitch-black mere feet from the entrance, as though consuming the light of the sun itself. My courage withered.

The bats made gleeful circles overhead before entering, followed by the wolves and the badger who sniffed the dingy air before trundling forward.

I paused just before the entrance, my legs a bit stiff from...the stairs of the solarium, surely.

"Don't tell me the heroine of the night—the one who defies princes and talks back to Death—is nervous about a bit of a walk in the dark."

"I won't tell you that then." I was proud that my voice only wavered slightly.

He offered his arm again. "Perhaps you can see with me, Dayspring. Let me show you."

My hand trembled traitorously as it reached for his arm. But I boldly stepped with him into the cave. And boldly stumbled over a stone. I reached for my lantern, but his warm palm halted mine.

"Not yet." His chuckle echoed like thunder in the cavern. He led us into the pitch black. "Now, give me your hand." My breath caught; my sight was now gone, and every touch felt like fire as I left the relative safety of his cloth-covered forearm for the heat of his palm. His fingers grasped mine. "With my magic, you'll be able to see with the shadows."

"That makes no sense," I muttered.

"Master, are you sure?" Jamison asked, his wings fluttering off to my left.

"Close your eyes, Dayspring, it'll be easier." I obeyed, but it was just as dark. "Feel the magic of the shadows, cool and thick, reaching with their fingertips and telling you of the world around us."

Nothing happened. A beat of disappointment. Suddenly, magic swirled through our linked hands, like frost on pine, scented and sacred. And then the world exploded into view around me. The colors were blue and red, the edges of everything lined by this contrasted light. The shadows moved constantly. It was like viewing a reflection on a slow-moving creek, but I could see the details of the floor, the path through the spikes of stones. I turned. I could see the details of the Shade's face and the haunted look in his eyes as he watched me in return.

It was wholly unfair that he could look more attractive in the contrasting art of the shadow images. A wayward thought wondered what the Shade's bonding mark would look like. I backpedaled quickly, back to mere admiration of statuesque features.

"The shadows become you as well, Dayspring. You look lovely."

The first step felt like walking on water, but the second was surer. The image in my mind functioned almost as if I had a lantern, the light from it circular and constantly moving with us in gentle waves. Soon, it was as if I was seeing with true light.

That foresty, magical sense of happiness fluttered within me again. I glanced over, suspicious of this new sensation, and confirmed—the Shade was smiling. It couldn't be that I could sense him, could it?

Quiet drips echoed against the stone, interrupted only by the tiny screeches of the bats or the wolves' claws clacking along the way. I found I could hold the image of the shadow as I opened my eyes, but it was disconcerting to see nothing when my mind was full of so much imagery.

The shadows highlighted little tubes on the cavern wall. The Shade squeezed my hand, and I opened my eyes. I focused and the tubes became wriggling lights that glowed in green and yellow, coating the wall like odd stars reflecting off a waterfall. I stopped and leaned forward.

"Cave caterpillars," the Shade supplied. Small one-inch caterpillars milled around the cracks and crevices of the cavern. Their many legs stuck out of pudgy thighs, much like their forest counterparts.

"They are adorable."

His eyebrow perked. "Most gardeners don't like caterpillars."

"I find them charming. Especially these, since they glow."

Tilting my chin up with his fingertips, the Shade added, "They also make a glowing silk." I looked at the ceiling and gasped. Strings of light and balls of nests latticed the stone, like constellations linked in a woven pattern across the top of the cave. Wriggly purple babies glowed within pink eggs.

The badger tugged on the Shade's pantleg, but he only spoke his mind to him. I saw warmth seep from the Shade's features as they hardened back to the lethal tension.

"Let's move on, Dayspring. We can sightsee next time."

The atmosphere around us thickened as well. The wolves stalked instead of leaping, the bats flew more quietly and perched between flights. The badger slipped behind us. At times, we had to squeeze through narrow walls and duck under low ceilings. The walk, aided by the endless dark, felt interminable, worsened by the twisting, pine-scented anxiety that I suspected was the Shade's.

The Shade cast a single shadow behind us, but the image was swept away by a rapid moving...something. Fear poured down my spine.

"Steady on, Dayspring."

"What was that?" I responded with a thought, hoping it would go through to him.

"It might have been nothing."

"It might also have been—"

"*Cat!*" A foreign voice interrupted. The badger stumbled backward, ducking his tail into a burrow and whipping out fierce claws.

The shadows whipped around us as the Shade tucked me behind him. Slowly, from the edge of the shadow's image, an emaciated, long-legged creature stalked toward us. Its head was the size of a wolf's, and its enormous eyes were slitted, rising above crooked whiskers and too-long teeth. The cave now smelled like a green and forgotten pond, ripe with upended fish.

The bats began dive-bombing the creature's head as the wolves took up posts beside us. One lingered to cover our backs. The creature raised its maw and yowled as it struck out, swatting the bats away from its face. I shivered and felt a warm fondness growing inside me. But I didn't feel any fondness toward the monstrosity. I glanced at the Shade, whose head was tilted to the side, curious.

"Really?" I asked aloud. "That? You like that?"

"I mean, she's kind of cute."

"I've seen dead things cuter than she is." He glanced at me quickly, and I stumbled over my words. "I mean, I can't think of any right now."

"I'm going to touch her and see if we can link."

"What? You'll get sick by touching her."

"She won't hurt me," he said, but I didn't believe him. "Just stay here and keep hold of August."

"August?"

He grasped my other hand and set it on the back of the large gray wolf's neck. "If anything goes wrong, August will protect you. I'm sorry about this."

"Sorry about what?" I squeaked, and then the Shade let go of my other hand. I was plunged into darkness. "Shade!" I whisper-shouted, ashamed of the panic laced within. The darkness was a being, pressing in from all sides, stealing the warmth from my body, and ripping away any sense of safety. Immediately, I was plunged back into the well I had fallen into when I was three. I shuddered and grasped August's fur tighter. I slid down the rock wall, a useless action as I couldn't run while sitting, but without sight, how could I run anyhow?

"*Steady, human. Your fear stinks.*" The low voice accompanied the wolf moving closer to me. August continued, "*The master has it in hand.*"

I nodded foolishly. A shadow slipped into my palm, and I grasped it tightly with one hand while the other petted the large wolf. My mind and body moved glacially. I realized I could see my hands as the paltry light from my necklace sent a glow onto the form in front of me. If only I had any magic whatsoever to help the Shade. If only the light from the necklace was mine to manipulate and to cast as I willed. The fear tightened, and the necklace stuttered. My fingers threaded through the fur, and tugged on the shadow, desperate to settle my rising panic.

I tried to lower my inner walls to hear what was happening. The Shade's thoughts began murmuring as the catlike creature made a continual moaning cry. "*Hello, my sweet, is it just you? You have lovely eyes. So bright. Won't you come a little closer? Those bats can go away if you'd like them to.*" He was crooning, and I had the strange wish to be the mangy cat. "*I have a little water, would you like some?*" Through his emotion, I knew he felt no fear. Perhaps a little caution. But it was hard to filter out the subtleties when I was panicking.

I heard water hit the rocks below. The yowling stopped, followed by a lapping sound.

The Shade was insane. No wonder he was surrounded by animals. He adopted every rabid and feral thing. Except spyrings, apparently, who did not want his love. My legs quaked in my crouch, and I regretted thinking about the spider-like monsters. Would we find those here too?

Suddenly, the fur was pulled from my grasp. I clutched the shadow to my chest. "Sh-Shade?" I yelped. I knew I was pathetic, but the emptiness was pressing in.

Only moments later, I jolted as warm hands found mine. The world exploded back into shadow view. The Shade leaned down, his brow furrowed in genuine concern, and beside him sat the ugliest monster I'd ever beheld, batting at the swinging hem of Death's coat.

"Aelia, can you stand?" I nodded and rose uneasily, but his firm grasp held me steady. "What should we call her?"

"The cat?"

His mischievous grin should be banned. A thousand unkind names filtered through my mind before I could hold them back. She needed a benign and simple name, one to undo the menacing gleam of her claws and the vacant hunger in her eyes.

"Bertha?"

The Shade chuckled. "Very well. Bertha will be part of our group now."

"Oh, so nice." I replied, barely holding back my sarcasm. Bertha took a tenuous step toward me and sniffed my fingers with cactus-sharp whiskers. "Hello...Bertha."

A juttering purr erupted from her, cacophonous in the small area, and she butted her whole head into my palm. The greasy sensation on my fingertips made me queasy. But she was indeed kind of...

The Shade finished my thought with a smug sense of satisfaction. "Cute."

Chapter Eighteen

The Way Home

We finished the journey up a steep incline. The light of the tunnel increased as did my pace. I rushed faster and faster, desperate to get back out to the sunlight. I felt a thread of sadness and a tingle by my neck, but I was too anxious to pay it much mind. Bertha paced beside the Shade, pleased by his pats on her head. I was as pleased to ignore her presence as she seemed pleased to ignore mine.

At the cave opening, I rushed out and dove into the warm, tall grasses. Panting in ecstasy and willing the sun to bake itself into my face, I lay, soaking in the rays of the sun.

"That bad, Dayspring?" The Shade leaned against the wall of the cavern, looking too casual.

I wondered for a moment if I should rise and brush myself off, returning to demure decorum, but the heat of the earth was too delicious, so I nestled deeper. "I've had worse days." I smiled back, the sting from that day not quite as sharp.

Bertha stayed in the shadows of the cave, and from here, her skin appeared nearly translucent against her glowing blue eyes. She gazed about with a wince and backed deeper into the darkness.

The Shade pulled out a satchel and a metal scraper. "Shall we?"

Lugging myself upward, I took his offered tool. "Let's do it."

Cloudy mossweed covered every inch of the cave's entrance. Part mossy netting, part long and tangled leaves, several stamens pierced through the mat and bloomed. The billowy, whisper-thin white flower quite resembled its namesake. The wolves took turns resting and standing guard, while Bertha seemed content to stay within the cavern. The Shade and I worked silently for a while, taking patches in squares so the neighboring plants could easily recover the losses we took with us. Whatever we dropped, the racoons were quick to pick up and drop in our bags.

While we worked, I felt a prickle of the Shade's curiosity. "Dayspring, tell me of your childhood."

I huffed a laugh. "You haven't heard enough?"

Too serious eyes found mine. "Never."

Clearing my throat, I picked a story at random. "When I first came to the castle, I was very nervous. We had been to various events at home—dinners and things—but being so young, I would be dressed up, showed off, and then excused while the adults talked. I remember being so tired, and my shoes were dirty from the dust of the road, but when I got out of the carriage, there was a boy just my age to play with. I hopped out. He sneered." I laughed. "Leon looked at the king with such annoyance. 'It's a girl?' he said. Well, obviously, I was. I curtsied. He gave the most awkward bow, and then we ran off to the back courtyard to play.

"This lanky, black-haired boy popped out from one of the sheds and scared us both. He laughed and laughed. From then on, during our breaks, Leon and I would always go and find this boy and play. I got in so much trouble with ruined tights, and scuffed palms, and bleeding knees. We climbed trees and fished in the castle ponds." I tucked in a whole bushel of mossweed, remembering.

"When Leon's magic first showed up, he sneezed and accidentally caught my skirt on fire! Thankfully, the other boy scooped me up and plopped me down right in the fountain." I giggled. "I got in trouble, of course, as if it was my fault I was wet, but the whole castle started a three-day celebration. Leon and I ate more sweets than we should and got so sick." While I talked, the Shade moved slower, and his brows appeared pensive. "After that, I never saw that other boy again."

I paused, discomfort whirling within me at his silence and stillness. "Well, I've told you enough about me. I think it's your turn."

"My turn." His tool halted mid strike.

"It's only fair."

"Since when is Death fair and the trapped maiden allowed to make such demands?" he grumbled. I snorted. The sentiment should have rankled under my skin, but I didn't feel trapped at all. He began hacking at the plant before him. "My childhood isn't a good one, Dayspring."

I set my hand on his tightly wound fist. "Please?"

He nodded once, and I released him. He renewed his attack on the mossweed. "My life is marked by lies and fear. My father didn't want me, and didn't want my magic to taint his perfect life."

"How could a father not be proud of his son?"

"He would have been proud of me if I'd had a normal magic or even an especially rare magic like light—anything but what I have. I have good memories of him until I was four. I remember that I once wanted to help stir the soup, but then I dropped the spoon, and Mother wouldn't let me help anymore—I'm sure it was because she didn't want me to burn myself, but what was a four-year-old to do? I was so furious, I plunged the whole kitchen into darkness. It was so brief that, at first, everyone thought it was a dark cloud or some weird solar eclipse. But as that prophecy you are so familiar with had just been released, any mention of darkness was the mark of doomsday for the kingdom. My tantrum sent him over the edge of reason. I was a black mark on his perfect life."

The steady hack, hack, hack, of his tool rattled the forest.

"And then..." I prompted gently.

"After that, he never touched me. Never looked at me except to correct me for oozing my black magic, as he put it. He hid me away, filling the house with luz and a thousand light fixtures to fight against my evil."

My heart ached for him. "But what about your mother? Surely, she—"

"She loved me as faithfully as ever. But when her second child showed signs of a different magic, Father sent me away." His eyes didn't meet mine.

I stilled. "What?"

"He put me on a wagon with Uncle Koll and forbade me to ever return."

"How old were you?"

"Nine."

How monstrous. He was just a boy.

"I was a scapegoat. Mother was getting sicker, and Father blamed me. He was also struggling to keep me hidden. So, I was forced to flee."

Waves of despair and rage prickled through my chest, both emotions enhanced when my fingers touched his arm. "It's not your fault."

His jaw clenched. "It may not be, but I paid for it dearly."

"Couldn't Uncle Koll seek help from the guards? Or seek peace and safety from the king?" I asked. Green eyes cut me to the quick, and I stepped back at the hostility I saw there.

"There was nowhere to turn, Dayspring."

Imagining a small and childlike Shade was too much. Water filled the base of my eyelids. As awful as he was supposed to be, it was becoming clearer and clearer to me how completely unfair the Shade's life and reputation had always been. I shook my head. "I'm so sorry."

His whole body turned, and the weight of his presence pressed heavily on my skin. "I'm not. I am who I am today because of those decisions. I'm stronger than I would have been under his thumb. My manor is full of life, and Uncle Koll thrives while my mother did not." His knuckle slid along my bottom lip, and his hand clenched before he tucked his palm against my neck. His thumb caressed my cheek slowly. "Without those actions, I doubt we would be together now."

Electrical tingles danced across my skin and shivered down my body. I swallowed hard. "My stay here hasn't been so awful."

The hard ice of his eyes softened, and I found myself melting as well.

I coughed once, feeling the weight of many mammal eyes upon us. "Well, shall we finish up and go home?"

A frisson of pleasure vibrated through my chest as he exhaled a low growl. His eyes flushed with shadows, almost a dark emerald, before lightening. He whispered, "Home."

I had nearly forgotten the rotten cave cat but when we reentered the dark, the beast pressed its oily skin against the Shade's legs, its purr more like rocks tumbling down a mountain than a gentle hum. Bertha was wholly attached to my...to the Shade. As my hand was laced in his hand on the other side, I started to think I might be attached too.

The way back seemed to pass much faster as I grew accustomed to my borrowed shadow vision, the steady arm to support me, and the fear of the slimy cat that propelled me to escape this cave. My fervor must have been obvious.

"Are we racing, Dayspring?"

"Obviously, I'm winning." I said, feeling a bit bold in the darkness.

"Obviously, I'm letting you win, as any gentleman would."

I tripped on a small stone. "A gentleman? You are Death, sir."

"A very polite Death, perhaps."

We turned another corner, and I stumbled again, the shadow vision shrinking around us. I glanced up to the Shade; his perfect lips were pinched too tightly. He caught me looking and softened them into his perfect smirk.

"Staring at me once again, I see. Well, look all you like. I'm here for your taking."

Behind me, Jamison let out a bitter-sounding chirp, and Bertha began a low, rumbling growl.

"Okay, okay, I won't look anymore." I said lightly, but the Shade's forearm tightened beneath my fingertips. The animals had all stopped. They stood as still as the stones around us. And they weren't looking at us.

At once, a dozen voices ricocheted in my mind. *"Ahead, Master."* *"They come." "So many." "Bigger than us!" "They smell of carrion." "Run, Master."*

"I believe it is time to race, Dayspring. An excellent call. Last one to the kitchen has to steal Uncle Koll's favorite ladle." The Shade gripped my hand and pulled me behind him. But the shadow vision was wavering, and my legs were tired under our packs. Even the Shade seemed unsteady and was limping more than usual.

A single screech echoed down the cavern behind us. My nerves zipped up my spine at the sound. A dozen screeches. Then more. I turned to look, but the way was still dark except for the hundreds of blinking red lights that glowed in the darkness. Blinking pairs of lights.

My voice wavered. "Shade?"

"I know." His voice was too tight.

"What are they?"

Jamison fluttered before us. "*Ground rats.*"

"Rats?" I imagined the mice I'd shooed out of the kitchen a time or two. "That doesn't sound too bad."

The Shade's hand spasmed in mine. "It is much worse than you could imagine."

My legs slipped out as we climbed a boulder, and I slid backward, slipping out of his grasp for a blinding moment. By the time he took my hand again, wrinkled dog-sized rats filled the cavern around me. Their red eyes squinted behind enormous noses and broken whiskers. Their bodies were covered in lichen, hairs protruding randomly through thick, scaly armor, dusted with pebbles and mold on to p.

Bertha prowled forward, her maw dripping saliva, clearly enticed by the horrible beasties.

"I should have grabbed the attack potions," I whispered.

"Caves are no place for toxic fumes. We'll handle this." He grabbed my hand and placed it on his back, under the shirt. I squeaked and was about to pull away, but he held my wrist firm. "I don't want you to be blind, Dayspring. But I need my hands, and you need to see."

Hesitantly, I set my hand on his hot skin. A flutter of his thought—*bad idea*—fizzled quickly away as the muscles of his back rippled while he shifted into a fighting stance. Beside Bertha, the wolves stood ready, the badger and raccoons behind them.

With one movement, as if they had the same mind, the rats dashed forward. Several swept past the larger predators and came careening toward us. The shadows glowed like hot metal in my mind as the Shade whipped them around lifting, throwing, and ripping at the onslaught.

Slowly he backed me down the path of the cavern toward home. Sweat beaded under my palm as the shadows wavered again.

Jamison landed on my collar, hanging onto my chest like a living necklace. *"Fellows. Give them insight!"* Half the bats dodged and ducked, pulling on ears or tails or whiskers. Their chirps competed with the screeching, and blips of information passed through my mind. They were reporting the rats' positions and movements, suggesting the next targets to the Shade, and their constant communication provided another type of sight. He worked in coordination with their instructions while moving me farther away. They must be talking to the wolves too as their movements became precise and well-tuned, smoothly integrated with the Shade's action.

After a final turn, the cave lightened. I spun and sprinted to the gate, pushing it open as I yelled, "Come on. It's open!"

The mammals poured out with the Shade who—after Bertha had cleared the door and hid in the shadow of a tree—slammed the metal gate. A shadow locked it behind us. The huge rats rammed against the bars again and again. I shuddered at the sight, which was even more horrific with my normal vision than with the shadow vision.

The ground rat bodies were pale and translucent, blood vessels pulsed rapidly beneath their skin. Glowing eyes gleamed through their pale irises, scabbed over and thickly lined with bristle-like eyelashes. Paws the size of my hands had claws nearly as long. Their bodies were emaciated, and their tails jutted out like skeletal lightning bolts.

My breaths came quickly as I backed away, not fully trusting the bars of the gate to hold. I ducked under the branch of a tree, only to have my hand pressed upward by a cold, wet nose. Bertha began to purr again, clunkily. One of the bats returned from the manor carrying a potion that the Shade poured over the lock. Bertha winced at the scent. Despite her repulsive appearance, I began to pet her back. She was a slice of comfort compared to the rats within the cavern.

The Shade slowly turned, his pointed finger tapping the air as he counted his creatures. Once completed, he walked past me and Bertha with a wink, tucking his satchel close to his side as he strode toward the manor.

I wasn't sure what I expected. For him to hold my hand, and ask me tenderly if I needed care? A rushed embrace and a blinding hot kiss? But none of those things happened. He just passed by, with a mere wink and it *bothered* me.

I stomped toward the manor in his wake, feeling petulant. Why was I following him like I cared about him? Why did I even stay here? I could be halfway to the ocean now that I was recovered. A gray wolf beside me gave me a hard look and a rumbling growl.

"Sorry," I muttered. Double-checking the barriers in my mind to prevent any additional leaking thoughts, I gave myself a good scolding. I needed to get my head on straight. He was just a man. One with shadows, a menagerie, a solarium, and a nice uncle, but still just a man. Someone I had used to escape, and who had saved my life, but did I really know him? Could I really trust him? He sounded so sincere as we cut the mossweed, but I knew he was keeping things from me. Furthermore, if I wasn't planning on staying, why would I even want to know his secrets? Why was I suddenly thinking that bonding wouldn't be as terrible as I'd once thought?

My mission was to help the queen, then get out of the mountains. I couldn't imagine a life within a stone's throw of my father and Leon. Not that life here was such a bad life. It just...it... Well, wasn't it settling to nestle into the first safe place I found? Wasn't it possible that the comfort I found here was just a trick of my mind, and one day I would look back and realize I'd gone from the frying pan into the smoky fire?

But the skin where his hand had held mine still tingled from the pressure of his touch. My fingers burned where they had spread across the fine planes of his back. He was as lithe as a mountain lion. I shook my head as I desperately tried to keep him in the frame he belonged: he was grumpy, as mercurial as a flashflood in spring. He was isolated and angry. My heartstrings argued back that he was just a wounded soul. But his wounds were not my responsibility. I didn't want to be burdened by another broken man's broken attention.

The Shade paused and turned around with a frown, but as I neared, the wolves who had been playing and tumbling threw up their hackles and spun toward the gate. "*Intruder,*" their minds said as one. Shadows burst from the Shade in waves as he moved supernaturally fast around the corner of the manor.

"*He's here,*" Jamison spat out. "*I told you he'd be back for her.*"

Chapter Nineteen

Decide

On the other side of the front rock garden, a man stood behind the arching black gate. I looked up from my miserable ruminations and locked eyes with the coal black eyes of the prince. His name slipped from my lips before I could stop it. "Prince Leon."

He ducked his head. "Lady Aelia."

My knees bent as if to curtsy, but I locked them with a test of my will. I would no longer bow a knee to the one who betrayed me.

The Shade glanced toward me, then stepped between me and the prince, blocking part of my view of him and the gate. "Leon, you've lost your entourage."

I hadn't noticed, but the prince *had* come alone. I frowned. What was he playing at?

"I didn't come to battle you." He leaned around the Shade until he could see me again. "I came to talk with Aelia."

The Shade crossed his arms, his shadows boiling across the ground beneath him, as agitated as he was. My chest tightened with anger, anger that I thought was his. "Then speak your piece and be gone."

The wolves were tense and crouched at the ready on either side of me. The gray wolf to my right had her teeth bared in restrained violence. Bertha slunk along the fence line, staying away from the sunlight, triggered into bloodlust by the tension of the others. Her eyes sparkled with fury.

I drew myself up even with the Shade, my ankles buffeted by shadows as my tunic swirled around my legs. "Prince Leon?"

The prince dragged a hand down his face. "I came to apologize—"

The Shade snorted and spoke in my mind. *"Too late."*

"—for everything and how it happened. I can't imagine how frightening it had to be."

"Most animals chased to death are frightened," the Shade murmured.

"I didn't mean for my men to hurt you."

"Just for your hairbrained seer to." The Shade stopped as I put my hand upon his elbow.

"I can't focus with you muttering," I thought to him.

"My lips are sealed."

The prince continued, "It's just...the prophecy seemed clear to us, I mean, to me. And you were the obvious cure."

"So obvious."

I smacked the Shade lightly. His chuckle rumbled between us.

"And so, I have to beg your forgiveness. My mother is worsening. My father is at his wits' end. Your father...wanes..." His head lulled forward and hit the gate with a clunk. "We need you, Aelia."

"Bet his mommy put him up to it," Jamison interjected.

But my attention was pulled by that long-held desire of mine. They needed me. I closed my eyes, fighting against the torrent within me, the longstanding ache to be wanted, to be useful. Perhaps now they would see me for me. Perhaps now, finally, they saw the value of my contributions...

"No. Still no. They need to value your person, Dayspring. Your whole person. Magicless, in a dress, in pants. In the morning. Late at night.

All of you. " I waited for him to finish the thought, I wanted to hear him say, "like I do." But it never came. The Shade's expression was a hard façade, only the shadows in his eyes betrayed any emotion at all. I shifted back toward Leon.

My childhood friend, the prince, looked worn down and haggard, his perfect hair mussed and frayed, and his jacket was missing a button. His leather shoes had lost their gleam as they trounced down the canyon to meet with me. Fool me once...

"What was the prophecy again, Prince Leon?" I asked quietly, tired of the games.

His brow furrowed. "The ruin of kingdoms from weak ones come. A sacrifice will make things right. Lest the deep reject the vile ones. Stars and sun turn black as pitch, the light must fight to cure that which has doomed us all to death and decay."

I frowned. "That doesn't even rhyme."

A door clanked open behind us. "That's because he forgot to say half of it." Uncle Koll strode purposefully down the stairs, his cane clicking upon the stone. "Poor form, Leon. I expected better from the one who claims to lead the nation with light and hope. You should add some truth in there too before it bites you in the rear." A wolf beside me chomped the air in response, and the prince jolted backward.

"It contains the important bits," he snarled.

"And yet, those were the same bits the king regent used to get rid of the Shade. Leon, you cannot use sophistry here. We don't stand on pretense or politics. Just tell the truth, boy."

Prince Leon's face grew sullen. "I don't remember the rest."

Then Uncle Koll's voice rose, clear and strong, echoing down the rocky canyon.

"The ruin of kingdoms from weak ones come,
but bind, entwine, and tie them some.

> As day from night, the brightness fights,
>
> A sacrifice will make things right.
>
> Lest the deep reject the vile ones
>
> that slink beneath and this way run.
>
> The stars and sun turn black as pitch,
>
> and light must fight to cure that which
>
> has doomed us all to dark decay,
>
> Still, love must reign and find a way."

Uncle Koll took two more steps down the front path. "That is the prophecy, is it not?"

Prince Leon pulled at his collar. "Yes, that sounds right."

"Does killing a faithful servant to the crown sound like love?" Uncle Koll asked.

A low blue flame lit in the prince's balled fists. "I love my kingdom. I love my people. I demonstrate my deep love for this kingdom daily as I reign. *That* is the love that will save us." He gave a furtive glance toward me. "We just needed to sacrifice one without...without power."

Uncle Koll's face was lined with sadness. "While I do believe you love your kingdom, I do not believe that murdering an innocent is ever the way to establish peace, restore hope, strengthen your people, or save your mother."

"She's dying." The prince's reply emerged as a broken wail, no longer hostile. Brokenness had even weakened the tension of his shoulders. "She's dying, and I can't stop it."

My heart shattered. My queen, the woman who had loved me, was dying. Because of me.

"Arrogant. Selfish. Self-aggrandized. Egotistical maniac!" Jamison's wings buffeted around my head. *"As if you were the creator and source of life and magic. Ha! Make the sun rise and fall, and then maybe I'll blame you. What foolishness."* The bat swept up to the

tall tower and ducked inside. Apparently, I had let down my mental blockade.

Prince Leon extended a hand through the gate toward me, but a snarl from the wolves made him pull it right back. "Just leave this place. Come with me. Come back home, Aelia."

Home. My mind drifted to Chef, the good memories of castle life, even of my father on a good day. Leon, disheveled and vulnerable as he was, reminded me of him as a boy. My friend. The friend who had tried to—

"Do what you will, Dayspring." The venom in the Shade's voice astounded me. He stalked up the stairs and threw open the door. "Get off my threshold, Leon." The shadows pulled the door closed behind him in a resounding crack.

I bustled after the Shade. "I'll be right back, Leon."

"But my mother!"

I held up a hand. "I know. Wait right here."

Rushing through the manor, I sprinted to the solarium and grabbed a box filled with the latest potions. I left one box for Uncle Koll, but this should be enough for a week or more depending on how sick the queen really was. I returned hastily and carefully to the gate.

Leon's gaze lit with momentary hope until he saw the box of potions. "You're not coming back, are you."

Of course not, but his guilt almost changed my answer. "N—I—Not yet, Leon. Take these to the queen. They should help for now."

His lips pulled back in a violent expression. "You stole these from your father?"

Offended, I pulled the box nearer to my chest. "I made these, Leon. I do not stoop to lying, thieving, or murder."

A flush of red stained his cheeks as his shoulders sunk again. "S-Sorry. Father—" Suddenly the prince's thoughts flooded into my own. *"I never should have listened to him. I can't handle the pressure from all sides anymore. First his demands, then Mother's..."* His thoughts faded into garbles.

"One day, you are going to be king, and you will have to follow your own code, Leon. Not his, not the seers'. Not the masses'. Your own values. Your own way. You can't keep being pushed around all the time and think you'll know yourself at the end."

"Easy enough for you to say. You're not a prince."

I raised my brow. "I'm in no-man's land, Leon. Not an accepted lady, not a servant...but I'm not useless. And I'm not hopeless either. If I can work on finding my own way, maybe you can too."

His thoughts slipped through. *"She's better than me."*

I waited to see if he'd say more aloud. But when he didn't, I reached for the gate which unlocked at my touch with a loud clang. "Take these to your mother. And tell her I love—I hope she heals quickly." I swallowed back the word, realizing the impropriety of what I was about to say. She wasn't my mother.

Leon had heard it anyway. "She loves you too, you know. Maybe more than me...especially...especially after everything."

I set my hand on his forearm. A wolf had snuck up beside me and growled at my action, ready to defend me if Leon tried to pull me beyond the gate. "She still does, I'm certain. It's not too late to change your course."

"But the seers—"

"I'm no expert, I admit, but they were wrong about many of the things that we blamed on the Shade. Maybe...they aren't all-knowing, Leon."

He hmphed.

"Maybe your father isn't either."

He pulled the box from my grasp. His Adam's apple bobbed. "Thank you for these, Aelia. I'll take them right to her."

The prince turned and headed up the canyon with heavy steps that moved quicker the farther he went. Eventually, he met his retinue and mounted his horse. I stepped back toward the manor, noting a swish of an upstairs curtain without a source as I made my way to the door.

The gray wolf neared again, tucking her head under my palm, as a single cub raced out from the manor and pummeled right into the wolf's legs. She bent her head and licked furiously all over. *"Mine. Mine. Mine. Mine."* She crooned at her baby. My smile was a bit watery as I walked through the front door. The bats had all tucked themselves up into the coffered ceiling and draperies and coat racks throughout the front room. A group of little foxes tumbled into the sitting room with yips as they played under the tired but watching gaze of two adults. The badger trundled past, looked me over, and gave me a nod before making his way into a closet with a burrow of blankets.

Uncle Koll came up beside me, taking it all in. Notably, there were no billowing shadows nor tortured souls here.

"I don't know where he went," I said to Uncle Koll.

"He might need a moment, Aelia. There's no excuse for him running off, as you know. But...he expects everyone to reject him. As his father did, as the people do, he expects everyone to follow suit. Deep within, I worry he might believe it himself—that he is unlovable."

"But the animals love him."

"Certainly. As do I." He looked at me thoughtfully, his gaze a soft brown as warm as his frybread and honey. "But he has spent most of his time defending himself from misunderstanding and hatred."

"I don't hate him!" I whirled to Uncle Koll. "He couldn't think I would hate him after all this."

"I very much think he could. He is confident, incredibly powerful, and a deep well of affection. But his inner circle of trust is very small, and it is hard for him to let anyone in at all." He tapped his cane. "I trust he will soften on his own and come to you. But you need to decide where you belong and who you want to be yourself. I don't want to see either of you hurt needlessly." Leaning heavily on his cane, he slowly clicked down the hall.

Chapter Twenty

Darkness Within

The queen was dying, the prince was broken, and the Shade was distant at best—angry at worst. Previously, anger had meant my father's harsh words, outbursts, and flailing hands. Anger meant pain and the shame of yet another failure to perform. At the castle, I would immediately work to settle the hurt feelings, soothe their anger with my sweetness, and placate them with some work or tea or a quick apology as if the conflict had been all my fault. When it came to th e fight, flight, freeze, or fawn responses to fear, I was definitely the latter. But look where that had landed me. Still rejected, still offered on a platter, and as unhappy as I'd ever been. Seeing Leon dredged up the memories of that night, of his royal public distance, of his brutal withdrawal of friendship. I still wanted what was best for him, since I could see who he could be, who he should be. My failing before was not seeing accurately who he *was*.

If I had accepted reality, and not brushed over it, would I have ended up at the seer's cauldron? Would I have been cast out earlier? Perhaps sent to the village to make it on my own? Only the stars knew, I supposed, what might have been.

Ironically, here at the manor, I finally felt flashes of myself, brief moments of joy and purpose, and less fractured as I was no longer passing out pieces of myself like crumbs from the last piece of bread. But was this my new opportunity to go back to the castle? To make things right with the queen? Leon had apologized after all, and he did look quite contrite, even if it still felt...insecure.

The prince had always followed his father, desperate for his love and approval. And who wouldn't? Stars above knew that I wanted my father's approval as well. As long as the king regent's edicts moved with the sway of popular opinion, it was almost too easy to explain away the injustice of Leon's actions. Especially as I considered the sweet queen I so deeply loved. The thought of her death was like losing my mother all over again.

Yet...I came back inside. I didn't follow Leon. And, if I was being honest, I didn't want to return to the castle. No one looked down on me here...well, except for Jamison. But he was a bat, and a bit of a grouch, and who really knew why he grumped at me anyway. The truth was, I wanted to be here.

I wandered through the halls, idly checking for the shadows that surely would be whipping about if he was as angry as the feeling in my chest suggested. When the hallway darkened at the end, near the room of books, I paused. I was more curious than scared, but I didn't want to fawn anymore when I hadn't done anything wrong in the first place.

I slipped down another hall, moving with purpose toward another window seat in the castle. He could calm down. And he could find me. I wanted to grow into this budding creature that felt more like me. I wanted to try something new, as nerve-racking as it might be. And certainly, I was not going to take responsibility for his emotions. I had enough of my own to muddle through. As I wandered past the dining room, I swore that my necklace seemed brighter. But then I noticed a few more of the lamps were on, enlightening the whole space. I peered at them. What was he playing at, lighting up the halls?

The Shade did always tell me to do whatever I wanted. So, naturally, I just had to figure out what I truly wanted. So...what did I want? I wanted to help the queen, of course. And to be with...Chef. And to stay. And to...be seen for me.

Sunlight streamed in through the window and filtered to the stone floor. Beyond the pane, a lovely green expanse of flowers stood in contrast to the red rocks around us. Across the garden was the gate, and I couldn't see any of the rats from earlier.

What an exercise of trust that had been, holding his hand, seeing through his magic. Surely, as connected as we were, I would have felt if he was as evil as the people claimed. At this point, I knew better.

A strong surge of emotion jolted me to awareness a moment before I felt his presence behind me.

"Rehearsing a route back to your prince, Dayspring?"

His voice was low and should have been sharper, but instead, it sounded full of morose acceptance. I slowly turned around. His steps were even and lithe, coiled and graceful. I felt hunted; I ignored the thrill. That couldn't be healthy.

"He's not *my* prince." Obviously. I'd already run away from him once.

The Shade huffed. His shadows were only a few feet around him, languidly moving even as his black brows darkened the green of his eyes. "He seems to think so."

I peered at him, offended until I realized I recognized this feeling *of his* in my chest. My lips pulled into a wide, understanding grin. "Are you... Are you jealous?"

He recoiled as if I'd slapped him. "Never."

I stepped forward again, hunting him this time. "Then why did Prince Leon get under your skin?"

"He didn't."

A step closer. "Then why did you huff off?"

"Death does not huff."

"Why did you storm inside?" I stood before him now, the shadows shifting my tunic as I turned my face toward his. My boldness surprised me. But I was done being walked on, done being prey, done with the past. Done with fawning. I knew in the core of my being that even though the Shade was angry—perhaps with Leon—his anger was not a threat to me or my person. His hands were still, his anger self-contained, even as I felt it boiling within him, and his words kept under control.

I reached a hand slowly to his cravat, moving the silk under my fingertips and straightening the end. He swallowed, and I glanced back up at his face. Tortured. Aching... Wanting?

"Shade?"

"I don't want him to take you." His voice was barely a whisper. "He had over a decade with you, and then he tried to sacrifice you. He doesn't deserve you." He hesitated as if considering his words. "He made his choice."

"But?"

"But you are not a possession, Aelia." His jaw locked as he gritted out the rest. "You have the freedom to choose, and I will not restrict that freedom. You may use your own discernment, a rare and precious thing. If you want to go, you may. You had a life there."

My chest flooded with pleasure and relief. The contrast between the men in my life had never been more obvious. This man was nothing like I'd expected him to be. But I still couldn't reconcile the man I'd met in the ballroom with the one standing before me. "Shade, why did you kill those guards?"

His face darkened further, and his irises flooded with black. "They broke in. They slaughtered the wolf cubs. The mother barely made it out alive despite killing one of the guards. Only one cub survived—her mother was the gray one that came with us today." And the cub was the one that had run out after Leon left. My heart ached. He took a deep breath. "They went after the other creatures, set the rooms on fire to smoke out everyone. They would have killed them all, destroyed the plants... And worse yet, Uncle Koll was in the upstairs kitchen baking. They blocked the door. He barely made it out alive."

Horrified, my own anger flamed. I would have killed them myself.

I wasn't confident if I thought it or said the words aloud, but the Shade peered suspiciously. "Oh, really? You would have?"

I nodded, though I choked as I imagined nearing that last brutal step. "That's awful."

"It was awful." His hand trailed down my shoulder, to my elbow, and pulled my hand into his. "You may think me a monster, Dayspring, but I only ever defend what is mine." His eyes flashed at that last word.

"I don't think you're a monster, Shade."

A wry eyebrow lifted. "Then what am I?" He paced forward, forcing me to take a step back. "A menace?" Another step. "A fiend?" My back hit the wall, yet again, oh so miserably trapped beneath the intensity of his gaze and the power of his presence.

I basked in it.

My necklace seemed to glow brighter, reflecting his eyes as his shadows crept around us and hid us from the rest of the world. Oh, what would it be like to stay here forever? My neck itched as I regretted for the first time that this man didn't have a bondmark. If only fate would be so clear.

"Penny for your thoughts, Dayspring?"

"Tell me what you want—like deep down, in your soul, want?" I asked. His eyes traced every detail of my face, his lips pressed together before parting—more luscious than before. I flushed, and I quickly added, "Emotionally."

He smirked, seeming to be aware of my thoughts. His dark voice dipped lower. "I want—"

I backpedaled, panicking. "Platonically, like from a family member."

"Really?" When I nodded, he continued. "I want..." His hand brushed past the mark on my neck and threaded through my hair, pulling me closer. My lips buzzed, hot with the breath from my tight lungs. "Lunch."

My breath left in an awkward exhale. "That's not emotional."

"What's an emotion?"

"Shade!"

"No tell me, I've heard of such things, but they seem mysterious and magical." He chuckled, clearly joking, yet I was unhappy. "Lunch meets both physical and emotional needs and is also mostly platonic." His eyes drifted down to my lips and back. "At least, it used to be platonic."

I laughed and patted him on the chest, pulling slightly on his collar. The heat between us intensified. I whispered, "And what if I took out the qualifiers?"

He leaned forward, his breath tickling my ear. "I know what I want, Dayspring." His shadows twirled, and his pine scent flooded my senses. "The real question remains: What do *you* want?"

My gaze fell to his lips before I dragged them back up to his eyes. "Firstly, I want to stay here." His smile was as radiant as the moon on the snow, the soft shards of light from my necklace glowed beneath our faces. "Secondly, I too would be okay with eating lunch." His other hand pulled on my hip, derailing all logical thought. "And fourthly—"

"Thirdly."

I ignited the few remaining brain cells I had left. "*Lastly*, I would be okay if you kissed me again."

He rolled his eyes and pulled back a bit. "Just okay?"

"Yes?"

"We only do all or nothing around here, Dayspring."

I paused, then closed my eyes before saying words that shouldn't be so difficult. "I want you to kiss me."

He moved toward me, and my lips burst with prickles of anticipation. His body crowded mine, the temperature of my skin between us as hot as the sun that beat on our clothes through the window. My breath hitched as he approached. His breath was minty; it tickled my cheek. My fingers twisted in the collar of his shirt. He came closer until...he dropped a warm kiss upon my nose.

The Shade pulled back, pressing his hand on the wall behind me. His breaths were ragged as he set his forehead on mine. Eventually he stood up straight and tugged on my hand. His emotions were a riotous mix within me. "Never kiss on an empty stomach."

"I'm certain that's not a rule," I whined as I pulled him back toward me. A sudden thought made me pause. *He doesn't really want me.* But that only elicited another laugh from the Shade.

"Oh, I want you, Dayspring, let me be very clear about that. But first, food. Then a nap for both of us after the stress of the day." He paused, and his touch was warm as his hands held one of mine. "I want you to be certain. I also don't want to play second fiddle to any other man. Not that you'd intentionally do that," he added when he saw me protest. "You have moved too often, too long under the whims and wills of other people. I want you to choose with your whole being, Dayspring, whatever that may be. I want to see you thriving, settled, and self-assured first."

I nearly stomped my foot. "I want this. I want the kissing—"

"My lips await." He squeezed my hand, flooding me with reassurance. "But I am a patient man."

I grumbled as I determined that I was, in fact, not patient.

Not patient at all.

Chapter Twenty-One

Trials

He did not, in fact, kiss me after lunch. Nor that evening. Nor the following day.

My lips shriveled.

Or they would have if I'd even thought about kissing him, which of course I didn't. Instead, I threw myself into making new potions for Uncle Koll to test.

The Shade, meanwhile, threw himself into helping me practice saying no.

"The only way to develop a full, heartfelt, powerful yes, is to say no." He said one morning over a breakfast of tiny quail eggs, lemon greens, and potato pancakes.

I sliced through the smallest fried egg I'd ever seen and pierced a matching-sized half of a sliced and salted cherry tomato. "That doesn't make sense. They are different words."

"How can you know where you end and someone else begins? You're a mushy, muddled mess." Jamison, ever helpful, was draped over a teacup on the table, lapping up black tea with a bit of honey. The thumb on his wings clutched the top, while the rest of the wings hung over the plate.

The Shade lifted his cup to toast the bat in agreement. "You do seem to shape yourself into whatever would please your audience."

Ouch. "First of all, Jamison, I'm a well-trained, cultured mess, thank you."

"Humph." The bat took a deep sip.

"Second of all, okay. Fine. Let's practice."

The Shade finished his tall glass and set it on the table. "Aelia, would you pass me the water, please?"

I immediately reached for the pitcher to refill his glass, thinking about boundaries and— "Sure."

"No."

I froze and frowned at him. "What? We already started?"

"The water is in the center of the table, halfway between you and me. There is no reason why I couldn't reach it. Try again." He clasped his hands beneath his chin, his elbow resting on either side of the table. "Aelia, would you pass me the water, please?"

My brows darkened my frown. "N...no?"

"A bit of conviction please."

"No."

"A little louder, more like Jamison, please."

That, I could mimic. "No, sir, you have arms and hands. Use them."

The Shade clapped once and reached for the pitcher himself. "Marvelous."

Ha. I rolled my eyes. "Oh, yes. I'm the epitome of inner strength."

He chuckled—a dark promise that, at every opportunity, he would ask more questions.

Sometime later, I was walking down the hall and Uncle Koll stopped me, asking me to come bake bread with him. But the first floor of the Solarium was looking very dry that morning and needed my attention. I almost said yes until Uncle Koll's wry eyebrow gave away that it was a test. When I passed, with a resounding no, he patted my shoulder and went on his way.

That evening, the badger asked me to open a hallway door. Only after I said no did I realize that the Shade had stored some dried meats in there, and the badger was just trying to steal more snacks. Maybe there was something to this *no* thing after all.

The rest of our hours were spent pouring over the tables in the solarium. Ingredients were mixed, leaves dried, herbs pulverized. My hands were constantly cramping and needed frequent stretching from the effort. The Shade now worked beside me every hour I worked, moment for moment. But he seemed more and more tired, while I felt enlivened and brimming with excitement. I cast him worried glances when I thought he wasn't looking.

Something about being surrounded by his shadows made my neck-lace shimmer brighter too. When I worked here in the manor, it didn't matter that I didn't have magic. No one cared if I was a noble or a servant, powerless or the most magical person in the land. The Shade and the animals never looked down on me for what I couldn't do. And, to my confusion and discomfort, they never treated me better if I did, served, or produced more. They just...accepted me.

To better utilize the nocturnal animals' help, we switched to working at night. Jamison would wake me in the evening, the Shade and I would finish breakfast quickly with Uncle Koll, and then we'd spend the rest of the night working on new potions. While I focused on new racerbristle potions, the Shade often worked on his healing potions and the sleeping potions as well as the toxic potions to replenish what had been used on the spyrings.

Uncle Koll was enthusiastic about the new racerbristle potions, despite some initial side effects. Once I'd added too much mossweed, and he started vomiting. Another time, I'd brought the dose down but trialed a hemty powder, and his toes went numb. The worst was when his skin turned green with swollen yellow spots after I used litten pine needles. It took several healing potions, a few days, and several dips in the shared hot spring before he returned to normal. The Shade brought us a few old potion books he'd stolen from the castle. The menace seemed wholly unrepentant for his thievery, but if it helped the queen and Uncle Koll, then maybe I could overlook it.

Many nights, the wolf pup and her mother joined us—at first sitting by the stairs, but as the nights passed, the pup grew more comfortable and less wary. The mother would sometimes fall asleep on my feet as I worked, her pup batting at my skirts in between rolling around and pouncing on shards of light.

A couple of weeks into this new routine, the sleepy Shade was suddenly sitting on the edge of his seat at our evening breakfast in the dining room. His gaze dashed from the table to the door, to the windows, to me, and back again to the door. I felt a buzzing tightness in my chest and prodded into his mind to see if I could steal a thought or two—he was a solid fortress.

Smiling as I held my teacup close to my lips, I said, "You might as well just say what has you so agitated. You look as if you might explode. But I can't tell if it's nerves or—"

"Excitement, certainly." He tried to pick up his spoon but overshot and hit his bowl of porridge, sloshing the contents. He pulled his hands back into his lap. "Perhaps I'll eat later."

The kitchen door swung in with the help of a raccoon, and Jamison fluttered in, carrying a box with a black napkin thrown over it. The bat deposited his package on the table and took up his post hanging from the coat hanger beside us. After he murmured his thanks, the Shade placed each hand around the small, palm-sized object. He cleared his throat. "So I've been working on a special project."

"In what spare time? When did you sleep?" I asked. At least, now I had a reason for his recent fatigue.

"Death does not need to sleep." I rolled my eyes, and he continued. "I... It's for you."

Pushing the parcel toward me, I felt a wave of fear, quickly masked again by the buzzing anxiety. Our fingers brushed, and I heard a quietly whispered, "*Please.*"

I studied him a moment, curious what would cause Death to say please before I untied the knot and released the thick black fabric. The object burst into blinding light, filling the room with searing brilliance. Several of the animals squawked, yelped, or squeaked, then dove beneath the table or fled from the room to hide from the light.

"Sorry, sorry!" the Shade cried. "Perhaps..." He reached forward and draped most of the thick black material over the back side of the square glass cube. "For the animal's sake."

My vision was dotted with echoes of the brilliant light. I released the hand that was pressed against my chest and reached forward to tap a fingernail along the edge of the glowing object. It wasn't hot at all. The glass square was filled with liquid light. Picking it up, I marveled at the amount of constant light—bright but no longer painful—that poured out.

"How is this possible? I see no flickering candle. And it's not luz."

The Shade shook his head, "Certainly not. I admit I've been working on this idea for some time, trying to uncover a new source to replace luz, but I was stuck. It was only when we saw the glowworms that I knew what I was missing."

I pushed the cube away. "There are glowworms in here? Innocent worms?"

"Dayspring, you know me better than that." He shook his head and reached to tilt the cube back. A cloud of light sloshed within the glass.

"I did study one or two, I confess—stars rest their tiny souls—but then I realized that with the right mix of ingredients and a lovely dose of glowing water bacteria that I could keep alive in my room, this will stay this bright for days. So far, it's lasted eleven days."

"That's so much longer than luz." I marveled. Luz had to be replenished daily. "But how do you restart the light?"

The Shade pulled out another glass cube, opened the top, dropped in a round morsel of sugar, resealed the top, and shook it. The second cube also began to glow, its intensity growing brighter moment by moment. "Between the sugar, air, and agitation, the whole process begins again."

"This is brilliant!"

"Obviously."

"This could change everything in Nuren!" I froze my animated hand motions. "This could stop the drilling and mining and smoke. It could help the queen. Help Uncle Koll."

His green eyes glinted. "They will have to find a new pretend enemy now."

"You could come back to the castle with me!" All warmth fled from his face, and I stumbled through my words, pressing him to understand how incredible this could be. "You would be lauded as a brilliant inventor and given high honor!"

The silence lay heavier than stones in a cave in. "So you do wish to return?"

My heart thudded; I felt instinctively that I had made a mistake, but I didn't know what it was. He didn't want the honor? "I wish to save the queen, as I always have. But Shade, this could save you too. Bring you back to the village. You wouldn't need to be alone anymore."

He threw his body up, knocking the chair back with a screech. "I do not need saving."

I slowly rose, my hand out as if to calm the agitated beast. "I didn't mean to imply you did, but what if you could return?"

"Return to the city that despises me. Return to those who betrayed the trust of a child? Return to the true monsters?"

I thought of Chef. "But they aren't all monsters, why—"

"Moon and stars, Dayspring! Every time I think you've made progress toward independent thought and healing from your own betrayal, you defend them again. Why would you go back to them?"

"Then why did you make this light, if not to go back to them?"

"I made it for my manor originally. Luz is not something I like to casually trade or purchase. No one *wants* goods or potions from Death." He sneered his words. "And candle making is tedious. But I couldn't figure out the key, couldn't solve the mystery until...you." He stalked toward the hall, turning his head for a moment. "Dayspring, I made it for *you.*"

He strode forward, shutting the door behind him. A small trail of shadows followed him beneath the doorframe.

My chest heaved as I sat heavily back into my chair. The fondness I initially felt for his kindness in making me a light was pierced through with confusion. Why was he so upset? Wouldn't anyone want a family? Friends? A place in society? I had spent over a decade trying to find my place. Surely any outcast wanted the same things. And certainly, the prince wouldn't continue trying to fulfill the prophecy with my death if I healed the queen. There had to be a place for someone brilliant and powerful like the Shade. If only I could understand.

"Well, I've not seen that kind of show this side of the moon." Jamison snickered from his perch. *"He used to glower more appropriately before your ill-fated arrival. Then he was"*—the bat shuddered—*"smiling all the time. This is better. At least he can see you for who you are."*

"And what am I?" I asked quietly, too wrapped up in emotion to snap back.

"A leech. A life-sucking leech who contributes nothing and takes everything." He fluttered his sinewy wings. *"For all the things shared between you, you'll never know him, not really. You'll never understand."*

I peaked a brow. "And you do?"

"I was there from the beginning. I was there when he fled under his father's wrath and his mother's cries. I hung from his lapel as he grew into a man. I have been with him as he thrived and faltered. I have had his ear...his thoughts...his friendship for over a decade. I know him."

"Then you'll know where he goes to sulk."

"I would."

Rising, I strode to the door and opened it wide. "Then you'll show me."

"I'll do no such thing."

"But you say that I hurt him," I said. Jamison nodded. "Then wouldn't you want me to fix my wrongs? Apologize? Stop him from hurting?"

The bat shifted, appearing uncomfortable.

"Isn't it honorable? Isn't it right?"

"Fine. But when his shadows sweep you off the parapet, don't say I didn't warn you."

"Always magnanimous, Jamison."

The bat flew and buffeted my face, sweeping down the hall at a pace that required me to nearly jog to keep up. He ascended a steep staircase, headed down a narrow servants' passage, and then went up again at the far corner of the manor. The tall tower's first floor housed a quaint sitting room, full of windows and four hardback chairs. I followed him up another set of stairs, endlessly circling to the rooftop above.

The cold night air pricked my cheeks, but the Shade stood there with his hands on the stone, staring off toward the bright tower of the distant castle. The clouds were mild tonight, and the stars showed through, beaming and flickering their delight in the night. The moon was a sliver, hanging low and distant along the horizon.

"The master, as requested by the lady."

"Thank you, Jamison," I said, my eyes fixed on the Shade.

"Enjoy the fall."

He flew away before I could retort. Something about so much rudeness in such a tiny body triggered a confusing blend of rage and mirth. But I turned toward the source of misery inside my own chest. I wondered for a moment at the fact that I wasn't afraid of the Shade. At some point, he had garnered my trust. And despite his tiny butler's threats, I knew the Shade wasn't vindictive. He wouldn't hurt me. He wasn't my father. So I stepped beside him, placing my hands over his.

After a moment's effort, I brushed away every shadowy brick I had created to protect my thoughts and emotions. I didn't have any magic. I didn't have strength in my muscles. And I wasn't particularly good at witty arguments. But I did have myself, and I would have to be enough. I had nothing to hide from him.

Through the touch of our hands, I only heard bits of his thoughts, but his emotions were a tumult of pain and anger and hurt. My eyes prickled in empathy. The shadows clung tightly to him, threading over our hands and up my arm. One seemed to caress my finger, and I lifted it in response.

"I'm sorry." *For everything I said. For not understanding. For hurting you.* "I'm here if you want to talk."

I looked toward the castle and considered my life there. It was one thing to be a loner in a room full of people. Had it been harder or easier for the Shade to be literally alone here? I thought of Chef and Uncle Koll and ceded to myself that we both had some support.

The Shade intertwined our fingers. "Any loneliness is always hard, Dayspring. I think it's worse when other people daily betray social rules and expectations. Or even family rules." His voice was hoarse, like gravel tumbling down a metal roof. He cleared his throat, which only removed a little of the roughness. "I'm sorry I left."

I nodded, silent, though I knew my thoughts and emotions were unguarded.

"Your thoughts are still safe with me, Dayspring." He turned his back to the castle and leaned against the stone, not relinquishing his hold on me. His thumb traced my fingertips. Sighing, he closed his eyes. "I ruined your present. I didn't even finish before I got offended and—"

"Ran away."

"—stormed, mysteriously and mercurially, like a very masculine man, away."

"Sure."

"It was exactly what I have been encouraging you *not* to do though. To face things. To address the past. Apparently, I hadn't addressed my own."

I squeezed his hand and brought my other hand on top of it. "I understand. It's not an easy thing."

The Shade shook his head. His hair was tossed by the movement, and a gust of wind filtered his intense gaze. "Why did you drop the barrier?"

"I wanted you to know everything, to know where I stood, to feel what I feel."

"Strength in vulnerability."

"It's the only strength I have," I sighed.

He tugged me toward him, and I stumbled into his warm embrace. "Dayspring, you're going to need to start being nice to my favorite person."

"But I am nice to Uncle Koll."

His wry eyebrow peaked. "If you continue to besmirch her, you will be encouraged ruthlessly."

I grinned, and whined, "Oh no!" Then it struck me that he had just called me his favorite person. My heart stilled, and my cheeks heated.

"Oh yes." The hand that had rested so hotly along my elbow traced my shoulder and pulled lightly on a strand of my white hair. "Aelia, you are gifted and smart. You are an endless well of kindness and forgiveness."

"You may cease your encouraging now, sir. I quite understand."

"You have a passion for every detail and small joy that you can see. You're positivity and light, while I have lived in the dark for so very long. I wanted to give you a small piece of what you had given to me. I-I noticed you cling to your necklace in the darker hallways, and walk from lamp to lamp to stay away from the corners. You shook so much in the cavern, I thought to abort the whole mission and carry you back out to the sun, where you belong, surrounded by your own essence." He turned toward the distant mountaintop, black on the dark blue sky. "I wanted you to have a vision of what I see in you, a light in my darkness, a tangible box of"—he chuckled, dragging a hand down his face—"of hope. When you wanted to give it away to those wyrm-cursed leaders of the castle, and the rude courtiers that hurt you, and the village that doesn't know what to do with your giftings, I reacted poorly. They don't deserve a shard of your light. They don't deserve a moment of your time or a thread of your thoughts."

He looked back over his shoulder until his gaze found the castle again. "I admit I also thought only of my own bitterness." His eyes glinted in the starlight they gazed into to mine. "But you only meant to restore me."

"I only want to help my friend," I said quietly.

He tugged me closer, his hand releasing mine to slide across my low back, sending exploding tingles up my whole spine. "Your friend?"

My mouth was as dry as flour. "Essentially a brother."

He scoffed and raised a brow. His fingers traced my jawline and swept the hair behind my ear, tickling the marking on my neck. How I wished it might be ours. I closed my eyes, trying to think of bunnies and spyrings and cleaning chamber pots…

The Shade laughed loudly into the night. "You forgot I can hear everything." He leaned forward, his breath tickling my jawline. "You forget I can feel everything."

Thoughts splattered around me as I became a puddle beneath the heat of his touch. My lip protruded. "That's not fair. When will you release all of your thoughts to me?"

His smile tightened before it sharpened to a charming smirk. "You're not ready for my thoughts, Dayspring." He shook his head, his black hair becoming unkempt in the moment. My fingers itched to touch it. "I'm not ready for my thoughts. I'll let you know when that time comes."

A pang jolted through our connection from some internal pain of his. I leaned forward, setting my chin on his shoulder as I rose on tiptoes to embrace him. "I'll be here."

He inhaled slowly before wrapping his arms around me in return. "I—"

"There you are!" Uncle Koll bellowed from the stairwell. "I wanted to show you!"

Uncle Koll pranced up the last steps and we jumped apart, mouths agape as he broke into a waltz with an invisible lady on the rooftop.

"Look at me!" And I did. He looked flushed and moved without a limp.

The Shade lurched forward. "Truly? Did it work so well?"

"This stuff is magic! Watch!" He fell into a city jig, one I had seen the servants do only after the nobles had gone to bed in a stupor and the musicians were relaxing in the kitchen. "I feel amazing. Better than I have in years!"

The Shade crossed his arms, falling back into a professional assessment. "We'll document how long it takes to wear off. And be on the lookout for unwanted complications."

Uncle Koll was not to be put off. He waved his hands, as though brushing crumbs off the table. "Sure, science, research, blah. But make me some more. I feel ten—no, twenty years younger!" He pulled the potion from his pocket. "Number 117. This is the one!" Uncle Koll passed the glass vial to the Shade and pulled me into a dance, spinning and laughing.

"Let's celebrate!" he declared. "I'll get the wine. And my pie should be cool by now."

"Everything is better with pie." I grinned.

"Come, come!"

I headed toward the step and saw the Shade take a small sip of the potion, shaking his head as he tucked it into his pocket. His eyes met mine, and he gestured toward the stairs. "Ladies first."

What did the Shade need with the potion?

He pressed me forward. "Don't forget to bolster your thoughts back up, Dayspring. But I'm always happy to hear all of you. Anytime." He smiled warmly at me as we meandered down the hallway. Just before the doorframe, he pulled me back. "And..." He dragged a hand over his face. "I think, if this potion works, we should bring it to the queen. And perhaps...perhaps we could also share the light somehow."

I leaned and pressed a kiss to his cheek. "We only do all or nothing, Shadespring. Not just perhaps. I want you to be certain."

He chuckled at his words being thrown back at him. "Let's do it."

"More work ahead." My fingers ached at the thought, but my heart leapt. Perhaps we could do some good and actually help the queen. Maybe we could help all the people, instead of being the end of the world that the prophecy claimed we were.

"More work. More time with you." He clasped his hands around mine. *Mine.* "I can't wait."

Chapter Twenty-Two

Not the Mines

Working on the potion felt more important than ever. Before, everything had been a trial and experiment, a giant maybe-but-probably-not-going-to-work moment, a held breath, but now that the potion was effective and safe, and Uncle Koll was thriving—and without yellow spots—we pushed to produce as much potion as we could. Since we could stop experimenting, we needed fewer racerbristles, and they began to recover nicely between their trimmings. The Shade—ever the menacing botanist—found a way to keep the cloudy mossweed alive around the cavern the spyrings had used to break through, and it soon covered every inch of the cavern entrance. Several of the animals worked with me all the time, constantly bustling through, watering, weeding, and cleaning up the dead leaves. The baby skunks rolled through our work regularly, bringing us a bit of laughter.

Uncle Koll had felt so good that he was always outside now and had taken over the landscaping. The rooms shook periodically when he used his earthen magic to reform stone, lift a rise, or carve a statue for the gardens. He made a stone pergola with intricate carvings from the red stone around us. For someone I first thought frail and weak, Uncle Koll was proving himself to be quite the loamer powerhouse. Every time the windows rattled, the Shade and I would just look at each other and laugh. His relief flooded through me. As he pinched off a leaf, he thought, *"I worried I was killing him by staying this close to the castle and the mountains...now he's full of power again."* He laughed aloud. *"Though he is so raucous as he plays, I hope he doesn't bring down the manor."*

Jamison and I settled into a truce of sorts. He glared and stood watch when he wasn't out catching dinner, and periodically, I heard him mutter something about smiling and propriety. But when he flitted around Uncle Koll in the evenings as the man danced through the dinner preparations, I knew the bat was as happy as we were that Uncle Koll was hale again.

Finally, we had finished creating a three-month supply box of potions—one for every five days—and a box of glass cubes, with instructions and dollops of sugar. The box was signed "Ever yours, the Shade." His amusement still flickered every time he pointed it out to me.

The final day came, and the Shade started us off with an evening feast. "It is a long journey through the earth to the castle," he touted as his reason.

"Through the earth? Why not go directly through the forest?"

"The forests are watched, and the gates are guarded," Jamison chirped. *"Unless you're trying to get Master's head on a platter instead of your own."*

I cast him a glare before stirring my peas. "Through then." I shuddered at the memory of our last expedition. "Doesn't mean I look forward to the dark and narrow."

"Thankfully, the mine tunnels are bigger and wider, and the monsters have likely fled the area."

"Or were killed by the soldiers," Jamison added. The Shade nodded grimly.

I hugged myself. "You know I don't like the dark."

The Shade sipped his tea. "But why, though?"

"Oh, I don't know. Being alone in the storms. Monsters under the bed. The howls of scary wolves and...once I was left in a well." The lone gray mother wolf that had wandered up gave me a concerned look. I petted the top of her head, my fingers threading through the fur right behind her ears. "Back at my first home. A group of boys told me I was the only one small enough to go down and save a cat that had fallen in, and of course, I said yes. After they lowered me down, they pulled up the bucket. I was there for hours and hours before someone found me." The room was still; the Shade's anger boiled in my chest, and even Jamison's jaw dropped with horror. "But I got out." I shrugged, trying to move everyone forward. "The dark is also full of beasts and ghosts."

"I admit, not even I would leave you in a well." Jamison rewrapped himself with his wings. *"Probably."*

The Shade set down his glass and looked out the window. The twilight sky was pricked with the earliest stars as the clouds reflected the last of the sunlight in pinks and purples. "Darkness isn't evil. Darkness is a cozy blanket, a safe place to rest. It's peace and quietness. It's cool water when the world grows too hot. Without the darkness, you cannot see the stars. Without the darkness, you wouldn't see half our friends." He glanced at me. "And every beautiful portrait uses the darkness as a stunning contrast to add depth."

"Some darkness is evil," I whispered. But I no longer pictured the Shade when I spoke the words. I saw a broken glass, dark amber liquid, and a deep red face that had been out too late, drowning too deep. Boys jeering and throwing stones at a girl in a well. Bloodlust in the eyes of a seer.

His face twisted in momentary pain as I shared my thoughts. "Evil is evil. But I promise, Dayspring, you never have to be afraid of me. I will protect you."

"From yourself?"

"From the prince. From the monsters. From everything."

"Your magic at full force can be a little scary." I picked at a button in front of me.

He reached across the table, his fingers tipped my head back to meet his gaze. "It can be used in this way, yes. But it will never, ever be used to hurt *you*. You are mine. Mine to safeguard. Mine to—"

His throat bobbed again as his eyes dropped to my lips. His gaze was a touch, a brand searing my skin. Mine to what? His thumb was soft as down as it touched my jawline. My heart ached with the blossoming feelings of—

A throat cleared. The Shade let his hand slip as he sat back. I busied my hands brushing off invisible crumbs from my skirt. The Shade leaned his elbows on top of the table, the picture of professional interest. "Yes, Uncle."

"The owls."

The Shade waved a hand of permission, and five owls flew into the room.

"*Fourteen to the north.*"

"*Ten in the ravine. And the dogs.*"

"*A regiment at the temple.*"

Their thoughts bombarded me simultaneously. Placing a hand on my head, I turned to the Shade. "What are they talking about?"

"I asked them to double-check the surface path. But as you heard, it would be impossible."

He had sent them for me. Gratitude warred with fear as I took in the box of potions at the end of the table. I was a coward. "Can you fly?" I gestured at his ethereal shadows that hung on his chair. "With shadow wings?"

He only chuckled. "Sadly, not quite." He closed his eyes with a deep inhale. "We go under then." He made plans for travel rations with Uncle Koll and sent the raccoons to pack up the potions before turning back to me. "Dayspring, go get some rest. We'll plan to leave in a few hours."

I nodded as Jamison flitted grumpily back to my room. I bathed quickly in the glorious water, locking the Shade's door and bathing in my sleep clothes, before I wrapping myself in a robe and leaving the hot springs.

My thoughts whirled with fears of the unknown beasties underground. I worried over what would happen if we were caught at the castle or if the queen was too far gone. I chewed on my inner lip as I dreaded more caverns, even though this time I had his box of light. His box of light. He was someone I had feared my whole life. I had avoided and hated him, even cursed him while doing my washing. And yet, my current thoughts of him were completely altered. He was nothing like the seers had described, he was nowhere near the menace the king regent had claimed. He was wounded and powerful, but he was also tender toward me and protective of his manor and all the creatures in it. And though I hesitated to admit it even to myself, I thrilled thinking of the Shade and his touch. I shivered in pleasure at the thought of his fingertips on my cheek and the warmth of his embrace. I pressed my eyes shut with the backs of my hands as I sat on the chair by the fire. I wouldn't think of his kisses. I would not recount in slow detail the brilliance of his eyes when he was mere inches from my face. I would not relive every soft embrace. I would not ache for his hands on mine. I wouldn't think of what they could mean.

"I never think of these things either. Only with every other breath." His thoughts were a deep lullaby.

I ran my hand along the beauty mark on my neck. The markings had lasted too long for it to be an irritated beauty mark, as much as I'd wanted to believe it. The rest of me had healed, but the tiny twisting swirls remained, black and as big as a teaspoon. Regret twisted in my chest for a moment before I tried to remind myself why bonding was bad, and besides, the Shade didn't have a matching mark. Perhaps, we could have a love match instead.

It was warm by the fire and I fell asleep.

Jamison called my name, then with a thump, he landed on my face, his wings splayed wide and grasped my ears. His beady eyes blinked at me. *"Lady, it's time."*

I sat up with a yelp, his long finely-clawed fingers grasped at the movement and pulled the hair on my temples as his feet pinched slightly on my lips. "Jamison!" He flew off before I could bat him away and snorted with a chirpy cackle.

"Do *not* land on my face!" I rubbed at my nose, still tickled from his fuzzy belly. "Say my name, squawk or squeak. But do not land on my face!"

He settled upside down on the lamp, looking wholly too pleased with himself. *"I only aim to be an effective servant of my master. And he bid me to wake you up."*

"I bid you to wake me differently."

"The master didn't specify. And I was effective. You are awake."

I tossed a nearby throw pillow at him before the reality of the next journey froze my chest.

Jamison shuffled his wings. *"You're afraid."*

I strode to the wardrobe. Afraid of getting caught, afraid of the caves, afraid to see my father, afraid to be seen by anyone. What if I had been utterly forgotten?

"Good," the bat said. *"You should be afraid."*

Debating which gown one should wear to climb through mines—and ultimately to see the queen again—I pulled out a black dress. Jamison snorted. I rolled my eyes. "Fine. You pick."

With a flap, the bat maneuvered over my shoulder. *"There. On the far right."*

A thick leather and canvas ensemble pressed against the wood. I removed it from its hook. "Jamison, these are *pants.*"

"They are."

"I'm a girl!"

"Girls have legs. Legs can wear pants."

"What would my father say?" I glanced at the outfit again. The elbows and knees were reinforced, and a thicker boned vest would protect my middle. It did look utterly practical. "Who cares what my father would say."

"Attagirl. Get dressed. I'll go ready the team." Jamison flapped away.

My shaky hands got the job done, and I was pleased with what I saw in the mirror. The warm tunic hung long over my thighs, and the gloves came with gauntlets and buckles. I also found tall leather boots that covered the front of my knee. I looked daring and coura-geous—and more things I would never have described myself with before. I turned to the side and eyed my legs. If Prince Leon could only see me now, he might kick me out of his court for the embarrassment. The lack of encumberment of my stride, however, traveled to my heart and I felt...giddy. Uncomfortable, perhaps, but—dare I say—unhin-dered. I grinned wickedly.

I nearly pranced my way to the entryway which buzzed with activity. The hallway was lined with two groups of animals—both day and night creatures on each side. The Shade sat in the middle, reviewing a parchment on the table as his shadow idly stirred his tea.

"Is everyone coming with us?" I asked as I sat beside him.

He glanced up. "Some will come, but most will stay. They are deciding amongst themselves who is going."

The wolves were engaged in a growling debate, the crows cawed and strutted away from each other in groups of five, and the snow leopard slumped in a lazy stretch before the kitchen door. I opened a mental window a small amount to try to understand their discussion, but it was too much. I slammed it shut, barraged by the cacophony. They could sort that out themselves. The table held three leather bags: the pink solution in one, and a mix of the other healing and toxic potions in the other two. A small pouch beside them contained the sleeping potions. Uncle Koll burst from the kitchen and set bags of food on the table. An owl dragged a carafe of hot water, and a small hawk grabbed Uncle Koll a mug of his own. The older man was also clad in leather gear.

"You're coming with us?"

His dark eyes gleamed. "Don't sound so astonished, young lady. I'm not dead yet."

My cheeks burned. "I didn't mean—"

"Ha! I tease, I tease. I've got to keep these old bones moving. Plus, you'll need my skill with the earth, as you all plan to be surrounded by it."

I shuddered.

"We'll go down the spyring path, I think. Jamison has reported that it connects with one of the larger mine shafts on this side." The Shade slid the map toward me. The three mountains reached to the top of the parchment, and various lines connected up and down and across the space beneath them. Three lines went to the surface of the mountain near the Shade's home.

"What are those?" I asked, pointing to the lines.

"Those are the tunnels that release the most of the smoke and acid I get blamed for." He pointed to a large green-shaded circle. "They mine for luz on the other side, but they must burn it near me to filter out the particulates that make it so bright." He cleared his throat. "I'd be glad if that would stop."

"We'll connect here," he continued, running his finger along the path. "Sneak past this section of the mine and slip up to the castle. There are two entrances on this side, near the back entrance of the dungeon."

I cleared my throat. "Where did you get this map?"

A snowy barn owl fluffed her feathers. *"I obtained it from the very chambers of the traitor king regent myself."*

"The traitor king regent?"

The Shade glared daggers at the owl, who clacked her beak twice irritably, and flew out the door.

"What did she mean about King Harold?" I asked the Shade.

Rolling up the scroll, he tucked it into his outer garment. "Pay her no mind, Dayspring. We must eat and run. I do not wish to be underground for long."

I could agree with that sentiment. I double-checked my bags to be sure I had the queen's potions, the snacks, the attack and sleep potions, and a carrier for my light box as I spoke. "Run to the castle. Drop off the potions. Race back home." I stood and grabbed my tea saucer before the pangolin could take it from me, then pushed in my chair. I paused. "I'm sure there's no way I can see her when we arrive, right?

I know that's foolish and dangerous, but..." My nail scratched on my palm. "Maybe we could make sure she's okay?"

The Shade took a slow drink before setting his cup into the waiting racoon's paws. Those who were going gathered their items and made their way through. "It is dangerous." I nodded, my eyes burning even though I had known the answer. "But it isn't foolish. It's kindness."

My throat clogged, and I swallowed past the ache.

"I cannot promise we can stop, Dayspring."

I waved a hand airily, casting about for a look of indifference. "But if we can..."

He stopped in the hall and took my hand in his, tails of leather from his bracelet tickling my wrist. The backs of my fingers could feel the warmth through his shirt and the beat of his heart. My eyes traced the fine tailored vest to his towering neck before fixing upon his chin. It was too frightening to look as high as his lips...or his eyes. When he lifted my hand and pressed his lips to my palm, I looked away, the mark on my neck burning as hot as an iron brand. I wished he could feel the same. My cheeks flushed, and tingles ran up my arm.

"I promise. If we can stop, we will."

His hand lingered, and he tugged on my fingertips as I stepped back. *Mine.* The word rumbled through me, possessive and hungry, but also safe and...well, it was nice to be wanted. I almost worried if he would want me when I was no longer helpful to him. But I knew better...or at least hoped...maybe he actually wanted me for me.

"I know what I want, Dayspring." His green gaze penetrated too deep.

I was afraid of what I wanted. Afraid of the attraction. Afraid of what it would mean to commit to one person. Even if he didn't have a matching bond mark, and even if that thing on my neck was mine, I was afraid because I liked him so very much. That kind of vulnerability was terrifying.

We made our way up the stairs. Three wolves, two raccoons, three bats, a honey badger, and a pangolin all waited by the gaping maw of the spyring tunnel. Uncle Koll and the Shade donned their packs. A pangolin passed me a lit lantern; her long claws patted my hand gently before she bumbled away on all fours. The family of skunks clustered under the racerbristles, and the room became uneasy and quiet. Even clearing the nerves from my throat seemed to startle everyone.

"I shall remain here to protect the manor, Master." Jamison bowed his head to his chest, as the Shade bowed back.

"Be sure you do."

He passed me the precious bag of potions, which I strapped over my shoulder. I'd already tied a bag of sleeping draughts and one of sleeping potions around my waist. He looked about the room, smiled at the lot, then climbed through the opening.

"Alright, Lady A, after you, if you please." Uncle Koll gently tugged at my elbow, guiding me forward.

The cavern was entirely too dark. "Perhaps you and the Shade should just go ahead without me."

"And let you miss the excitement? Perish the thought, young one."

"Boring is nice too."

He smiled warmly at me. "Mankind was not made for boredom but for risks. The right risk at the right time is worth all the stars in the skies."

I stepped onto the rocky earth, clutching the glass square of light like a lifeline. My heart pounded against my ribcage, desperate to return to my safe room and my safe bed. I wasn't brave or courageous.

A cool shadow wrapped around my hand and tugged gently. *"You do have a choice, Aelia. But I know you can do this. And I'm here with you.*" The shadow tugged again. *"One step, Aelia. That is the key. One step, and then another."*

"*It's dark*," I whined, embarrassed at my whimper.

"*I am the dark*," he whispered back. A shiver threaded up my spine. *"You do not need to fear me. Together."*

One step. Then another. Down the tunnel. Into the gloom and darkness and rot and webs. One step and a thousand more. And then, we would save the queen. Together.

Chapter Twenty-Three

Caverns and Chaos

The rocks were slick. I slipped down the narrow tunnel, stumbling at times, ducking at others to protect my face from the wayward webs. My courage wavered, but a gentle clink from the precious package of potions bid me onward. The thread of shadow still held my hand while the lightbox showed the way brilliantly. But beyond the reach of the light, the cavern was darker than black. The sounds of the cave expanded until we all stood in a large atrium. The sounds of dripping echoed down several endless passages. My back ached as I stood upright, and I shook the remaining spiderwebs off.

The wolves stood at attention facing away from us humans in the center. They sniffed, their ears turning and twitching, then they all rested back on their haunches. From a distant corner, a pale, ugly cat slunk into view and joined the team. Bertha had returned for the adventure.

"Good to go then," the Shade said as he pulled out his map, then indicated with his hand. "To the left, if you please." The Shade offered his elbow, and I took it, grateful for the grounding touch. The cavern was just small enough that the edges of light caught on shining mineral veins, which threaded through the gray stones, while the distant walls remained dark and hazy. My eyes constantly tricked me into believing that there was movement along the walls at the edge of the light.

We walked quietly, the crunching sound of sand on stone the only noise as our group traveled underground. Nothing stirred. Soon, between the fatigue and the boredom, the walls became only walls, and the sounds mere murmurs of a sleeping mountain. No creatures attacked, and my tension loosened.

Uncle Koll tapped my shoulder. His voice, though low, echoed in the dark. "Did I ever tell you the time that Sh—"

The Shade cleared his throat.

"—that the Shade used his powers to cheat in a game?"

I pursed my lips, intrigued. "You have not."

"Well, the first time he discovered them, he was four. He was helping to make some soup, and we thought it was just a storm cloud when he started to cry. But we discovered that shadows were his magic type when he was around five. That's still very early—as you know—for magic to show itself." It was common for magic to develop between ten and sixteen years of age, maybe seven if they are stronger. Five was nearly unheard of. My horrifyingly old age of twenty was impossible. "We were playing King's Castle, and his washer had just knocked out my galer. But then I noticed that tiny shadows had shifted my pieces off the board. I told him he couldn't do that, and he was so upset he kicked the board and screamed. The whole room blackened, and I thought I'd gone blind! Poor soul scared himself too, and he tripped and fell over the chair he knocked over. Thankfully, I caught him. We sat there as he settled down, and the shadows reabsorbed into this tiny, sobbing little boy on my lap."

Uncle Koll chuckled, the sound mixed with amusement and sadness. "Scared us half to death. And it certainly scared the maid who dropped the tea tray."

"I can imagine. I wasn't taught much about shadow magic. Except that there was only one." And that he was evil. I squeezed the Shade's arm, happy to have corrected that assumption.

"Oh certainly, shadow magic, light magic, even the elemental magics can have their nuances," Uncle Koll continued. "But the shadows scared his father, to be honest—terrified him, more like it. Thought people would judge him."

The Shade's voice rumbled in the cavern. "The beginning of the end."

Uncle Koll hummed his agreement. "The Shade was his own sort of trouble. Take a mischievous five-year-old, give him tangible cords of shadow, and you get many a disgruntled chef as a cookie starts floating off the table and out the door." He laughed, casting a very sharp side-eye at the Shade. "Or moving chairs out behind their favorite uncles as they are about to sit."

The Shade smiled with an edge of orneriness.

"Is the thought magic...yours then too?" I glanced up to see him nod. "Did that show up at the same time?"

His eyes were evergreen in the light of the lamp as they met mine, and his lips pressed flat in thought. "I'm not sure when that arrived..."

Uncle Koll shook his head. "He always seemed to have a second sense about what was going on—even as a child. I'm not sure if that came with knowing people's thoughts or before. Shadow magic can certainly be a tangible thing, but just like a human shadow is a representation, shadow magic extends to thoughts—the representation of the inner person. Though I suspect it's why you often played alone or with one or two others. You were easily upset in large groups of people."

A pang of loneliness struck me. His loneliness? It would be hard to hear the thoughts around you as a child—good, bad, ugly, and otherwise. The more people, the more thoughts. "Must have been overwhelming."

"It was," the Shade agreed. *"Now I'm pleased to only hear you,"* he murmured into my mind.

I rolled my eyes. *"And Uncle Koll."*

"I've heard his thoughts my whole life. I'm glad to hear someone new."

"My only appeal—novelty." I said quietly, forgetting to think it.

He stopped and let Uncle Koll walk ahead of us. The man was now carrying on about some other dinnertime disaster the Shade had caused. The Shade placed his other hand on mine. "You have many appeals." His eyes took their time looking me over, each glance a caress. "For example, you have very nice leather boots."

I snorted and pushed us forward. "You gave them to me."

"Maybe, but you are wearing them. I wouldn't look nearly as delicious."

"Is it snack time?"

"Are you on the menu?"

My cheeks heated, and my thoughts—as well as my heart—stopped beating. What is the game I had fallen into, and why was I enjoying this? Grinning, I tucked the light away and reached into my pouch. I pulled out a piece of dried meat, holding it in front of his mouth.

"To satisfy your hunger." My gaze seized upon his lips. His eyebrow quirked as he smiled back. Without realizing it, we had stopped walking again. He grabbed the food with his hand before kissing my fingertips, one at a time. The Shade splayed open my hand and placed gentle tingling kiss upon my palm. A shadow pulled back the edge of my sleeve.

A wolf growled, and I startled. I turned to see him standing on defense, his hackles raised and teeth bared toward the tunnel. Screeching reached our ears right before a chant of *"Food, food, food"* ricocheted in my mind. Many things were coming this way. Spyrings.

Not again.

"Time to run, Dayspring."

We sprinted down the path, clattering legs close behind us. The Shade pushed Uncle Koll forward, throwing up a barricade of shadow behind us. Several too-long pinchers slammed into the wall and started to reach through. Sweat beaded on the Shade's brow. The manor animals kept pace with us as we turned left and right. Bertha frolicked in delight, looking back as if she wanted to return to the spyrings.

"How are you running and blocking?" I shouted.

"He's always had a keen mind," Uncle Koll began, "once when he was fourteen—"

"Later, if you please!" The Shade took a sharp right. "The bats are ahead. Listen in your mind for them."

My boots pounded, and I was thankful that skirts weren't slowing my escape this time. I imagined the shadowy room and inserted a window, which opened to let more thoughts in. Several small voices began chirping. *"Here, sir. Here!"* and *"Turn, now! Turn!"*

The voices were extremely helpful. The sounds of the spyrings grew distant, and I slowed, heavy with fatigue. The bats fluttered ahead, offering new instruction for the Shade. Everyone walked now, cooling down after our sprint. The Shade still panted, as if he'd exerted even more energy than when he had fought the prince. I wondered if he needed a snack. Perhaps I could grab him some. Perhaps he could kiss my fingertips again, or...

"Shut the mental window, Aelia!" Uncle Koll cried out.

My face flushed, and I mentally slammed it shut.

The Shade's chuckle echoed around us, growing even as the echoes reverberated his mirth back to us. "Perhaps add a gossamer curtain as a filter? Allow others' thoughts to come inside without letting your thoughts leak out?"

I held my burning cheeks in my hands. "Certainly. So sorry."

Uncle Koll approached, wheezing, and patted me on the back once before bending forward, hands on his knees, as he dragged in air with noisy breaths. "Not at all. I just don't care to be distracted while running from certain eight-legged death."

The Shade stood at attention, the rapid rise and fall of his chest pulling at his leather vest as he scoured the cavern. I added curtains to the windows in my inner room, hoping it would work.

"*Silence.*"

"*Nothing here.*"

"*They retreat, sir.*"

Each bat spoke over the other. The Shade dropped his shoulders and looked toward the ceiling. He looked exhausted.

Uncle Koll's brow furrowed. "Rest, son. You know—"

"I do."

Uncle Koll just nodded.

The Shade dragged the back of his hand against his forehead as he rolled his ankle to loosen it. "Lucas"—he saw my confusion—"the bat behind us, says the spyrings are retreating."

Uncle Koll smiled and pulled at the whisps of his whiskers. "Thank heavens. I don't know how much longer I could have—"

A raccoon screeched and tumbled backward followed by his friends. The wolves jumped to their feet, turning, spinning, facing...everywhere. Only Bertha sat back and began to calmly lick her thin paws with her pitch-black tongue.

The clattering began once again, this time loud and from every corner of the cavern. The spider-like creatures poured out of holes that were tucked away from the light, crawling and dripping down the walls.

"Above, sir. Above!" a bat cried.

I snapped my gaze upward. Hundreds of spyrings drifted down like volcanic ash. Lower, lower, on top of our heads.

The Shade grabbed my hand and took off toward one of the tunnels to the east. "Uncle, can you—"

"With pleasure!" Uncle Koll lifted his left hand, tossing up a stone slab like a door across the nearest tunnels and blocking the way. A set of shadows whipped before us, lifting, tossing, and slicing through the spyrings that charged us from the front. Bertha jumped up to bat spyrings out of the air, tumbling with them until she had ripped off a claw here and a leg there. The wolves tore through the spyrings on our flanks while the other creatures tucked between us and Uncle Koll. The raccoons displayed uncommon violence when a spyring fell before them. The Shade's tug pulled me with him into the next tunnel.

"Collapse it!" the Shade shouted.

With a grunt, Uncle Koll turned and planted his feet in a low squatting stance. The final mammals, including Lucas, tumbled into the tunnel or flitted in on thin wings, then Uncle Koll swirled his arms and threw them toward the floor. The tunnel behind us collapsed in a tumble of boulders. When silence reigned, my shoulders fell slack with relief.

"Well done," the Shade said as he petted the ugly cave cat.

"Thank you, my boy. Feels good to stretch my magic again."

The Shade smiled. "Shall we be off then?" He offered his elbow, then turned back. "Uncle?"

Uncle Koll was still squatting. "Well, ha! It seems I have gotten down...and now...I cannot get up."

I rushed back to help lift him—unnecessarily, it turned out, since the shadows wrapped him and lifted him aloft, while I...guided...kind of.

I laughed, feeling awkward and presumptuous. "Looks like you don't need me."

The Shade's expression turned hard, his green eyes glinting in the light. "I don't need you to help lift." My soul ached. I knew it. "But that does not imply or even suggest that I don't *need* you." A wayward shadow slipped past my cheek in a sweet caress. "I need you very much."

Uncle Koll walked through the shadow waving his hands. "Yes, yes. True love. Star crossed. Et cetera, et cetera. Please save the wooing of your lady for outside. I have no desire to remain here while you two figure this out."

The shadow drifted to my palm and tugged, and I grasped it until it led me to the warmth of his own rough hand. "You need me?" I said stupidly but hopefully, knowing I was begging for attention.

"Like water. Like sunlight."

I pressed my lips together. "Are you a plant?"

"Come *on*." Uncle Koll demanded as he stormed ahead. Our eyes met as we traversed forward. I watched as the sharp edges of his face flickered in the lamplight. His dark brows pulled down in determination, his jaw scruffy and begging to be touched. My fingers burned with anticipation. But I held back. This man had been kind when he could have been cruel. He had been helpful when he could have abandoned me. And certainly, he cared for my wounds when I showed up mostly dead on his doorstep. He helped me make potions, and perhaps even a near-cure for the queen. He made me a lightbox because I felt afraid. Certainly, this man meant much more to me than I had expected.

I sighed, long and deep. Indeed, I liked him. I was a fool, but I liked my evil shadow overlord very much. And not even because he had saved my life or housed me. I had come willingly—pursued, certainly—but even before my life was on the line, at the ball, he had felt like a safe haven. The Shade had already claimed me as his, perhaps I should make him mine too.

The mark prickled on my neck.

Perhaps I would.

Chapter Twenty-Four

Badness and Weakness

We paused for several minutes, trying to determine which cavern we were in. These walls were spiraled, almost like the inside of a shell, smooth and inhuman. My hands dragged along them, confused. Where were the tool marks from the workers? The other cavern had clearly been cut with hammers and chisels. Even loamers, who would do the bulk of the moving, relied on tools for the finer work. What had made this? A natural vein, perhaps?

"Can you use your earth magic to determine how much farther we have to go?" I asked Uncle Koll. "Would that help us determine where we are?"

He shook his head. "This far down, I can feel...too much. The earth is like cheese with holes in it. Or water with bubbles. I feel the voids and fullness, but I cannot reach the surface. Below us is hot."

"Hot?" The Shade turned sharply.

"Extremely hot. My palms are sweating. It's starting to run down my back and into—"

The Shade clenched his jaw. "We don't need those details, Uncle."

"I don't like hot. Let's get out of here." Uncle Koll pointed along a green line on the map. "Assuming we are here, let's head that way."

Goosebumps prickled my arms. Assuming seemed a bit treacherous. But the bats ahead of us had reported no new spyrings, so on we went.

We walked for what felt like an hour. My feet ached, and my brow began to sweat as the air around us continued to warm. "Is it only me, or—"

"Not just you, my dear. We are in deep trouble, I think." Uncle Koll placed one palm on the wall. "If anything, we are much deeper than we were before."

A left, then right, we went up and down, and then we entered another spiral cut tunnel.

"These walls are so odd." I said, running my hands over the waves on the surface. "What tool carved them?" The men shared an uneasy look. "What?

Uncle Koll pulled at his collar. "It's nothing, my dear."

"That look wasn't nothing." He waved his hands and walked away. "What aren't you telling me?"

The Shade sighed, "I'm not sure it will help you—"

I let go of his arm. "I'm not a delicate flower. I am not going to wilt or break. I don't want you to keep something from me."

He quickly kept pace. "I'm just trying to protect you, Dayspring."

"I don't...I don't want protection from information. If I'm attacked, sure, use your willowy tendrils to slap things about"—the Shade looked affronted, but I pushed on—"but you either trust me to be an adult and able to handle it, or you don't trust me at all. You can't expect me to choose or react wisely when I don't have all the information."

He groaned and wiped a hand down his face. "It's not a matter of trust. It's that...your life has been unfair, and you seem to have carried everyone and neglected yourself. You were responsible for those around you to your own detriment. Can't I wish for you to live without the burden for a little while?"

I paused, sorting through whether I was offended or grateful for his comment. His sentiment was fine, but... "But you can't decide for me. I have to be free to be able to choose." I swallowed with difficulty. "I think...there's a small chance that you're right"—he chuckled—"but if I'm to figure out what is mine to carry, then it's not fair for you to shield me from every harm."

His other hand flared to the side. "We are surrounded by harm. I clearly trust you. I let you come."

I caught his gaze in mine. "Then trust me a bit more." I turned toward him, pleading with my gaze. He tilted his head as if battling with himself.

He huffed out a breath. "There's that rumor—"

"A prophecy," Uncle Koll interjected.

"—a rumor told by old ladies."

Uncle Koll guffawed. "Fair."

The Shade continued. "And the prophecy you know says: Lest the deep reject the vile ones that slink beneath and this way run. Et cetera, et cetera."

I nodded. The Shade swept his hand through his black hair. "Well, in one version I found quite on accident in the king's study, the first line read, 'Lest the deep reject the vile *worms*.'" I blinked, slow to understand. "Uncle Koll senses the earth shifting below us in a single line. Moving in one direction. Constantly. A long, winding, moving *thing* that isn't earth."

I glanced at the older man who looked worried. "I'm not certain, my dear," Uncle Koll said quietly. "I can't tell if it's something made of the mountain that will not affect us in the least, or..."

"A beast," the Shade murmured.

Cold like ice slipped down my spine. "Oh." I rubbed my arms. "But that's okay, right? You've got your powers, and Uncle Koll—"

"A massive beast. Monstrous. I'm not sure I could drive it back," the Shade said.

"Especially—" Uncle Koll started.

"Especially with our animal friends in tow. It's not safe for them," the Shade finished.

Uncle Koll stopped and turned, his eyes burning toward the Shade. "It's not safe for anyone."

The Shade conceded with a nod.

"Perhaps." I cleared my throat. "Perhaps we could go back? Try on the surface, then?"

"Perhaps. There are ways back through the tunnels, to be sure, but..." The Shade paused as we passed a dead spyring on the ground. Upside down, its legs curled around its body. It had been dead long enough that its usually acrid scent was weak in the stale air. "But we don't have fire power to help keep away most spyrings like the prince and his men." He stopped as the tunnel turned sharply downhill. He restarted, his voice quieter. "And the surface, as discussed, is also treacherous."

"Also, I did collapse that one tunnel," Uncle Koll supplied. "Making the map quite inaccurate now."

A rumbling groan shuddered through the very air around us.

"*Whooooooooooooo aaaaarrrrrrreeeeee yoooooooouuuuuuuuuu?*" A sound deeper than thunder hissed and scraped through my mind. Bertha stood, arching her back as the ten hairs on her shoulders stood on end. Her eyes seemed to glow in the light, and her translucent skin paled even further.

Uncle Koll set his hand upon the wall, and his eyes widened. "Run again, please."

The animals kept pace as we sprinted down the incline. The vibration of the floor buzzed through my shoes and shook my spine with each step. The sound felt heavy, and I covered my ears. The wolves whined.

Uncle Koll stopped and pushed against the wall to our right, shoving it aside and creating a hole. He grunted, the muscles in his arms flaring with the effort. After a clatter of falling stone, he led us into another tunnel. This one felt like it ran upward and had been carved with squared off tools.

"Faster, faster!" Uncle Koll shouted above the groaning, thunderous din. He picked up a lagging pangolin, as the raccoons climbed onto the backs of the wolves. The bats screeched around us.

"Giant." "Hot." "Help us!" The bats cried in my mind.

The Shade was visibly limping but threw a tendril backward for what seemed like minutes. Then he whipped his arms toward his chest and pulled two bats to himself. He clutched them against the leather of his chest as we continued to run.

The air was sweltering. The smell of eggs rotting in the sun burned my nostrils. My thighs ached as they protested any more steps before us. The Shade heaved himself up the steep turns of the tunnels with his hand on the walls, grimacing with each step. I tucked myself into his side, one arm wrapped behind him, my brows pinched in concern.

His smirk was tired. *"Thanks, Dayspring."* Even his voice in my mind sounded weary. For too long, we dashed and wove through endless corridors, and by degrees, the air cooled again, the scent shifted back to soil and dust, and the rumbling faded behind us. The Shade slowed further.

"Uncle Koll?" I called out to him in my thoughts and was relieved to see him turn in concern. He fell back to the Shade's other side, slinging

the Shade's arm over his shoulders. We slowed to a fast walk, but even this proved difficult for the Shade.

Uncle Koll sputtered a few cut off sentences before he said, "You know, if you'd just—"

"I know." The Shade sounded resigned.

Uncle Koll huffed.

I frowned, ready to argue again when the Shade cut me off. "I *will* tell you, Dayspring. I will. Soon. Some things I can't tell you yet, but I will. I promise. Right now, I just need you to trust me for a little longer."

Trust was a tender, budding seedling, but I did. "Okay."

His weight collapsed slightly in relief. "I will not harm you." His voice was quiet, but his words were heavy. "I will do everything I can to give you what you deserve. To give you your freedom."

I squeezed his arm. There was nothing I could say.

Uncle Koll harumphed. "Let's get out of here." He pulled out a vial of the healing potion we'd made earlier that week. He held it out to the Shade, who tried to wave it off. Uncle Koll palmed it to raise a craggy finger. "Do not start with me, boy. If you hope to run through the castle in an hour, you must recover what strength you can. Unless you want to—"

"Fine." The Shade tugged the pink potion from Uncle Koll's grasp. "I'll take it."

Moments later, his limp disappeared, and his weight lifted from my shoulders. The cold air of the tunnels felt icy in his absence. Uncle Koll nodded his approval before leading us to the left again. The ground flattened and darkened. The rock looked almost glassy, worn down from thousands of steps taken by the workers as they'd plodded in and out of the cavern. Tools and trash were cast along the edges. Ahead, a track began with no sign of a cart.

A sharp chirping sound startled me, and I looked back for some new monster. Soon more chirps sounded, growing until I recognized it. Nighttime grasshoppers.

We were finally at the surface.

"Well, it's not the dungeon entrance we'd planned for, but hopefully, they won't be looking for an attack from within the mines," the Shade mused.

The wind blew the dusty, earthy air from my lungs, and I nearly clapped with glee to see the stars. Perhaps we'd have to go back home this way, but I hoped upon hope to take a long route above the surface instead.

We emerged from a cavern high on the back face of the western mountain, where the castle perched above us. The wagon road before us turned sharply, elbowing down at frightening angles toward the village and the twinkling lights of the city. The distant mountain—into which the manor was carved along the canyon walls—was still dark in the pre-dawn light. Below us, the castle rose from its stern foundations with white columns, high arching windows, and massive patios.

The sight stirred a chaotic mess of emotions within me: relief to be above ground; hesitance to return to the place where I'd been so badly hurt; hope that I might see the queen; fear that I might see the prince; and dread at the thought of my father. The Shade squeezed my hand. I was not alone.

Bertha remained behind in the cavern as we headed down a deer path behind the craggy trees. In the east, the sky was barely lightening. A distant boom rose from the far mountain. The mesa was obscured with a haze of something even darker.

"Looks like the prince decided to attack after all," the Shade muttered.

"The smoke traps were a good idea. If you weren't there fighting back, it would be a dead giveaway you weren't at home." Uncle Koll scratched at his beard. "I wasn't sure those trip wires were safe with all the creatures milling around."

The Shade huffed. "They are much smarter than the prince."

A weak defense rallied in my mind, but I stuffed it back. The prince was his own man; I wasn't duty bound to defend his honor, only my own.

I slipped on a rock, and the Shade caught my elbow. The back garden gate of the castle gardens loomed ahead. "I take it you got in this way before?" I asked.

A dangerous grin sharpened his features. "Last time—if you re- member—I used the main door of the ballroom. I wasn't going for subtlety."

I remembered it well: the fire, the smell, the shadows, and the burn in his gaze. "Thank you for saving me that day."

The Shade's brows pinched together, and he clenched his hand. Anger that smelled like pine and burned like charcoal filled me—his anger. "The prince revealed that day what a fool he'd become. These little spats, pseudo-battles, aggressive coups, assassination at- tempts—fine, he can do as he wishes, and I will respond—but to billow flames at his own people?" He paused, pulling me to a stop. "At you?" He shook his head and continued walking. "Unthinkable. Poor leadership at best. A complete failure at worst."

"I would have died."

"You would have." His lip twitched. "That was the second time I wanted to kiss you." I stumbled on a stone. "I'm glad I didn't have to wait too long." I stammered through a few false starts before he continued. "But since then, it's been a remarkably long time. I hardly remember what your lips were like. Did you taste like radishes? Or was it bark? Or perhaps cave dirt?"

I stifled my laugh and whacked his arm. "You are just trying to distract me with such charming descriptions. It's no wonder we haven't kissed since then."

"Ah, so you've decided. I'm glad you keep thinking of kissing me."

I paused. "Wait a moment. What was the first time you wanted to kiss me?"

"When you were lost in my woods, and August was trying to scare you out."

Of course. He was the forester.

"You were covered in pine needles and dirt, and I have never seen anything more kissable."

I flushed. "I...certainly am not thinking about kissing you right now."

But the Shade seemed to see right through me, even when my mental barriers were up. I had thought entirely too long about wanting to kiss him. I needed to think about something else. Something important—like measuring potion ingredients, or the meaning of life and happiness, or even the color at the edge of the rainbow. Instead, my memory of that harrowing experience was solely focused on that one world-ending kiss. Surely, I'd been delirious with blood loss, but that memory was seared into my very marrow.

The Shade leaned forward. His head angling toward mine. "Well, if you do ever think of it again, let me know."

Uncle Koll growled beside us. "Young man, if you don't focus, I'm going to feed you only carrots for a week!"

"Fine. But only because it would be distracting to kiss her with you standing there."

Uncle Koll rolled his eyes.

"Ready, Dayspring?" He reached out for my hand.

"I'm ready," I lied.

The impenitent Shade stood proud as we peered through the fence at the back of the gardens. Three guards paced the parapet of the castle, while another two strode corner to corner along the sides.

It was time to break into the castle.

Chapter Twenty-Five

A Brief Castle Break-In

U ncle Koll gently shifted the dirt beneath the edges of the gate. Arms of soil wrapped around the base, lifting the structure up until the hooks of the hinges slipped out of their holds. The shadows caught the door silently, and together they set it aside so we could sneak into the garden.

The world darkened hazily as the Shade returned the gate and obscured us in inky clouds. My steps were unsteady on the broken tiles of the garden path. But as it was not yet dawn, the grounds were quietly lit by the clouded moon, and we slipped silently toward the castle doors.

I paused with my hand on a cracked fruit tree and looked at the animal menagerie around me. All the pangolins and wolves scuffled around my feet; the bats circled above us.

"Won't we stand out?"

The Shade looked about. With a tip of his head, he commanded the pangolin and honey badger to stay by the gate with one of the bats, which immediately flew up and hung from the tallest peak of the arch. "These can stand guard." He instructed most of the wolves to stay in the courtyard, while the dark one with bright yellow eyes came with us

.

The dried skeletons of fruit trees around us reached toward an ashy sky with craggy black arms. They were as dry and desiccated as the desolate forests I'd scavenged while searching for a cure for the queen. Pots stood dried and empty. Dead stalks of plants and flowers, caked with ash and black slime, folded onto the cracked soil below. In a hundred steps, we would reach the back door.

Another explosion boomed in the distance.

"I'm glad the prince is having a good time at the manor." Uncle Koll scratched his beard as he slunk behind a dry wall of shrubbery. "It's convenient that he's out of the castle today."

The Shade chuckled darkly. "I may or may not have sent a threatening letter."

I put my fingers to my forehead. "You don't have to antagonize him all the time, do you?"

The Shade's smile turned as feral as the wolf's. "No, but I do enjoy it."

The black wolf slunk forward between us, its claws clattering on the stone tiles below. We froze as one of the guards looked up toward the mountain above us. Then as he turned away, we rushed ahead and ducked under the arching doorway.

Uncle Koll jostled the door. "Locked."

A sliver of shadow brushed past me, weaving its way through my fingers before threading into the lock and snapping it open with a click.

"You would have been so handy when I was a hungry little girl trying to sneak into the kitchens," I muttered as I led the way inside, pausing as we entered the small gardener's room strewn with abandoned shovels, rakes, and aprons draped with dust and spiderwebs. The gardeners had long since given up on landscaping, scraping by with the vegetables and fruits grown inside the solarium.

I turned down the servants' passage. The castle was eerily quiet. Down the hallway, I could hear the gentle clatter of early morning breadmaking. My heart ached at the thought of Chef. The Shade reached over and squeezed my hand, his eyes curious and kind. I squeezed back before entering the servants' quarters.

We snuck past rooms whose inhabitants still snored the night away, slipped through the narrow threshold, and crept up the far steps. I patted the pack on my side. The clinking glass reassured me that the potions were still there—the bottles of hope. I paused beside a closed door, a hallway entrance to my father's workstation.

I looked at the Shade. "Can we try to see her?"

His eyes unfocused, I assumed checking in with the other animals. "Everything seems quiet. The guards haven't altered their course. But if we need to go, we go quickly."

I carefully leaped and hugged him, being sure not to clank the potions much. I led away from the door to my father's room and toward the back passages of the royal suites. We came to the final stair, and I put my ear against the door at the top. No sound came from the other side. The queen's attendants would join her in a couple of hours as the sun began to rise, but they usually left the queen alone through the night since she got the most rest in the early morning hours.

I felt a squeeze in my chest—nervousness—but this feeling wasn't mine. I looked back at the Shade. His fist pulsed, tapping on the side of his leg, and his jaw muscles feathered as he clenched them. I reached toward him, but he brushed my hand away.

Unduly hurt, I turned toward Uncle Koll, who looked paler than before. One hand was on his chest as the other fussed with his shirt sleeve. He glanced over at me, dismissing the question in my eyes with a shake of his head. My eyebrows furrowed with confusion, but I opened the door with a click. I peered in, listening for trouble. The smell hit me first—much worse than I remembered. The room was saturated in that sick, sour, rotten smell that came with the queen's sickness. Uncle Koll's breath shuddered. Nothing else in her room stirred.

I approached her bedside. Her thin frame looked more skeletal on the bed than when I'd last seen her; her eyes were sunken, her face resembling an empty skull. The pillows were fluffed, and the blanket tucked in around her. She looked more like a child than a queen. One of the potions I had sent was half drunk on the bedside table. It had kept her alive, but only just.

The words breathed out of me in a whisper, an ache unable to be restrained. "Oh, Your Majesty."

Her eyes fluttered. I held my breath, torn between hoping she would awaken, and terrified of disturbing her. Slowly, her lids lifted, and she regarded my face. Her green eyes fixed on mine, sharp and clear. I stepped into the thin moonlight that streaked across her bedding so she could see me better.

"Aelia?" Her dry voice croaked. The Shade inhaled sharply. I stepped toward her and grasped her hand. "Your Majesty, I'm sorry to wake you."

"You left the castle in uproar." The queen swallowed hard, and I offered her a sip of water from her bedside table. "Everyone is certain you are dead. Leon won't tell me what's going on. The seers all left the castle and have been sending messages by pigeon. Where did you go, my dear? I've been so worried."

I smiled at her. "I'm not dead, thankfully. And in fact, I have been very busy." I turned and brought my bag to my lap. "We brought you some new potions." I stacked them at her bedside. "I think they'll be stronger. We were able to come up with some changes in the ingredients, and I think..." I glanced up at her face and stopped short. Her eyes were wide and frozen on the Shade behind me. She had become as still as death, although her chest still moved with each breath.

The queen's gaze flickered to Uncle Koll. "What—"

"Oh, don't worry, Your Majesty. They came with me. They've been helping. The Shade...he's..." I paused my babbling—the words stuck in my throat as I watched tears well up in her eyes. "Your Majesty, don't cry. You're safe." I reached for a handkerchief to dab at her cheeks.

"Koll." The queen's whisper was ragged. Koll? I twisted to look back at him.

"Gemmie." Uncle Koll said, his voice stripped and raw. Queen Gemaline Aura Grace often went by Queen of Grace, but no one called her Gemmie. Uncle Koll's cheeks glimmered with his own tears.

"Sha...ade," the queen stuttered, turning to study him. The Shade nodded, his eyes soft and glassy, his Adam's apple bobbing. His hands were folded in front of him, his thumb rubbing the other. What in all the lands was happening?

Uncle Koll pushed past me and cupped her face with his hand. The queen gave a small sob. His thumbs brushed her cheek, and he reached back to me for a potion.

"Gemmie, can you drink this?" The queen smiled a bit, and Uncle Koll brought the potion to her lips. "Just a bit more, my dear."

The queen coughed as she swallowed the potion before smiling brightly. Even the darkness of the room lifted at the sight. "It's good to see you."

Her frail hand drifted past me and toward the Shade. One beat. Two. Then the menace of our nation, the embodiment of Death, stumbled forward to take her hand. "My queen."

"My son."

My gasp was too loud for the quiet room. I studied his face as his emotions flitted through me, affection and pain, betrayal and...love.

He swallowed again. My mind whirled. The Shade was the queen's son. She wasn't crying because she was afraid. She was crying because... I stepped back, giving them their space. I was so confused—the stories said that the Shade had caused her sickness, that his shadows were there the day she fell ill.

He turned his head slightly, his green eyes glowing in the cast of the moonlight. *"Of course, I was here that day. And every day before that when I could sneak in as she was worsening. I was that boy you played with, Aelia."* His eyes closed in a picture of anguish. *"But I was too young, and I couldn't stop the sickness. And Father blamed me."* His hand squeezed around his mother's small frail fingers. *"Even though it was the mining—and the effect the mines had on the earth—that had made her unwell in the first place."*

"But how could you leave her?" I whispered, too overwhelmed to remember to project my thoughts. The Shade's pain lanced through me, and I felt instant regret—I didn't mean it so harshly. The queen glanced between us, then fixed back on the Shade.

"Did you—?"

"No." He looked away. "Not fully."

She nodded and regarded me again. "Why not?"

The Shade just shook his head.

"Aelia, come here." Her command was a whisper but lost no power in its quietness.

She attempted to sit but collapsed back against the pillows, fixing me with her gaze. "No matter what happens, Aelia, you must know that he didn't do this to me." She wheezed. "He could never. And Aelia, no matter what, no matter what you think you know or what you have been shown before, now you must trust yourself when it matters most."

"Trust myself?" I repeated, confused at why that would matter at a time like this. At her insistent stare, I agreed. "Okay."

"Promise me."

"I promise, Your Majesty."

The queen released a long sad sigh. "I am so tired of being tired."

Uncle Koll set his hand on the bedding over leg. "These new potions should help, Gemmie. They helped me."

If the Shade was her son, then Uncle Koll...Uncle Koll was her brother.

"Mother, I have a gift." The Shade reached into his pocket and withdrew the box with the four lights. "The instructions are inside."

The queen held the glowing glass up toward her face. "My son, this is remarkable. How did you make this?"

The Shade blossomed with pride. "It was actually Aelia who inspired me when we—"

"*The prince. The prince!*" A small voice burst into our minds. "*He's not at the manor. He's there! He's coming. I'm—*" Jamison cut off the connection with a squeak. He was nearby? But where?

The Shade stiffened, his eyes deadly and worried when they met mine. The Shade bent down to kiss his mother's cheek. "I'm sorry, we must go. Leon is here. I'll finish the story another time."

The queen smiled weakly. "Come back soon, my dears. And Aelia, don't forget." The Shade still held her hand, his body tightened like a string on a bow.

"Shade," Uncle Koll warned. "We must go."

He whirled and stalked across the room. "Look at what he let her become." I gave a fleeting curtsy to the queen and tripped after him.

"My son. Family is still family." The queen's voice croaked and stopped the Shade mid-step. His fists pulsed. Around him, the floor broke into fractals of shadow, the tiles seeming to smoke as the Shade started again, every step leaving a hazy footprint. Waves of icy shadows poured off his shoulders, and his eyes blackened. My heart ached with emotions that weren't mine. Grief. Regret. Guilt. Anger. The last one boiled the strongest.

I set my hand upon his arm. Glancing at his contorted face. "Shade, let's go home."

He blinked once, though the billowing darkness still shrouded him. His voice crackled like walking over thin ice, desperate for a lifeline. "Say it again."

I slipped my hand into his. "Let's go home."

A pulse of anger. "But the prince. The king. They are doing this to her."

"They will be here tomorrow. And the next day. We aren't finished yet. The potion will help her while we fix the rest."

He turned to me and pressed his palm against the mark on my neck. Waves of his agony flooded through me. Violent pain ripped through us. I turned into his touch, begging him to feel what it could be: Comfort. Safety. Hope. His thoughts were a torrent.

"We have done what we came to do," Uncle Koll murmured behind us.

His nostrils flared again as the trumpet sounded from the entrance. He nodded, then took my hand. *Aelia first.* "Get us out of here."

Chapter Twenty-Six

My Father's Workshop

We bolted down the servants' passageways, but voices ahead echoed down the stone. Then I heard three long gongs of the bell to rally the guards. The Shade's blackness deepened the natural shadows of the servants' corridor, but I wasn't sure how it would stand up to the guards' luz lights or keen eyes. A cacophony of stomping footsteps forced us to duck into a supply closet, too small for the three of us and the wolf.

We held our breaths as they passed. The Shade called mentally for Jamison, but there was no response. The hall went silent again, and we rushed into the corridor, racing toward the back garden. But additional voices—louder voices—stopped us. Diving down the right hallway, I ran into the only place I knew we could hide for a moment. My father's workshop.

We came through the doorway and sprinted down the corridor. The Shade was limping and his breath becoming more ragged.

"Don't worry about me, Dayspring," he muttered when he saw my worried expression.

I pushed open my father's door, ushering the Shade, Uncle Koll, and the wolf into a room lined with jars, herbs, oils, and candles. Clicking the door shut behind us, I pressed my back against it and let out a slow breath. The Shade began picking up various canisters and tilting the substances within.

Uncle Koll sat heavily in the chair. "Can you reach the others?"

The Shade nodded. "The wolves stationed at the gate have hidden farther up the mountain. The bats are watching. The others are hiding for now."

"Jamison?" I asked.

The Shade just shook his head. "I haven't heard him since his first missive."

I rubbed my hand on my chest. I didn't want to worry about that tiny, annoying bat, but I was. When had he wormed his way into my affection? The Shade clacked his teeth twice—he was worried too.

"Okay, so"—I pushed up off the door and came to lean on the desk—"the other side of this hallway goes toward the kitchens. We could go there. I know Chef will be good to us, but—"

"The guards will be everywhere," the Shade finished.

"We can't stay here." Uncle Koll pointed around the room.

The room door shut with a bang. The Shade shoved me behind him, his shadows curling around my shoulders as he faced off with the intruder.

"No. You cannot." The speaker was wrinkled and bent, his eyes sunken, and the lower lids dark and scabbed. I hardly recognized him.

"Father," I breathed.

He glanced at me, his expression both unreadable and showing a thousand emotions at once. "Aelia."

The Shade stiffened, took three strides forward, and then punched my father across the jaw.

"Shade!" I squawked and rushed after them.

The shadows picked up my father and set him back on his feet. He rubbed his cheek, but there was no fire in him. No fight. His shoulders slumped.

"What were you thinking?" I asked as I tried to brush past him, but the Shade stuck out a hand.

"I'm thinking I'd like to do more than that." The Shade's sharp finger pointed at my father. "You let them take her. You didn't protect her when it mattered, and you didn't love her well before." Instant tears sprung to my eyes, a lifetime of emotion on the brim. The Shade continued. "You should have done better. Been better."

Each word struck my father like a blow, though the shadows and the Shade's fists had stilled. My father...cowered. His small frame shrunk into itself, and I saw nothing left to fear. He was a broken, pitiable man. Disgust mixed with the residual ache in my chest.

My father shook his head. "You're right." Icy prickles covered my skin. "I should have...should have."

"You didn't," the Shade said, the shadows boiling around him.

"I should have stopped the prince somehow."

"You're a coward."

My father shriveled. "Yes. To my shame. I've thought it a thousand times, considered a million ways I could have done anything besides what I did."

"Which was nothing." The Shade's hand reached out to me, and I grasped it. His emotions flooded me at the contact, my heart surging with righteous fury demanding justice.

My father put his head into his hands. "For so many things, Aelia. So many...I'm sorry."

The Shade felt unwilling to forgive him. My previous self was ready to stop the tension and make it better, but I wasn't that person anymore. He had apologized before and hadn't changed. I was so sick of hurting. And yet...what was forgiveness but freedom for the one who forgave? What was forgiveness but a means of letting me loose from every ache and bond my father had pinned me under? The Shade, mercifully, held his tongue.

I glanced around the room for the alcohol bottle but saw none. Even his emergency supply under the cabinet was gone. Empty potion bottles lay on the floor in the corner. All drunk or...I hated to hope again for him. I cleared my throat. "Why did you do it? Why didn't you love me more?"

His shoulders sagged. "I did love you—do love you. I just didn't see how much until you were ripped from me—until I thought you were dead." He pulled back his sleeve, showing the scars on the back of his hand, the bond mark he had burned away all those years ago. He closed his eyes, and a glowing leaf emerged beneath the twisted tissues. "I thought losing your mother was the worst pain I would ever experience. But I didn't know the depths of agony until I lost you too." A wave of unease slipped from the Shade, but father continued. "We were bonded. So young. She was my everything. When she gave you to me, I knew I had it all. But then I lost everything."

Bonded. Bonding to someone meant giving up part of yourself, sacrificing the best part of you for another. And if one died, the other would wish they had died also. But Uncle Koll had responded so differently to that pain.

"Your mother was the very air I breathed, Aelia—the ground I walked on. When she left us, I was unmoored, a desiccated husk of a man. But there was you—you needed me. I didn't...I didn't want to care for *anything* ever again. I wanted to work and to die, but you and your persistent affection awoke my shriveled heart, making me want to care for something again."

The scoff escaped before I could stop it. I looked down at the fingers in my grasp.

"Tell him, Dayspring."

I bit my lip. "But you didn't care, Father. You were...mean. Drunk." My throat threatened to close. "You hit me."

My father had the decency to look horrified. "I was a fool."

"Even when you lost Mother—you said you lost everything—but you still had me. I was here. I was trying...trying so hard to win your affection."

"I was blind and stupid."

The Shade scoffed. "And cruel."

Father cringed. "That too." He heaved a breath. "I thought I was doing okay. But when you looked at me at the temple—when your expression was not one of horror, but of acceptance, as if you already knew I was capable of this—I knew the slime I had become." He scratched his arm. "I quit drinking. But without you, there isn't enough potion. The queen's health is failing. The hope of our nation is failing."

"We gave the queen a potion, Father. One that is better because of the Shade—because of his help." I tilted my head to the bottles in the corner, one still containing a drop of the pink liquid. "Did you drink her potions?"

His head sunk farther into his shoulders. "I'm a weak loamer—my earth magic is minimal—but I still felt the effects of the earth's sickness. So I started taking the potions too."

I didn't know I could be more horrified. No wonder all the herbs I found were never enough.

"I'm sorry for this also. I started drinking both the mead and the potions to numb the pain, then to ignore the sickness, and finally to hide my shame from it all." Father looked at the Shade and dipped his head. "I owe you many things, sir. Thank you for protecting her when I didn't."

Wicked shadows whipped around the room—menacing, but never touching my father or his things. "And what will you do now?"

My father stood as upright as he could. "Now, I'll help you escape."

Uncle Koll let out a slow breath. "The only correct answer."

A shadow from behind my father slipped back to the Shade and returned the knife in its clutches to the sheath on the Shade's hip.

"You were going to kill my father?" I thought at the Shade.

"I was thinking about it. If he threatened you, I had to disable him." He shrugged. *"My plan was more about maiming him. He's a healer—he would have recovered."* Turning toward me, he pinned my eyes with his, the shadows around him causing the green to glow. Aloud, he said, "I refuse to let him hurt you again."

My smile was a bit wobbly. "You can't protect me from everything."

"Watch me."

"Stubbed toes?"

"I'll destroy the floor that tripped you." He shook his head. "Or maybe just carry you everywhere."

"Splinters?"

"Burn the trees."

I snorted at the image. "The prince already does that so well."

He raised his eyebrows. *"May I punch him too?"*

I gave him a sad scoff. *"Maybe, but not today. Today, let's get out of here."*

Dark shadows filtered across his green eyes as the muscles of his jaw feathered. "Dayspring, I—"

A boom preceded the shaking of the entire castle. The ground below us buckled, and dust rained down from the ceiling.

The Shade clasped his hands to his head. "Uncle, something is here—"

A loud blast shook the walls around us again. Uncle Koll rubbed his hands. "I can feel it."

Father pulled a cane from the wall and peered out the door. "To the kitchens then. A recent shipment came for the village. We could put you on the cart as it leaves. You can escape."

"They'll search it," the Shade said.

"Not if I'm driving," my father answered with a disgusted sneer. "I'm the prince's loyal dog."

The Shade turned to me. "*Your decision, Dayspring. I'm with you.*"

I squeezed his hand, a flood of warmth blooming through my heart. No one had ever looked at me with such affection, much less *respect.* And no one had ever actually waited for my decision. "It's not a bad plan." He raised a brow, and I spoke more confidently. "Let's do it."

Chapter Twenty-Seven

Run or Fight

"Come this way," my father shouted as he rushed to the back wall of his workshop. He tugged on a book, and a secret door clicked open. My lips parted. My father looked sheepish. "This, uh, this leads to the wine cellar."

Of course it did. I stomped past him. At least the wine cellar had a front door in the kitchen—and it was, admittedly, a fine escape route. A huge bellow rumbled before distant screams screeched against the rough stone. A single line of booted footprints cleared a path through the dust on the floor—the steps my father had taken toward the thing he loved more than me.

As the pain surged, a shadow slipped gently against my palm. "*Dayspring?*"

I tried to stifle a teary sniff. "*It's not fair.*" A stone fell into my hair as the hallway rumbled. "*I shouldn't have to forgive him. I shouldn't be asked to be the better person again. I shouldn't have to make peace after everything.*"

"*Dayspring, I am not a pinnacle of forgiveness.*" His shadows caught me before I stumbled, as the earth heaved beneath us from whatever was going on outside. "*But forgiveness isn't about them. It's about releasing yourself from the grip he has on you. He may not pay the price*

*of some just punishment, or suffer like you have, but you don't have to be
consumed by it or be beaten under it anymore. It's in the past. The scar
remains as a marker of when you were hurt but you healed."*

I whimpered, pain twisting my chest at his words. I knew he was
right, but that didn't make it easier to hear. I shifted and tried to deflect
the weight of the conversation. *"Could you forgive the prince?"*

*"I'm certain that I don't know what you mean. Death doesn't for-
give."*

My laugh came out a bit sad as I wiped my eyes. At the end of the
hall, my father pulled a luz wall sconce to open yet another doorway.
Wine bottles were stacked on either side before we pushed through
the other door into the kitchen. We all fell in and tried to rush to
the outside doorway, threading through the chaos of servants and
panicking staff. One woman stood on a stool and commanded them
all.

Chef. My lips split into a grin as I took her in—in all her flour-coat-
ed, ladle-wielding glory. Her gaze caught mine, and she froze. Tossing
one last command, she leapt with unexpected grace and rushed to me,
wrapping me up in her embrace.

"Child, I have missed you."

"I missed you too, Chef."

She patted my arms as she pulled away to examine my face before
taking in my companions. Her eyebrow rose in suspicion as she saw
the Shade. We must have looked absurd: my ailing father, a scrappy
Uncle Koll, the glowering Shade, and a black wolf rushing through
her domain. But she pinched her lips and tilted her head to the side
toward the exit. "And now, dear, we need to get you out of here. The
castle is under attack."

Uncle Koll asked, "From what exactly?"

"A monster is all I can gather." Chef shuddered and pushed me toward the door. "It came from the mountain—a beast of the deep. Lord Ramsha, if you do anything right, get her out of here. Go home, if you must. Just save our girl." She spoke of home to my father, but instead of my old home by the sea, the word conjured a dark manor with a dreamy solarium.

Uncle Koll caught Chef's hand and flourished a bow and a kiss. "Don't forget to save yourself, madame."

Chef's stoic features flushed a glorious ruby, and she bopped him gently on the head. "That's enough of that. Go on now."

We rushed outside. The sky swirled in ribbons of black. Distant thunder rolled while the clouds brightened in waves from the prince's fires. A roar rumbled from the other side of the castle. My father lifted the cover of the wagon and ushered us all inside. The Shade offered me his hand, but as I took it, a scream rent the air. My head flipped toward the noise.

"*Inside, Dayspring.*" He pressed lightly on my back to urge me forward.

I climbed into the wagon, tucking myself against the wolf's furry side. The tower wall burst out, and stones fell in the distance. The roof of the tower fell slowly, landing in a heap on the cobblestone street. After covering our view with a tarp, my father climbed into the driver's seat and took off down the path that led away from the castle. The horse clopped quickly at first, but soon, we were surrounded by panicking people, and we slowed considerably.

"We'll get you to safety, to start," the Shade muttered. "I'm not sure the manor is far enough away, but the animals will protect you. Then, I could retu—" He winced as we heard another scream.

My breaths grew shallow. I turned back to the castle, peeking between the cover and the wall at the home of my youth. And we were just...fleeing. I turned to the Shade. His knowing expression told me he read my thoughts. The green of his eyes swirled with shadow, and his jaw clenched.

"We can't just leave them," I whispered. "There are good people here. The queen is here!"

A spark of mischief flit across his face. "What are you saying? Don't you want to go where it's safe?"

"I'm saying..." I reached forward and grasped his fingers. "I have a home at the manor, not the coast. And being safe isn't everything. What did Uncle Koll say about risk earlier? Mankind was not made for boredom but for risks. The right risk at the right time is worth all the stars in the skies." The Shade leaned toward me to reply, but he was interrupted as Uncle Koll's cry cut him off.

More rocks fell from the tower and the castle wall striking the side of the wagon and panicking the horse. My father tried to steer us straight, but with a crack of splintered wood, the wagon tilted to one side, dumping its contents—and all of us—to the ground. My landing was softer than it should have been as I found myself wrapped in the embrace of shadows and two strong arms.

People sprinted around us in the dusky morning light—too early for the sun, too cloudy even as it rose—jostling one another as they fled from whatever was on the other side of the castle. We had grabbed the battle potions from the manor. Though I might not have magic of my own, I wasn't helpless anymore.

"Let's go save your mother," I declared, pulling him to his feet.

The Shade's expression turned fierce. "After you."

Shadows pulled Uncle Koll upright. My father brushed himself off and caught the reins of the horse, steadying him before unlatching him from the wagon. Masses ran around us in the dim dawn light, shoving past each other to escape.

A long, loud bellow came from the far side of the castle. An enormous open-mouthed worm emerged behind the shattering tower. Six tiny eyes glittered on each side, and its gaping maw revealed rows upon rows of teeth that whirred in circles—first one way, then the other. A spinning cave of death. The worm was easily twice the size of the tower and nearly as long as the castle itself. Its massive body writhed and wriggled. Its skin looked as thick as leather but was devoid of any plated armor. Rolls of skin whorled around the creature, much like the twisting marks in the stone tunnels from earlier—this creature must have made them.

"*Death. And pain. And death.*" The voice was lower than thunder and buzzed against my skin like a lightning strike too close. It sounded familiar—the voice in the cave.

The Shade pressed me behind him. "Well, Dayspring. There's your caterpillar."

I squawked. "What?"

"You said you liked caterpillars."

"This is *not* the kind of caterpillar I was referring to!" I grabbed his hand before shouting behind us. "Father, go home if you'd like. We are going to stop that worm."

We rushed up the road through the crowds. A flame came from a balcony and blasted the beast's neck. Its head turned and battered the tower, collapsing the top few levels.

"What is his weakness, do you think? Maybe I could just ask him to go home?" I shouted.

"*Death. Pain. Death,*" the worm moaned in our minds.

Uncle Koll panted beside us. "I don't think it can be reasoned with."

The Shade laughed. "Hello, dear sir, could you please return to your place of slumber. It's breakfast time."

"Okay, okay. Fine. Overwhelming force then." I veered through the castle gates. "Why am I leading? You know this place as well as I do, *Your Highness*." I threw a glare his way. At least the Shade had the decency to look mildly sheepish. But he waved me ahead.

"To the ballroom." I ducked through an unguarded door into a library, then we rushed down a back hallway until we reached the steps leading from the kitchens to the back of the ballroom. The larger castle halls were faster, but I didn't want a forward-thinking guard to take hold of the Shade before he reached the front lines.

The far ballroom wall was in shambles—the pristine stone floor now covered in debris. Several soldiers cared for the wounded, and the northern wall had a new gaping hole to the courtyard below. A large boulder sat in the center of the room—perhaps it was what had made the hole in the wall. The prince stood on the dais with three galers on each side, hurling gusts of fire. The galers' wind made his flames grow larger, carrying them toward the beast and wrapping them around it as the creature bellowed in agony. The worm's tail lashed forward and knocked down an outer wall of the courtyard. Soldiers filled the garden. Most threw spears, though a few dared get close enough to stab the worm with their swords; like the arrow shot from the window, each spear fell harmlessly to the ground.

"Uncle Koll?" the Shade asked. "Are you well enough?"

"Maybe, yes. I took my potion this morning."

He nodded. "I have my bag of poisons. Aelia, do you still have those sleep bombs?"

"Does the moon rise in the east?" I teased, holding up the small satchel of potions.

He kissed my cheek. "Only when you're here, Dayspring." He took the bag. "Stay safe." Then he stepped around the doorframe and toward the prince. Uncle Koll and I ducked inside, waiting along the wall.

One of the soldiers raised a panicked voice. "The Shade! The Shade!"

The prince whipped around, one hand still casting a flame at the worm. Sweat beaded his brow. A soldier pushed off the wall and strode between them, his sword raised. "There you are. My men said you laid a trap but didn't actually appear."

"Leon." The Shade nodded a greeting, ignoring the soldier before him. "Nice to see you again so soon. Need a hand?"

The prince's face contorted in vitriol. "Not from you."

"I have sleep bombs."

The prince paused, clearly fighting with himself.

"We should battle together for the queen. For Moth—"

"Fine, fine." The prince interrupted that critical word. With a wave, the prince called off the confused guards. "Let him through."

The Shade strode forward—past the worried guard—and climbed the three steps to stand beside the prince. Shadows burst around him, and several guards startled and stumbled back—one even falling to the ground—but the Shade ignored them, directing individual tendrils to retrieve the sleep bombs from his own pouch.

"Make it mad, will you?"

"It's already mad," the prince responded but flicked a hand toward a guard all the same.

The washer sprayed the beast with water from the fountain. The prince turned and threw fire around the blast, boiling the steam, which hit the worm's side. The monster bellowed again, rows of serrated teeth spinning as spit and pebbles flew out of its mouth.

"Excellent." With a grunt, the Shade threw the shadows, sending each of the eight sleep bombs into the gaping maw. "Each one could knock out twenty men."

The worm writhed, throwing its face to the sky in a high-pitched, marrow-rending scream. Those in the room stumbled, clutching their hands to their ears. After an endless moment, the worm turned to the balcony, all twelve eyes peering forward, and lunged.

The prince and the Shade dove off the platform in opposite directions. The worm rammed the dais between them and slid partway into the room. Its soulless gaze pinned me as it slowly withdrew. Grabbing a luz lamp from the wall, I stabbed it into the eye nearest me. The worm groaned again and thrashed, shoving me, Uncle Koll, and a table into the wall. One eye was now closed, but the others glared with heart-stopping malice. My blood filled with ice.

It wriggled back out of the room. The Shade wrapped its neck with a shadowy collar, and the prince attacked it with fire. Uncle Koll lifted discarded stones and pummeled the creature as archers tried to take out the rest of its eyes. The creature rose, then dove forward again, its teeth spinning within its mouth as it bored through the center of the balcony—biting out a chunk of the thick stone as if it were cheese. The structure creaked, and a crack formed between the balcony and the main room, splitting it in half.

"It isn't very sleepy, Shade." The prince shouted as he tucked himself against the wall.

The Shade was visibly relieved when we made eye contact; I was still safe against a column. I smiled reassuringly. Then, with a vibrating crack, the damage to the balcony became too great, and in one terrifying moment, the Shade, the prince, the galers, and the balcony collapsed to the ground. I screamed as I lurched forward, wishing I had my own magic to wrap around him and draw him to me.

Uncle Koll caught my shoulders. "Trust him, Aelia. He's capable." But his eyes were laced with worry, as we ran to the edge.

We looked down as the dust settled. The balcony looked like a broken hill before the beast. The eerie light of the early sun, filtered through black clouds, cast a yellowed sallowness over everything. The debris cleared around the center of the balcony, and the Shade, the prince, and—to my surprise—many of the soldiers rose to their feet, relatively unharmed. My breath escaped in a whoosh.

The stairs of the outside entrance now lacked a back wall but remained attached to the castle—though it creaked under the shifting weight. The worm circled and bore down on the men below. Fire, shadow, water, and wind swirled around the creature, driving it backward—up the mountain and toward the cavernous cave it had apparently burst from. The worm reared up again. This time, Uncle Koll lifted a hand, pulling up a wall of stone from the collapsed tower to shove into the creature a couple feet to the side. It was just enough to save a swordsman on the ground below from a death blow.

"Pain and death!" The monster screamed again; the agonal wail felt like my skull was splitting in two. Even the Shade clutched at his head. Leon stepped in front of the Shade, deflecting the tail of the worm as it whipped around with a punishing blow of flames. I saw Father appear in the courtyard. He picked up a bow from a downed archer and seemed to be firing with some accuracy.

He hadn't left after all.

A yowl like a woman screaming, echoed from the gaping cavern. At the edge of the ballroom, where the wall had collapsed, hundreds of spyrings poured into the village. Bertha snarled again, pouncing, ripping, and sprinting between the spider-like monsters with glee.

"At least someone's having a good time," Jamison muttered beside me, flitting haphazardly in the air.

"Jamison!"

Relieved to see his grumpy self, I offered my hand. He perched upside down and panted. His little body trembled in exhaustion.

I scratched at his fuzzy cheek. "You worried me, you silly bat."

"I flew the whole way here to warn the master. The manor attack was just a ruse." He took in the scene before us. *"The princeling should be out here fighting anyway. This is an absolute mess. I mean, look at it. The curtains will need to be cleaned twelve times to get all that smoke and dust out of there."*

"Yes. The curtains," I said dryly. My focus returned to the Shade as he sprinted around the outside edge of the castle yard. I worried my lip, wishing again I had any magic of my own. The wolves and badger clambered over the crumbled wall, heading off the spyrings that had made it into the fray. The monsters were closing in now. I grabbed a broken curtain rod in my free hand. At least if they made it up here, I could whack them.

"So you've returned." The low voice made me jump, and I sprang back toward Uncle Koll. King Regent Harold came to stand beside me, his two galer guards tucked beside him, arms at the ready to defend and protect their leader.

"Not for you." My boldness surprised us both. His eyebrows flew upward, lost in his graying hair. I continued, "We brought new potions for the queen. And we stayed to save her and the people."

The king regent frowned and slowly turned to take in the scene before me. "The Shade and the Savior working together."

Jamison hissed at him from his perch on my finger. I tensed, ready to grab him should he try to attack.

"Surely you mean to imply that the Shade is saving your other son and your castle, and not something else," I answered drily. The king regent flinched. I watched as the Shade lifted up a wolf to toss him onto the worm's back, biting at the hide that seemed impenetrable. "He's doing more than you are." I curtsied with no little sarcasm. "Your Royal Highness."

A sneer curled the king regent's lip as he stepped closer. At first, I thought he was going to threaten me, but then I realized his frown was mere curiosity. "I liked you better when you were quiet."

"My time with the Shade has been enlightening. I found my voice. I found a place I belonged."

"You always belonged here, Aelia. You are your father's daughter, a noblewoman."

I scoffed at the idea. "Magicless, I had no place here."

The worm dove, striking the upper side of the castle again, which jolted the whole structure. We stumbled. When we regained our footing, we both stepped back a few paces from the collapsing edge. Leon and the other guards were showing signs of fatigue, but nothing seemed to do much more than thwart the creature. "Your sons need you, Your Highness."

"I-I can't."

"You won't."

He tilted his head back and forth before he held his palm between us. Thin, hazy black shadows filled it and spilled over like fading black steam to the ground. "I have"—he swallowed hard—"weak and sinister magic."

I blinked, shock freezing my muscles in an icy bath. "You have shadow magic?" His cheeks flushed, and he looked guilty. "I thought you were a galer!" I stepped closer, gesturing wildly to the courtyard. "You abandoned your son *who was a child* who has the same magic?"

"Wind magic is an easier ruse when we all act together. Who can tell who is doing what with that invisible magic?" He pulled at his collar. "And certainly, the people could never know about the shadows..."

My jaw dropped farther. "You lead a kingdom who believes that the more powers someone has, the higher their rank and standing. You abandoned him." He nodded slowly. "You let me believe I was an aberration and an embarrassment."

"I *am* embarrassed, Aelia. The nation's leaders should be the strongest of all."

"One's strength doesn't come from magic powers, Your Highness."

He shrugged and looked before him. "Certainly, magic is needed here today, to fight this creature."

The mountains and caverns seemed to belch more black clouds, obscuring the early dawn. More spyrings—as well as those awful translucent rats—flooded out of the cavern and were met by the mammals and guards. But our side was becoming overwhelmed. The worm belched projectiles of rocks that slammed into the castle's walls. The king regent and his galers as one raised their arms to block any from striking us inside. They moved together perfectly—such a coordinated deception.

A seer began to wail the prophecy from the street. Her words were broken in the cacophony of the battle. "The ruin of kingdoms from weak ones come...lest the deep reject the vile ones...the stars and sun turn black as pitch and light must fight to cure that...dark decay. Still, love must reign and find a way."

King Regent Harold regarded my disdainful expression. "The people needed to see me as a strong leader—when Gemaline got so sick, and I needed to step into the role of the king. When I married her, especially since it had been a love match, I had a certain expectation to fulfill. The opinion of the masses has toppled better rulers than I. And I must maintain peace and ensure their compliance even if it's through omission, Aelia."

"I have respected you my whole life, sir. I have been grateful for the roof over my head, my friendship with Leon, and access to education. Because of that education, I know that this stance will lead to your downfall. The people will find out. They'll also find out about the Shade and his parentage. But unless you do something right now to stop that beast, you won't have a kingdom to rule."

He held up his hands in a posture of surrender. "What could one person do against a beast like that?"

Uncle Koll patted my shoulder. "We are better together."

The king regent looked over at his...brother-in-law. "Koll."

"Harold." Uncle Koll had never appeared more tense.

Before us, the scene was in chaos. The mammals and the Shade were pushed back to the top of the crumbled balcony mound. Leon had climbed up an archer tower to try attacking from a different angle. His flames were still scorching, even though he looked exhausted.

But something wasn't right; I could see through the Shade's shadows.

"Uncle Koll, is something wrong with the Shade?"

Chapter Twenty-Eight

Freedom of Choice

I watched with increasing horror as the Shade whipped his shadows around the courtyard, pushing, shielding, and battling the worm. It wasn't like the morning he'd fought the prince at the manor. His shadows weren't as dark or thick as they'd been when the prince attacked us, or during the ballroom fight. Their reach wasn't as far. Their lines seemed almost whispers as opposed to the ferocious and indefensible force of nature I'd come to know. In between attacks, the Shade was heaving deep breaths.

"Uncle Koll, what is happening?" I asked, turning my back on the king regent.

He was silent. I turned to him, but he was watching the Shade, his brow furrowed and his lips pressed tightly in unspoken words.

"Uncle Koll, why isn't he fighting at full strength? He's usually better than this."

"He's fighting with everything he has." His voice was quiet, the acceptance a death knoll.

We watched as the worm bore down again, and the Shade ducked to the side. A shadow barely caught him, and his head whipped hard toward the ground.

"Why is he so much weaker now? The prince looks tired, but his magic is just as strong."

Uncle Koll dragged a hand over his face. "Oh stars, he'll hate me."

"What is it?"

Jamison flitted overhead, hovering before me. *"You did this. The master is suffering from half a bond."*

Half a... "What did you say?"

"When you came to us...he bonded himself to you to save your life." Uncle Koll's hand clasped my arm. "That's why you can hear the creatures. That's why the marking is distinct but seems to bother you. It's incomplete."

I touched my neck. "But I had the mark before I came to you."

"Master said he'd seen you in the forest when you were trespassing. He noted your clumsiness even then."

The Shade had been the forester...and he had caught me, placing his hand on my neck. That was our first touch, and though I'd had a tiny dot there before, it was when the mark had first expanded like a twisting bloom. It was, even now, a black whisp curling up and curling down—not full circles. Was the mark...if the Shade was the boy from my childhood...had it started forming then? But the Shade didn't have a matching bond mark.

Jamison continued. *"That's why he's weakening. It's why he's been limping. He continues to feed his magic into you, but there's nothing going back into him. As I said, you are a leech."*

Cold flooded my chest. He'd bonded with me. "Why would he half-bond, and why didn't he tell me?" And where was his bond mark?

"You'd have to ask him that. But if I were to guess, I'd say he was unwilling to steal any more of your freedom after you'd already sacrificed so much to others. He wants you utterly whole and unbound, as you told him you wished to be. He would rather die so you would be untethered—and therefore free to choose—than think you had to choose him against your will. Against your conscience."

"He's such a fool," the bat hissed.

I whirled to watch this man—this idiot of a man—throw everything he had at the worm. The prince had been knocked off the tower, but he looked okay. He struggled to heave himself back from the battle scene; a soldier ran to pull him toward the wall. The Shade stood alone in the center. He knew he was weak and had gone anyway. I remembered him trying our various potions, but they must not have worked. He wasn't weak because the earth was sick. He was weak because he was giving his strength to me. No wonder I had healed so quickly. And now, he was going to lose. *I know what I want.* The memory was as clear in my memory as if he were saying it again in my ear.

What did I want?

Bonded. Enslaved. That's what a bond had always meant to me—a connection where, if you lost them, you lost everything. If you lost your partner, you lost your will to live and your will to love ever again. But that hadn't been true for Uncle Koll.

"You said it was worth it?" I turned to him, searching his face for the answer. "To bond even though you lost her?"

"Every second with her is one that I would never exchange for anything in the world. My loss is great, because my love is greater, Aelia. Love is worth the risk."

The Shade was willing to die for me. He knew how I felt about bonding. He knew the pain caused by my father and the loss of my mother. He knew the half-bond would save my life, but I hadn't known fully what I was agreeing to. At that time, I wanted him to save me from everything, including death. He had acted. And now he stood alone, fighting off a creature he could never defeat by himself—one that, though blistered and angry, didn't seem to be slowing in the least.

Galers fell as the worm's tail slammed them to the side; yet the arrows kept missing its eyes, and the Shade fought on in the center of the hill. His shadows only reached treetop height, a fraction of his full power. They laced above him, shielding him and throwing what they could at the worm.

He glanced up to see me standing on the balcony before facing the worm again. *"Aelia,"* the Shade panted. *"I think it's time for you to run. I can't stop him. You've got to go. Run to the coast."*

He sounded so hopeless, alarm burst through me. *"You have to come with me. I'm not going alone. We'll evacuate the village and start over."*

"Of course not. You have Koll. You have a future. I have to keep you safe." His voice was exhausted but firm.

Mine wavered. *"I need you alive. I need you with me."*

Another blast from the worm shoved the ball of shadows he had whipped around him deep into the cracked balcony, creating a round basin. As the shadows faded, the Shade's head was low, and he rested on one knee, his hand raised above him.

"Koll, he's going to die. How do I save him?"

The older man looked me over carefully. "Are you saving him because you are compelled by guilt or responsibility? By your need to help? Or are you saving him because you *want* him? A whole bond would strengthen his magic and give him a fighting chance, but don't do that just because you want to help. Very few people have looked at him and wanted him for himself. Don't save him just to disregard him like the others. Go to him because you care for him. Bond with him because you love him—and only for that reason."

I had lived my whole life for other people, helping, serving, catering, fawning. I served my queen. I served my father. I bowed my head and curtsied and kept silent. I chose every outfit for someone else's approval. I said yes to things I didn't want and had never learned to say no. Now that I had found myself, I knew what I would do. I chose this. For me. My necklace sparked with a pulse of light.

Without another word, I bolted down the wall-less stairwell that wrapped outside the castle wall to the courtyard. The ground looked perilously far on the unsteady stones. King Regent Harold cried out but didn't stop me with his galers. Bodies of creatures lined the patio, rocks and boulders littered the way, and I stumbled countless times, but I couldn't slow down. I had to reach the Shade before the worm killed him. So I could tell him how I really felt. So I could complete what he had started.

He saw me sprinting across the rubble of the courtyard.

"Stop her!" the Shade cried to our minds.

"Aelia, no!" my father cried. He picked up his rate of shooting, trying to distract the worm as I worked my way to the center of the crumbled balcony. The Shade turned, and fury burned across his face. His shadows reached for me.

"Pull me to you!" I cried.

"I told you to run."

I gestured at my body. *"And I listened! I'm running!"*

"Blasted woman." A whip of his hand brought the shadows around me. With a tug, they flew me to him. I wrapped my arms around his neck as the shadows writhed around us, guarding us, shielding us. A dense circle of darkness wrapped around us. A boom from above shoved us downward, the worm, presumably, beating us down. The shadows seemed to strengthen as the Shade gritted his teeth.

"Dayspring, you foolish creature." The worm slammed into us again. The Shade winced; pain from that hit to his waning magic cut through me now that we were touching. "You have to get out of here. I can't hold it back much longer. My magic—"

"Why didn't you tell me you had bonded with me?"

His eyes flew wide, and as his focus faltered, a rock landed beside his feet. "Seriously? Now?" He glared toward the castle. "My uncle is a dead man."

"Sure, yell at him and Jamison too. But why didn't you *tell me*?"

"Because I wanted you to be free to choose, free to leave, free to—" He raked a hand through his hair. "Free to love. If I told you, I knew you would return the bond because of some predetermined nonsense about being nice and helpful. You'd choose it for my sake. I wanted you to choose me because it's what *you* wanted. We should have had so much time"—his breath hissed through his teeth—"but we're here now, and I can't beat this creature, nor woo it." Of course, he'd tried to befriend it. "I'm going to let you go so you can be truly free, even free from this half-bond." A half-bond that would break at his death.

"Would you choose it again?" I stroked a finger down his cheek, the tip of my finger following the lines of his lips.

"I would choose you and die here a thousand times to be with you for even a moment. Your brief stay has brought more light to my black heart than I ever thought possible. Why do you think I call you Dayspring? You are the sun, and I am a winter wasteland desperate for life." He paused. "You are not my prisoner or my servant or some passing amusement, which is why you need to go, Aelia. Let me save you! The world needs your light."

Hope glittered in my chest. "What's your name?"

"What? Shea."

I blinked twice. "That's it? You'll just tell it to me?"

"You never *directly* asked." He chuckled. "It wasn't much of a leap to my nickname, was it?" He smiled, that glorious half-hitched grin.

I giggled. It was an impossible, defiant giggle—despite the whirl-wind of death and shadows around us. "Shea, I choose you—for me. Selfishly, greedily, demandingly. Because I love you. I say my most enthusiastic, heartfelt yes—to all of you."

He gaped and pulled back slightly to argue. "Aelia—"

I pressed my fingertips across his lips. "I'm going to kiss you now."

I leaned forward, threading my fingers through his locks. Then I pulled him down, crashing my lips into his. My hand rested on his chest, my fingertips touched his collarbone, and his heart thudded against my palm. His arms wrapped around me, one hand graz-ing my ribcage, the other gripping my hip, pulling me toward him. White light exploded between us as my necklace beamed. Heat ripped through my chest and burned its way around my heart. My soul sang. The mark on my neck tingled pleasantly. And when we finally pulled apart, the Sh—no, Shea—pulled up his sleeve and tugged on the top edge of his leather bracelet to reveal a swirl: two arms thinning as they spun once, twice around itself in a widening circle. His completed black bond mark. His fingers tickled my neck as he traced what must have been a similar pattern. So that's where his mark was.

Brightness burst between us, but it wasn't from my necklace alone anymore. Looking down, my hands glowed, my skin bright with its own light. Shea gaped. Hot white heat burst from two points in my back, streaking outward on either side like sunlight through storm clouds. I turned and saw impossible wings that arced behind me. I had magic. Light magic. I laughed.

Shea's shadows, now as dark as night, contrasted like darkness around a candle flame. They reached forward, danced along the edge of the brightest beams, wrapped about my ankles, slid through my hair, and traced circles along my spine. His emotions, awe and conten-tment, flooded through me with the strong scent of forests in winter.

The bond was complete. He was mine, and I was his, and no one would take him from me.

"The power of a full, heartfelt, powerful yes." Shea smiled. "I knew it! When we played hide and seek as children, I swore you glowed in the dark! But then my stupid father and idiot brother and those ridiculous nobles drained you dry. You poured out yourself for others for so long, Dayspring." He cackled. "Look at how amazing you are."

A wrenching cry ripped through the wonder. The worm was pulling back. Its eyes clenched shut, and it whipped its head back and forth. Shea dropped his shadows to the ground to see what was happening and held my hand. My light burst brighter at the contact.

"Too bright. Too much light." It wailed. *"Give me what's mine, and I'll go,"* the worm cried. What's his? Shea looked behind us. His irritation vibrated under my skin.

The prince and a group of soldiers were closing in behind us, rallying for another fight. Shea pierced Leon with a glare. "What did you take?"

The prince shifted his grip on his pommel as he stood at the ready. "An egg."

"An egg?!" Shea cried, the shadows boiling along the ground in wild waves at his agitation. "You stole an egg? Is it alive?"

"It is. We were going to study it and raise it...you know. For science. For the kingdom's defense," the prince replied weakly.

Rolling his eyes, Shea turned back to the worm. "We will give you your young," he said. "Then will you leave?"

The worm swayed his head back and forth. *"Stop destroying my home."*

Shea added, "She wants to know if you'll stop digging." Oh. She was a mother worm, of course.

"She has my word," the prince cried back.

"Mine too!" The king regent had stepped forward to the edge of the broken balcony. "Leave us in peace, beast, and we will leave you to yours!" he shouted. The worm growled at the king regent, who stumbled back into his galers.

"Very well." The worm held still, lowering her head until she lay not twelve feet from us, her uninjured eyes glaring at Shea as she waited. The rest of the creatures from the caverns held still as well. The cloudy sky was lightening by degrees. The badger stood atop of the wall with a long spyring leg dangling from its mouth. The crunching echoed in the stillness. As we waited, my glow settled slightly, still present but not blinding.

Several long moments later, a massive egg was rolled out from the stables by twelve soldiers, with several ropes holding it onto a wheeled platform. Pitch black, impenetrable shadows raced across the courtyard and lifted the massive object, waiting for the soldiers to drop the rope. Then the shadows delicately set it before the creature.

"For the mother worm. May you go in peace," Shea said.

We stepped back as the worm lunged forward and grasped the egg as tenderly as a toothy-vortex ever could. *"May you keep your word."* She rumbled as she dove back into her caverns. She screeched, apparently calling to her creepy minions, and they all fled back into the darkness.

Shadows billowed, stretching around the castle, looking for stragglers. They wrapped the entire castle and filled the courtyard. Soldiers shifted uncomfortably as they brushed by, but when no more monsters were found, the shadows retracted back to Shea. With a smile, his hand slipped along the small of my back, and he pulled me to him. The happiness in my chest bubbled up again, and my skin brightened by degrees. I felt a little sheepish—definitely uneasy with this new magic. Shea felt my discomfort and kissed my temple.

"Shine brightly, Dayspring. Don't hold back."

I smiled, unable to restrain the shine now. Shea's shadows traced the beams of light, thrilling and vibrating the very center of my soul. "Kiss me, Shea. Don't hold back."

Shea leaned down, his breath tickling against my lips.

"Wait." I stopped him with a hand to his chest.

"Wait? What? Why?" Annoyance filtered through the bond.

I tugged on his collar. "You never said it."

"Said what? Oh." He planted a quick kiss on my lips, brightening the light around us. "I think you're kind of okay."

The Shade, a being of darkness and shadow, swept me backward in a glorious kiss. Our magic danced together—a beautiful mosaic of power—before he answered. "I love you, Dayspring. I have liked you since we were children, and I have loved you since you stumbled into my manor, and I will love and protect you forever. Every night needs day, every shadow is born from light, and every darkness needs a spark of hope." Shea smiled. "You are my perfect match in every way."

His lips met mine in a gentle fervor. Our emotions threaded together, woven in a contrasted tapestry of magic. *My magic.* His touch was gentle. Mine was not. I pulled him closer, wrapping my arms more tightly around his neck. I had chosen him, and I would never let him go. The clouds were thinning as the sun beamed at us from the horizon. We pulled apart, and a prickling discomfort made me fully aware of our audience.

Shea peered over my shoulder at Leon.

"Ready to talk to them?" I asked.

He grinned. *"There's a choice? Then no. Let's make a run for it."*

I snorted even as I shook my head. It was time for him to come home and be acknowledged as a hero, or better yet, accepted as a son. Already, a great defense of my bonded partner rose within me. I had no idea what my—this light—my *magic* could do, but there was no way I would let them harm him ever again. He deserved their love, but today, I would settle for their gratitude—for saving their sorry, greedy lives.

Chapter Twenty-Nine

Restoration

T he silence left by the worm's flight was absolute. Scattered pebbles fell off the castle, echoing like a rockslide from the mountain face. A sniffing archer was as loud as the whipping wind. Soldiers rose to their feet and stumbled onto the patio. The dawn light shimmered over the mountain peaks.

The prince strode toward us, proudly walking despite being exhausted and depleted magically from the battle. Shea, rejuvenated from the bond, didn't limp in the slightest.

"Shea."

"Leon."

I looked between the two, the familial traits impossible to miss now that they were standing so close. Of course, they were brothers.

Out of the corner of my eye, I saw movement. An archer was aiming at Shea, who was distracted by Leon. Rage filled me. I extended a hand toward him as the man loosed his arrow. Light—searing hot and focused—zipped across the space, and in seconds, incinerated the arrow. The clatter of the arrowhead hitting the stone shattered the silence.

"The battle is over," I said loudly enough for all to hear. "The Shade is not your enemy."

Leon waved off his men and set his hand on a guard who'd raised a water whip in response to my magic. "Lady Aelia is right. Stand down." He studied me warily. "So it seems that you had magic all along."

I raised a brow. "So it seems." I thrilled at the idea of my magic; not only was it useful for scaring off cave beasts or never being afraid of the dark, but now, perhaps I could defend myself as well. Shea squeezed my hand, his pride almost matching my own.

Doors swung open with a clatter, and the king regent strode forward, a small woman at his side.

Leon stepped toward her, hands out as if he could catch her even from this distance. "Mother?"

Queen Gemaline, for the first time since I was ten, *walked* toward us, though she leaned heavily on her husband's arm. Her attendants and a scowling seer flitted behind her, wringing their hands, sloshing a glass of water, and worrying. All of the soldiers in the courtyard watched her slow progress across the stone; they collapsed to one knee, bowing when she had stopped before us. I beamed at her. Our potion had actually helped.

Keeping my hand linked in the crook of Shea's elbow, I curtsied as usual. Leon bowed his head politely to his father. But Shea…Shea stayed rigidly upright, his glare locked with the king regent's. A thousand emotions flitted over King Regent Harold's face, but the queen had only one—pure joy.

She stepped forward and nearly stumbled, breaking Shea's battle of wills as both he and Leon caught her by her arms.

"My boys. My wonderful, strong boys!" She pulled them into her embrace. Whispers began among the men. "I am so proud of you."

Shea never broke eye contact with his father. Tension knitted his shoulders together as the shadows that cast around his feet eddied, ever at the ready. The manor mammals slunk behind us, poised and watching. Even the men seemed to hold their breath.

The king regent dipped his head, closing his eyes for a moment. "Our sons have saved us. The kingdom owes you their gratitude and respect."

Shea took a deep breath and leaned back on a heel, pulling me closer. "The kingdom also owes Aelia a great debt."

King Regent Harold crossed his hands in front of him. "Too true. The kingdom is saved by light and courage once again."

Turning to the gathering crowd of villagers who had made their way out of their houses, the queen signaled to a galer to carry her voice. It only wavered a little. "Today, we have witnessed the cataclysmic end of a foreboding prophecy that we spent years preparing for. We'd even sent away our firstborn, to ready himself for this day, to grow in strength for the monsters that would come. He has played his role perfectly. As it is written, 'Stars and sun turn black as pitch, and light must fight to cure that which has doomed us all to dark decay. Still, love must reign and find a way.' Truly, the love of these two"—she indicated me and Shea—"and the light of the rare and powerful lumos mage, have saved our people from the monsters of the deep."

The king regent glanced my way, raising his brow. She had skipped over the first line: 'The ruin of kingdoms from weak ones come.' For over a decade, I had thought that weak one was me. The ruin of kingdoms had actually come from the deep mining of a greedy and weak king regent, who was afraid of his magic and his powerful son. He would have ruined his wife's kingdom as he worked in her stead, and she was too sick to stop him. His own weakness was not one of magic, but of character. He nearly killed us all.

She cleared her throat and continued. "My sons have worked tirelessly for our good and the protection of the kingdom. My Shea has researched healing tonics to restore our people and our lands, found a light source that does not require anyone to disturb the creatures of the deep, and my Leon has defended us bravely from those beasts of the deep along with his wonderful work making peace with our neighboring kingdoms. Together they will bring our kingdom into a new era."

"Together?" Both men coughed out the word simultaneously.

The queen, frail and tiny, but with pink cheeks and a spark of life that gleamed mischievously from her green eyes, smiled at them. "Together."

Awkwardly, the people began to clap—no doubt whiplashed from their long held belief that the scourge of the deep, the menace of goodness, and Death himself was suddenly not...and heralded as a hero instead. As the crowd grew, so did the volume of the cheers. The city was saved. A prophecy fulfilled. Light had won.

King Regent Harold, swayed on the opinion of the people, shouted next, "Together we will rebuild and restore. Please see your head of village to compile a list of needs. With my queen healed, she will rebuild this kingdom even better than it was before." He regarded his queen fondly, brushing her shoulders with his thumb. Despite anything else I felt about him at that moment, at least he loved his wife.

The queen smiled, then turned her back to the crowd, her voice dropping to a murmur. "Well boys, that potion was something, but I'm exhausted. Please help me leave gracefully."

The queen positioned herself between them and began her return to the castle. I stood uncertainly, even as Shea looked back at me.

"May I have the honor?"

The king regent stood before me with his arm out. I clacked my gaping mouth shut, curtsied for good measure, and with cheeks flaming, took his arm. He had publicly acknowledged me—an honor among my peers—after everything. At long last, I had the king's attention. It was remarkable how little it mattered to me now. What was once something I strived for daily now seemed so paltry compared to what I had found in myself, what I had found at the manor, and what I had found with Shea.

"Thank you for saving us," he said as he waved to the people.

"You are welcome, Your Highness."

We ducked through the doorway, side-stepping the already busy cleaning maids. He paused, his gaze lingering after Shea. "I broke him, I think, when I sent him away." He coughed once. "It broke us all. It worsened my queen, poisoned my first son against me, and ripped out the heart of my second son. Leon loved him as a boy." My heart ached for the entire family. He continued. "I was a fool."

"A fool is one who, seeing the right path, takes another." I swallowed. "If I may be so bold, you may have been mistaken, but there is still a right path before you."

I braced for the backlash for my brashness, but the king's eyes remained contemplative. "Even so, Aelia. I'm glad you didn't die at the temple."

I doubted I would get any other apology from the king. "I am too, Your Highness. For her sake."

He faltered in his steps, regarding Queen Gemaline as she made her way through the halls of the main floor. "For her sake, I would do anything. Yet I could not save her." His hand pulsed on mine. "But you did. For this, I am in your debt."

I smiled. "I'm sure we can think of some way to repay it."

Chapter Thirty

Light at the End

T he castle restoration went slowly, but since the mining stopped, the smog had filtered away, and the earth returned to rest. The potion was widely distributed to all the loamers, and those who'd left the kingdom returned in droves. Through the next few weeks, the healed loamers systematically collapsed caverns to separate the worms, spyrings, rats, and humans. The prince unveiled a new policy regarding mining, instituting a new team led by Uncle Koll, who would mine responsibly for the prosperity of the kingdom without harming any loamers, the earth, or the creatures within. The fire battles had ended, and washers began to rehydrate the dry earth around the castle, while loamers worked to recover the soil.

The village and the queen alike were thrilled with Shea's new light source. The bacteria was easy to reproduce, and the cubes were a wonder to children and adults. People still walked cautiously around the Shade, uncertain if the dark lord would suddenly flip and kill them all, but they were softening to him bit by bit. It helped, I liked to think, to have me at his side, beaming—literally—and happy. No one had ever been afraid of me.

My bond with Shea and our glorious display of magic had intimidated some, but my newfound power—and my close association to the king regent and queen—had thrown me into the center of public attention. Everyone who had previously disregarded me, belittled me, or bullied me suddenly wanted me to be their best friend. I was the tamer of the darkness. The pinnacle of the kingdom of light. I was even dressed in fine gowns, much finer than I was comfortable with, but I hoped with time, I would get used to all the attention. Everyone watched me. Most whispered about me. But it didn't feel like the harsh judgments I'd always received before. Not that I trusted flattery any more.

As for me, I just wanted to spend time with Shea and steal moments eating cookies with Chef in the kitchen. We split our time between the manor and the castle at first, needing our own quiet time at night, while we helped to reunify the kingdom and mollify the people during the day. My quiet moments with the queen were now limited to allotted tea times, as she flitted around with Jamison—making up for a decade of motionless bedrest by never ceasing her work. She was tireless and grew stronger by the hour. Between her and Jamison, the castle was whipped into shape.

My father seemed to recover some, the potion and the healing earth were both effective treatments, and he looked healthier than he had in years. It also helped that he had continued to avoid alcohol. We spent most days apart. He continued making potions using the new recipe Shea and I had created. But even that need would hopefully fade as the earth fully healed. I waited to see if he would prove himself trustworthy.

Prince Leon and Prince Shea held an uneasy truce, but I caught them playing a game of cards last evening and they had laughed like tentative friends.

I now stood on the edge of the ballroom, dressed in an enormous deep purple gown, like dusk just before twilight, with lines of silver that caught in the new shealights. Queen Gemaline and Jamison were bustling around the ballroom. He hung from her shoulder tassels, repeating her orders to the creatures, as they went about bossing and directing the servants and soldiers alike to prepare for a ball.

Our ball. Shea's and my bonding ball.

Though the bond was complete, the rights and covenants had to be shared formally. I had about an hour before the room was filled with nobility and commoners.

Soldiers lined the newly finished balcony, and the courtyard beyond was strung with lights, ready to welcome the whole city in celebration of the return of a son, the saving of the kingdom, and the recovery of the queen. Owls hung lanterns, and the queen stepped around a pangolin that waddled awkwardly toward a lantern with a light cube. The castle was filled with many such helpful creatures. I wasn't sure Chef was entirely thrilled by the raccoons yet. But she did like them better than the lords and ladies.

My shadowy prince was...well, he wasn't entirely pleased by the nobles' attention. I think he might have been happier as a menace than as a highly sought-after power player in the courtly games. While there had been discussion of having both Shea and Leon split certain royal duties, to his delight, the queen placed him in charge of the forests, creatures, and mountains and the defense of the lands. The queen had strongly limited the power of her husband as she recovered her full strength and political power. And while part of me wished there could be even more punishment for what had been a poisoned reign, I had confidence in the queen—and Shea—to keep things honest.

Tonight, Shea had mysteriously disappeared. Hiding, no doubt, from forced pleasantries. I tugged gently on the bond, which pointed somewhere near the garden. Happiness filtered through, and I suspected he was playing with Bertha. The best part about her was that when she walked at my side through the castle, no one approached the ugly cat. Shea and I both appreciated that kind of reluctant respect.

Someone stepped in front of me, snapping me back to the present. Prince Leon was bowing, much lower than I warranted.

Quietly, he spoke, "Aelia...I...I feel terrible about everything."

I patted my dress with my fingers, waiting. "Define everything, please."

He slowly rose, his hands fidgeting before him. "Oh, that whole business at the temple."

"Where you tried to sacrifice my life, and had your men chase me down and shoot at me like a deer?"

His face flamed red, and his voice sounded stuck on the ball of guilt in his throat. I waited patiently. He scratched at his neck.

"That business?" I prompted.

"Yes, that." He tugged his collar and fixed his cuff. "I am...sorry. Very sorry. I—There's no excuse. I abused your friendship, and I placed a higher value on my bitter desperation than your life. I listened to Father and believed a version of the prophecy that...that was mis-applied." To his credit, his shoulders slumped in shame. His emotions fell from him in waves as I dipped quietly into his mind. He was being genuine. "I deserve no mercy."

My eyebrow peaked and I squinted at him. "Maybe jailtime with the seers who manipulated the ceremony?" At least those crones were under investigation—a small victory.

His jaw worked. "Yes, maybe that." He shifted, uncomfortable for a moment, then his shoulders slumped again. "If that feels like justice, then I will sit under your judgment."

I mulled over his words for a moment, recalling that day in the temple in vivid detail. The pain was etched in my soul, even as the scars had faded. My mind raced to the present, flashes of my time with Shea, of our completed bond. "You designed my death to serve your own purpose. You and your father abused a prophecy to fit your goals." He nodded slowly. "But even before that, you didn't protect me, you used my friendship for your own comfort and not mine, and when others laughed at me, you never stopped them." Shame burned his cheeks. "I always believed in you. So for now, I will withhold judgment." I snorted. "We also know your father wouldn't let you rot in jail. Leon, you have a choice before you—a choice about what kind of leader, and what kind of friend, you want to be. You were wrong. You deserve a consequence you will not receive, and you certainly do not deserve my mercy or friendship." The line between his brows deepened as I scanned his face. "But I forgive you. I know who you once were, and I believe you can be better."

He looked shocked.

"I forgive you." I repeated. "I miss my friend, Leon. Do the right thing and show me who you can be. Discernment is rare, Leon, but more precious than luz. Fight for what is right, for the vulnerable, for the weak. That is how you become a good king."

He nodded. "I will." He bowed again. "Aelia, thank you. I can do this. And maybe one day, I can earn your trust again."

I grasped his hand in mine. "I hope so."

His face was determined, and as he walked away, his steps seemed a little lighter and his head held a little higher. I glanced over to see the queen watching us. Her proud smile warmed my soul. She brought her fist to her chest and bowed slightly. I returned the motion.

"*Dayspring, where are you?*" Shea's voice sounded agitated.

"*Ballroom. Why? You're supposed to be here too.*"

"*Come outside.*"

Winking at the queen, I gracefully swept to the stairwell. The door shut, blocking the ballroom light, but my magic shimmered, highlighting—oh my. Uncle Koll and Chef stood before me. In each other's arms. Flushed and looking sheepish. They jumped away from one another like they'd been burned.

I stuttered, "Uh. Okay. That's...yes. Bye."

Rushing down the stairs, I heard giggling from both people behind me. I shook my head. If I was able to find happiness, I hoped that they would too. Several floors later, the door at the garden clanged open, and the late evening sunlight turned the world pink. Shadows tumbled at my feet. My glorious, thunderous Shade stood casually leaning against the wall. Bertha was rolling around with a knitted ball.

"Finally." He paced forward, stalking me to the other side, where he backed me against the stones. "I don't like sharing you. We're leaving." He ducked his head against mine and trailed kisses along my jaw.

I laughed, breathily, desperately trying to remember why we couldn't just leave. "The ball."

"Don't care."

"The bonding ceremony."

"Don't care."

"Your mother will be there."

His kisses paused. "Okay, I do care, but we leave at seven-fourteen."

"It starts at seven."

"Perfect."

The kisses found their way to my lips, and my whole being glowed. A deep chuckle rumbled from his chest as I pulled his vest toward me, hungry for more.

"It's not very easy to sneak away when you light up the night like a beacon," he murmured, his breath hot against my face.

"Stop making me blissfully happy."

He tilted his head back, his hands filtering through the light that beamed from my shoulders—cast out each side like wings, though intangible. Yet somehow, I could feel him—his touch, his shadows—like his whispers across my skin. Delicious goosebumps prickled down my arms and back.

"You are mine." The world around us blackened to nothing as he encased us in a dome of shadow.

I grinned. "And you are mine, but I'm not sure a ball of blackness in the corner of a garden is more subtle. It's sunset, not midnight." The laugh escaped me, free and wild.

His fingertips caught my chin and tilted me toward him. "I'm going to kiss you now." His green eyes sparked with desire.

"Not if I kiss you first."

Our lips met. The light burst out between the arms of the shadows. Newly sprouted seedlings turned and rose, growing toward the light, while the garden below exploded with plump buds. I was fully and finally alive. I had looked Death in the face and...

I kissed him.

The End.

To see scenes from the POV of THE SHADE. Go to my website and join my newsletter.

www.AloraCarter.com

Ties of Frost

Thank you so much for reading my book!
Next in **Tethered Hearts**:

Available March 14, 2025

Find it on Amazon!

Selina R. Gonzalez incredible story: Ties of Frost.

A self-reliant wyvern shifter. An extroverted ice elf. A deadly curse.

Wyvern shifter Zidra and ice elf Kyrundar are members of a sacred order of elite warriors—and, according to Zidra, bitter rivals. While she seeks to prove she's the best without aid, Kyrundar believes their friendly competition makes them ideal partners. Then Kyrundar follows Zidra into a trap, and his distraction costs her everything.

When Zidra is struck by a lethal ice curse, only ice magic can save her. Yet Kyrundar can't remove the curse, and as long as the curse is affecting Zidra, she can't shift. Worse, a side effect of his aid is a heartbond neither of them wants.

Despite years of misunderstandings and recent resentments, they will have to cooperate to survive assassins and find a reclusive healer who can destroy the curse and the magical bond. But if they discover the accidental heartbond isn't a catastrophe after all, will either of them have the courage to admit it?

Find it on Amazon

Tethered Hearts Series

Tethered Hearts

Ties of Legacy by Melanie Cellier

Ties of Starlight by Celeste Baxendell

Ties of Deception by Alice Ivinya

Ties of Bargains by Tara Grayce

Ties of Death by Constance Lopez

Ties of Shadow by Alora Carter

Ties of Frost by Selina R. Gonzalez

Ties of Dust by Deborah Grace White

Grab the whole Tethered Hearts series on Amazon!

Acknowledgements

Friends, I cannot begin to express how thankful I am for the team that surrounded me during the last year and more that I have been writing this book— nor how terrified I am of missing someone since it's been such a long journey. If I do, please write me immediately so I can fix this and thank you as I should.

To my parents, who watched my babies so much that I could finish all the editing here at the end, I do not think I could have done it without you.

To my alpha team, Constance Lopez, Deborah Grace White, Phi Pilgrim (who got an pre-alpha copy as well missing 6 chapters, oy), Jacque Stevens and Sara Lawson. I needed you so much to make this book go from a hot mess to a tangible book.

To my beta team, Kate Stradling, Auntie Lolo, Robyn Sarty, Lyndsey Hall, Bethany Aich, Hailey Rodriguez, Sarah Metcalf, Nicola Wilkinson, Kim Rayburn, Nic Page, Dayna Clark, and again Phi Pilgrim, the details that you added made the clanging gong sing like... like... one of those singing bowls. The resonance of this story hits so hard because of you.

My ARC team has been PHENOMENAL – your reviews are a daily joy to me, and I'm so encouraged by your emails and messages. I'm so thankful that you picked up the truthchimes I tried to stike, and felt anger, danced in joy, and bit your nails with me through this book!

I'll also thank my husband again here, who, though he thinks in zeros and ones and pigeons, he is still a better salesperson of my book than I am.

Phi – you get a third special mention because you were CRITICAL to the functioning of this MAS and the saving of our sanity. Thank you for your work and your friendship.

Thank you, thank you, thank you to the authors of this incredible series. Besides this series literally not happening without you in it, you have also been professional, pleasant and enjoyable teammates. You've been nothing but kind to Constance and I, and I am so thankful.

To my other author half of Conra, Constance Lopez. Thank you for dotting all the T's and crossing all the eyes, and making sure my crazy ideas not only are edited right (as they aren't earlier in this sentence), but also come to fruition. You are a gift I didn't ask for and one that I'm never letting go now. You're adopted and can't escape. You're welcome.

And lastly, I'm thankful to God who shows us that he remembers the ones forgotten, downtrodden, rejected, hated, misunderstood, and betrayed. He is always near to the hurting. He is the ultimate light to overcome all darkness, and the ultimate peaceful rest from when things get too uncomfortable. I'm so grateful that goodness, and kindness and slow-to-anger are traits that belong to my God. Thank you for the chance to write books, and be in this community.

Again – if I missed you it's because I have dropped so many plates this year, and please let me know so I can rectify this immediately.

I'm the luckiest, most blessed author.

Sincerely,

Alora

Also By Alora Carter

*The Awakened Prince -
Clean Sleeping Beauty
retelling with romance,
snarky animal compan-
ions, evil vs good and love
conquers all*

Written with Rachel Rener, this heart warming story is worth reading and rereading again and again.

Free on my website when you join my newsletter!

1983. Dam Failure. Can Titania find her purpose when everything she planned is swept away?

www.ingramcontent.com/pod-product-compliance
Lightning Source LLC
Chambersburg PA
CBHW052029240626
47153CB00006B/2010